RHETT C BRUNO
TITANBORN

TITANBORN

©2018 RHETT C. BRUNO

Published by Aethon Books LLC.

Cover Art by: Jasper Schreurs

Cover Design, Print and eBook formatting and cover design by Steve Beaulieu.

CHILDREN OF TITAN

- Book 0: **The Collector**
- Book 1: **Titanborn**
- Book 2: **Titan's Son**
- Book 3: **Titan's Rise**
- Book 4: **Titan's Fury**

PROLOGUE

Somewhere outside New London, Earth, a tall, lanky Ringer named Nash stood within the cargo hold of an unmarked transport shuttle. Although he was human, three centuries of living on Titan had stretched his people's bodies and bleached their flesh. He wore a white armored suit with an orange circle painted on the chest. His helmet was off, revealing a soaring forehead, a long, tapered jaw, and a sanitary mask pulled tight over his mouth.

Across from him stood a Ringer many years his senior. He was equally tall, but unlike Nash, he was dressed in nothing but an unmarked boiler suit, and his sanitary mask was covered in grime. Bloodshot eyes appeared even redder against his ashen skin, but they were resolute.

"When our ancestors fled Earth with Trass before the Meteorite struck, I bet they never thought any of us would return," Nash said.

"Or be enslaved by the very people they left behind," the older Ringer replied. "Perhaps they should have gone farther."

The older Ringer shook his head. "It wouldn't have helped. There isn't a star these Earthers won't try to reach one day."

"Let them. Soon the Ring will be free."

"If they don't wipe us all out first."

Nash pursed his lips in anger, but before he could say anything else, the older Ringer stepped forward.

"Enough," he said. "We have to stay focused."

Nash groaned, and as he did, someone else stepped into the cargo hold from the shuttle's cockpit. This one wore a matching suit of white armor, only it had no orange circle, and the helmet was on, complete with a tinted visor that blocked the face. He was shorter than the others by at least a third of a meter and was holding a small metal cylinder with blue light emanating from slits on the sides.

"Is it finally ready, Doctor?" the older Ringer asked. "I'm running out of time."

"Yes," the Doctor said through a vocal distortion device. "Are you?"

"As I'll ever be."

The Doctor handed him the tube, and the old Ringer inspected it. He ran his fingers along the sides, but when he reached the flat top, the Doctor stopped him.

"Careful," the Doctor warned. "Don't worry, my employers assure me that it'll pass New London scanners."

"It better," the older Ringer said with a snarl. "We're putting a lot of faith in you." He switched the device into his left hand.

"It will. You remember where to use it? We don't want casualties."

The older Ringer hardly paid attention to her. "I'll do my best."

"Good. You get that right where we planned, and they'll never see your men coming."

The older Ringer stared into the Doctor's black visor for a few seconds, and then the two exchanged a nod. The Doctor turned around and marched back into the cockpit.

"Our people won't forget this," Nash said after the Doctor was completely out of sight.

"They will," the older Ringer countered. "Nobody will ever speak my name because what I do mustn't be remembered. What comes after will be."

Nash's lips started to tremble. Tears welled in the corners of his eyes. "I won't forget," he said. Nash spread his arms and rushed forward to hug the older Ringer, but he bowed out of the way.

"You shouldn't risk it," he said.

Nash froze for a moment, then grunted before he decided to embrace his older comrade anyway. They touched their foreheads together and held each other there until both of their cheeks were wet with tears.

"From ice to ashes, Alann," Nash whispered.

"From ice to ashes," the older Ringer repeated. He backed up and stared down at the glowing device in his left hand. A glimmer touched in his sickly eyes. He was ready.

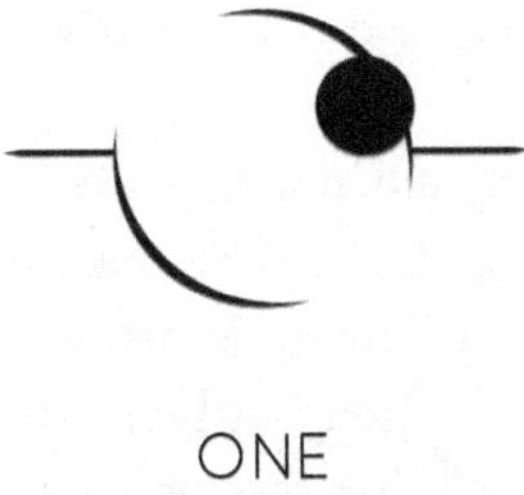

ONE

THE DAY WAS A.D. August 29, 2334, three hundred years after the Meteorite crippled Earth. In a little over three months' time, I, Malcolm Graves, would help spark a revolution. I didn't know it at the time. I didn't even consider it a possibility as I crept through the dark, cavernous hallways of a mining facility on an asteroid named 92-Undina. I was focused entirely on the job at hand.

One of the mining chiefs on Undina had decided his wages didn't match his labor, and he was becoming a problem for my employers at Pervenio Corporation, who happened to own the entire mine. I have no problem with a man asking for more credits if he thinks he deserves them. Hell, I can't even count how many times I've done the same. But this rabble-rouser, Yev Tavar, had inspired the entirety of Undina Mining Sector D to stop working, overthrow the security team stationed there, and shut down all hangar access. With food and water stores in their sector able to last around six months, waiting out their less-than-peaceful strike was not a viable option.

Undina was an M-type asteroid that was unbelievably rich in valuable metals. Pervenio Corporation had drawn it into a close orbit around Earth a few years back when they were selected to build an Ark for the coming Departure, though not without complications. Three centuries ago, a moon-sized Meteorite had nearly wiped all life off Earth, so people remained skeptical about keeping asteroids nearby no matter how lucrative they were.

Seemed foolish to me not to have brought it closer to a spaceport or land it on Luna. Undina wasn't going to miraculously change its orbit unless someone with a lot of credits wanted it to. But the United Sol Federation—USF—still made the rules when it came to protecting Earth, even if the corporations that really ran Sol didn't care for them. A few handshakes under the table with the Assembly, however, and Pervenio Corp bent the rules as always. At the expense of every Earther's sense of safety, Undina orbited closer to Earth than any asteroid mine before it. No more than two days outside Luna by modern ionic impulse drives.

For those reasons, and I'm sure a few more, my employers were eager to get Undina back to running at optimal conditions. That was where I came in. As a collector working for Pervenio, my duties consisted of cleanly settling their issues before they grew into something worse. The bounty on Yev Tavar was ten thousand credits—dead or alive. A nice haul for what appeared to be a routine "eliminate the instigator of a workers' strike" contract. I'd dealt with plenty in my time. Offworlders never seemed to be satisfied with their lot in life, especially those dwelling in the hollows of asteroids.

I crept up to an emergency hatch within the cramped tunnel that bridged together mining sectors C and D. The passage was so squat that my hair scraped across the craggy ceiling, and the musty aroma of air recyclers in need of repairs filled my nostrils. They clicked and whined like beasts in the darkness. I stopped in front of it, reached into my pocket, and removed my lucky charm: a small figurine of an old Ark Ship named the Barsamin. A coruscating line down the center indicated where it'd once been cracked in half before I fused it back together. I raised it to my lips before returning it to its proper place.

Then I knocked on the glass portion of the hatch. As I did, I slid my right hand down to my hip and drew my long-barreled, collector-issued F-3000 pulse-pistol from its holster. My baby.

"This is Aaron Duvell, minin' chief of sector C," I lied into the two-way intercom built into the airtight seal. I put on my best underprivileged offworlder twang.

"You can't enter," a raspy voice responded.

"We're standin' with you, didn't you hear?" I continued. "We got the security officers pinned down and need help gettin' rid of 'em. They still got their guns."

Another lie. A Pervenio security team and I had already locked down sector C and ensured that the strike didn't spread there. I'd been careful, however, to leak news that riots were occurring throughout Undina as miners chose to stand alongside Yev Tavar. There was no better way to appeal to the sense of narcissism inherent in anyone willing to start a near-futile rebellion, no matter how small it was.

"Wait here," the man on the other end said. A few minutes went by in silence before the hatch rose a few inches. The dissidents had destroyed the control console on my side so only they could operate it. A pale hand poked through the narrow opening by my feet. "Show us your ID."

I pulled open the flaps of my faded brown duster and withdrew the ID card of the sector C mining chief, Aaron Duvell. It hadn't taken much convincing to get him to agree to help turn in his comrades—just a few extra credits and a promise to end all the discord that threatened his livelihood. I placed the card in the rebel's open palm, and he immediately reeled it in.

Another few minutes passed, and then the hatch flew up into the ceiling. Two miners with pulse-rifles awaited me on the other side, but my gun was also raised. As soon as the opening was clear, I planted a bullet in the arm of one of them, causing him to drop his weapon. The other panicked and squeezed his weapon's trigger too long and too hard. The recoil from the rifle had the untrained man shooting at the ceiling, and I'd already bolted forward to arrive safely beside him. I smacked him in the side of the head with the butt of my pistol and watched him crumple to the rocky floor. Then I quickly turned and kicked the other miner in the head so that they were both unconscious.

There was no reason to kill any more workers than I had to. Those were the express orders of Director Sodervall at Pervenio. Laborers were cheap, but transporting new ones wasn't. That was why we didn't switch off their life support in the first place and end things in a hurry. That, plus the fact that we had no idea where the security team Yev Tavar had displaced was being held... if they were still alive.

"Sorry, boys," I whispered as I knelt and deconstructed both of their pulse-rifles.

When I was done, I pulled my spotter goggles down over my eyes and set them to thermal imaging. The confined, rocky tunnels in the bowels of Undina were dark, especially since I'd cut the main power to the sector beyond the emergency access I came through. All they had beyond that were a few small generators, which they would need to sustain their food supply. Breathing was all I'd allow them to do until this was over.

I delved in deeper, indistinct voices echoing down every branch in the cramped service corridors I passed by. I ignored them. My spotters picked up the heat signature of a miner approaching, carrying a light-torch. It didn't illuminate much beyond the few meters in front of his face, so I couldn't tell whether he was armed. I didn't intend to give him a chance to show me. I tucked myself into a small nook in the wall and ducked down so my duster, which matched the dark hues of the rock, covered most of me.

As he passed my hiding spot, I sprang out, wrapped my arm around his neck, and dragged him to the ground. I squeezed just hard enough that he couldn't cry out, but not so hard as to kill him. This, unfortunately, had me close enough to get a whiff of him. He smelled foul, like he hadn't showered in over a week. Somehow this Yev character had convinced all the miners in sector D to settle in for the long haul and do everything they could to conserve water.

After thirty years as a collector, it was my experience that most self-appointed leaders never attained that kind of clout. I never cared to ask how much Pervenio was paying these people to spend their lives in the mines, but what Yev was demanding must've been quite appealing if his followers stood so adamantly against the most powerful corporation in Sol.

"When I let go, I'm going to ask you a question," I whispered. With my other hand, I raised the barrel of my pistol until it was pressed snugly against his temple. "If you try to call out, I'll splatter your brains all over this rock, and not a soul will ever know. Clear?"

He gagged, but I felt him attempt to nod. I loosened my grip a bit and allowed him to gasp for air. Once he had his fill, I grabbed his jaw and spun his head around to face me. The young man's whole body quaked.

"Now," I said. "Where is Yev Tavar?"

The miner tried to speak, but only a few incoherent words came out. He was petrified. I'd seen the same expression he wore on countless faces before. It happened when simple, hard-working men were stirred into a cause they never had any intention of fighting for.

"Only one of you needs to be removed," I explained. "Take me to Yev, and I'll make sure you get his old position."

That got his attention. His eyes went wide, and his lips started to slow in their trembling at the thought of becoming the mining chief of sector D, as high a position as you could get on an asteroid mine like Undina without wearing a Pervenio badge on your chest.

"He's... he's holed up in the refectory," the man stammered. "They're counting supplies. P...please don't hurt me. He forced us to do this! We never had a choice!"

That excuse was another on a long list of things I'd dealt with too many times in my life. "There's always a choice," I growled.

I yanked him up by the collar of his dusty boiler suit and shoved his light-torch back into his hands. "Now take me," I ordered. I pushed him far enough ahead that I wouldn't have to smell him but could keep my gun aimed squarely at the center of his back. He glanced back nervously over his shoulder a few times to see it glinting from the shine of his light-torch.

We wound our way through the labyrinthine tunnels of the sector D service passages until we reached a tall ladder leading to the living quarters. I sent him up first and followed only once I was sure nobody was waiting with a gun. At the top, the ceiling was taller, and when we emerged, I could feel my body grow heavier. The artificial spin Pervenio Corp had provided the asteroid gave it simulated g conditions barely a fifth of Earth's. It was still enough to have my old legs feeling sore from climbing.

"It's right up here," the man said. He was getting calmer, but I could still sense an edge in his voice. I hoped it wouldn't cause him to try something stupid. I took no pleasure in killing those who didn't deserve it, but I'd been around for far too long to let remorse get in the way of catching my targets. His life rested securely in his own hands.

"Grant, is that you?" someone hollered from up ahead, through the dim outline of a tall entranceway.

I lunged forward and grabbed the arm of the miner I now assumed was Grant. I leaned in close to his ear, making sure to push the end of my pistol hard against the center of his back. "Stay calm and respond that it's you," I whispered.

He swallowed audibly. "It's me!" he shouted.

We were close enough to the refectory's entrance for me to recognize where the heat signatures of those inside were coming from. A few held light-torches, likely all pried off the hoods of mining crawlers. The two by the entrance were positioned in a way that told me they were carrying more of the guns they'd no doubt stolen from the ousted Pervenio security team.

Grant took a step forward, but I stopped him and ripped the light out of his hand. "Thank you, Grant," I said softly. "You've been smart today." He went to reply, but as soon as he did, I knocked him in the back of the head. He folded over onto my open hand, and I gently lowered him to the ground before pressing onward.

"Took you long enough, Grant," the same voice from earlier groused. "Still no word from sector C?"

I remained quiet, busy planning my route of attack as I got closer. When I reached the point right before their lights would reveal me, I fired a disarming shot at each of the miner guards' shoulders.

Screams filled the room. Voices in every direction shouted things like "It's one of them!" or "Shoot him!"

Anyone in the refectory with a gun unloaded blindly toward the dark tunnel I'd emerged from, but not before I was able to sprint out unseen and duck down behind an upturned table. They were making it too easy. I waited until they had to reload and was careful to remember which of the handful of heat signatures were shaking from firing pulse-rifles. They were incapacitated in short order when I leaped out of cover and flanked them.

I felt young again. Not many missions called for taking on a group of armed combatants these days. When I first started out as a collector, little rebellions broke out all the time, on all the many colonies popping up around the solar system. Credits rolled in faster than I could count, but the more the corporations sank their talons into the solar system, the less wild it got. Presently, most of my assignments consisted of hits on poor saps who thought they could steal from Pervenio and get away with it. It got tedious.

"Look, boys! We ask to negotiate, and they send in one of their killers!" a new speaker bellowed. It was the only one who didn't sound the least bit terrified, which I deduced meant it was their brash leader, Yev Tavar.

The headlights of a mining crawler flashed on, flooding me in a radiance so bright that I had to yank up my spotters. The vehicle consisted of an oblong operating cockpit sitting atop six spindly legs, like those of a spider. With those, it could easily clamber around the walls of the hollows blown open for mining where there was essentially no gravity, and use the blades set along its front to carve out minerals into the storage basin attached to its bottom. The vehicle's engine roared to life, and it charged at me.

I stood my ground. Bullets fired from the rifles of the other miners pinged off tables or whizzed by my ears. I aimed my pistol at the crawler's cockpit as long as I could, until I could see the face of the man within it. I squeezed the trigger right before I dove out of the way. The vehicle promptly slammed into the wall behind me, its legs still thrashing.

Now that I was back in darkness, I was able to escape the

sights of the remaining miners with guns. I hit one in the kneecap and two others in their collarbones. When the last one fell, the only sound that remained were the moans of the injured. The others had either fled or hid in the shadows, waiting for the fight to come to a conclusion.

I hurried over to the crawler and climbed on top. The control console in the cockpit flickered as its legs began to die out. A circular gash pierced the center of the glass, and Yev Tavar lay in the seat behind it. Blood leaked out of a wound in the center of his chest. Using the external controls, I popped open the glass lid, then ripped him out. He squealed in pain as he tumbled over the side of the vehicle.

"I'll applaud you for a solid fight," I panted as I hopped down and knelt over his body. "But you couldn't have thought this would work."

"Better..." He spit up a glob of blood. "Better to try. One day, you and all those Pervenio bastards will pay for how you treat us. All I wanted was a fair negotiation."

I tapped him on the forehead with the barrel of my gun. "You lost your rights to negotiate when you murdered the security team posted here," I said. I got tired of giving the same speech to every *righteous* dissident.

"Murdered?" He started laughing so hard that blood sprayed all over my coat. He raised his shaking right hand and pointed to a generous exit leading out of the refectory. "They're alive. Through there, tied up in the hangar."

"How kind of you. Maybe for that, I'll let you have a quick death."

"We'll... all have one now... because of you."

I watched his gaze sweep away from my face and down toward his left hand where a hand-terminal was concealed. It didn't take me long to realize what he meant. I shot him right between the eyes, but not before he was able to key a command.

The exterior hangar of sector D opened without first depressurizing.

It was a neat trick, hacking into the hangar controls and syncing them to both his own hand-terminal and the mobile generators they were relying on. One that would require at least some level of expertise. I know I should've seen the device in his hand, but clearly, the directors had missed something when they'd briefed me on him. No lifer in a mine should've been capable of something so complex.

A loud whistling tore through the refectory. My body was towed along with it, more forcefully with each passing second. I grabbed hold of one of the mining crawler's heavy legs before my own were thrust into the air. With my other hand, I clutched Yev's arm. The squeals of the miners he'd decided to take down with him echoed as they too were yanked into the air and through the opening.

Tables, chairs, light fixtures torn from the walls; they all flew by me. Even the substantially sized mining crawler screeched across the steel floor. I'd have followed everything else through the refectory's exit and across the hangar into the vacuum of space if the crawler hadn't rotated so far that its long side wasn't able to squeeze through.

I found myself pinned tightly against the vehicle by a pressure so violent, it felt as if my rib cage was going to cave in. From the mess hall, a knife zoomed toward me. I'd have closed my eyes if I could, but the blade glanced off the Ark figurine in my pocket and twirled out into the hanger.

After that, I watched a few bodies, including Grant's, be sucked out through the space above the jammed crawler, but somehow I managed to hold on to Yev without passing out. My hand slipped down his arm until I was able to locate the hand-terminal within his clenched grip. I snatched it before releasing him to the great vacuum.

I couldn't pull my arm back in front of me to see, so I started blindly keying at the screen of the device. It didn't matter what I pressed. If I didn't do something fast, there would be no oxygen left for me anyway. A roar of agony gathered in the bottom of my throat from having my body tugged on as if I were a children's doll being fought over by two jealous brothers.

When it was almost too much to bear, I must've stroked the correct key because the deafening howl of air being sucked out into space suddenly quieted. The mining crawler plummeted, and me with it until I sat against its fractured chassis, wheezing. My limbs were so sore that I could barely feel them, let alone move them. My Ark figurine lay half out of my pocket. Since I was too weak to grab and lift it, I tipped my body over and kissed it a few times.

"Can't get rid of me that easy," I wheezed. I kissed it one last time, then nudged it back to safety. My daughter always said it was lucky, and I hadn't let it out of my sight since the last time I saw her.

From halfway on the floor, I had to use my shoulder and the hauler to slide my spotters down over my eyes. I searched for the heat signatures of anyone else who'd somehow survived. I couldn't find a single one.

I imagine the miners of sector D would've spaced Yev right at the beginning of the strike if they'd known what he was going to do just to hit Pervenio Corp in the wallet. As if any single man could affect that.

Offworlders... the bastards never learn.

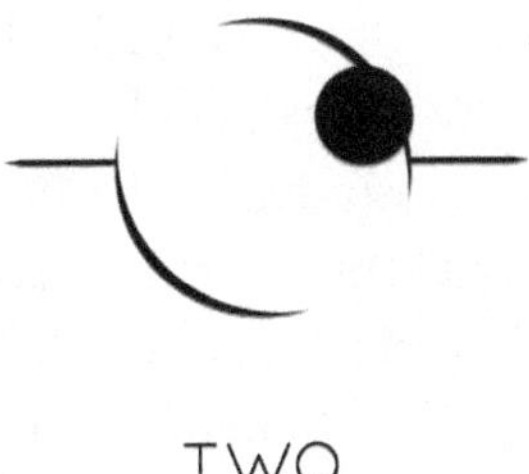

TWO

FOR THE FIRST time in a long time, I was on vacation. Well, forced vacation to be more precise. At least that was what Director Sodervall called it. After cleaning up the mess on 92-Undina, that was to be my punishment for what happened. He demanded I take some time off to "relax under the pleasant g conditions of our beloved homeworld." Like I was some sort of old man.

Sure, what happened on Undina could've been avoided, but it had nothing to do with my age. No one can predict the shit that happens on a job. If Pervenio had provided better intel that mentioned Yev used to be a programmer on Mars for Venta Co, then maybe I would've been more cautious with him. Still, there was no way to ignore a death toll of nearly fifty—including the ten security officers that Yev Tavar was holding captive—due to the hangar opening. Not to mention that an entire sector of the Undina Mine had been rendered in need of heavy repairs.

Thirty years of loyal service kept me from having the ten thousand credits I was owed rescinded as a result, but it wasn't enough to change Sodervall's mind about me needing a break, no matter how ready I was to get back to it.

"Take a week or two to get your muscles right," he'd said through my hand-terminal. "We'll send you to New London. It'll be M-Day when you get down, and there'll be plenty to drink."

He knew me too well. I wasn't the kind of man to say no to a drink. I fought him as much as I could to keep up appearances, but in the end, it was an order, and I had no other means of getting assignments without directors backing me. So I swallowed my pride and hopped onto a shuttle bound for the capital of human civilization: New London, Earth. At the very least, I had a shiny new pile of credits to spend, which would make the punishment of being stuck in New London on M-Day more bearable.

Shortly after arriving, I settled into a suite at the most luxurious Pervenio-owned hotel in the city. I thought about catching up on some much-needed sleep, but the whole situation had me too irked to lie still. Instead, I decided to brave the unruly crowd of Earthers flooding the city for M-Day and find a place to get a glass of whiskey where I wouldn't be sweating by the time I ordered it.

It was a tall order. The streets were mobbed. M-Day, the day that commemorated the exact moment, three centuries ago, when the fiery Meteorite crashed into Earth, was the most important holiday in all of Sol, especially for anyone who grew up on Earth like me. Hell, it was the only holiday for us, and people would come from all over the solar system to fill its largest city to celebrate the fact that, even though Armageddon had come, humanity endured.

Men would dress in their finest tunics and the women in sparkling gowns that matched the vibrant hues of their made-up faces. Most of them probably couldn't afford their extravagant getups, but on M-Day, every Earther in New London got to pretend they were a part of the wealthy elite. They'd get drunk, they'd get merry, and they'd get a little too brazen for my taste.

I'd worked security in New London when I was younger, so I knew what it was like to flash a badge at a crowd of drunken Earthers who felt like they were invincible. Those were a few of the innumerable reasons that M-Day was my least favorite time to be on Earth.

The crowds were the worst part, though. It took me a few blocks of scouring the upper-level walkways of New London to spot a bar that looked like it had enough room for me to squeeze in. Even then, I had to step over the legs of a passed-out drunkard and push through a row of market stands to get to the door. I shook my head as I passed the vendors selling artifacts from pre-Meteorite Earth; everything from broken tech to utensils. Buying garbage like that was another thing people did on M-Day, though I'd wager at least ninety percent of it was counterfeit.

The bar was a tiny place called the Molten Crater. It was tucked into an alley across from the maglev rail station cutting through the center of the city. Only half the sign remained lit. For the life of me, I couldn't recall whether I'd been there before.

It may have been less crowded than any other bar, but hundreds of Earthers were packed inside. Booths running down the long wall were overflowing, the fabric of the seats stained and shredded from people standing on them, lying on them, or worse. The profits from the holiday were always worth the inevitable repairs. Every so often, the entire crowd glanced up from their drinks at the bright view-screens bolted to tin-paneled walls, eagerly waiting for the broadcast of the M-Day address to commence. By my count, it wouldn't start for another hour or so.

I weaved my way across the room, which reeked of spilled beer mixed with whatever else happened to be on the filthy, faux-wood floors. Everyone who noticed me stopped what they were doing to sneak a look.

My loose duster was purposely pulled open just enough to reveal the pulse-pistol dangling from my belt and a sliver of the Pervenio emblem printed near the shoulder of my shirt. I always chose to wear the gun on Earth as long as it was permitted. No Earther would bother me if they thought I was on duty, even though I wasn't. Half of them were probably nervous I was going to put a bullet in the backs of their heads over something foolish they'd done years before. People have a way of thinking their mistakes are far more significant than they really are.

Once I finally made it to the bar, everyone quickly returned to their conversations, as if nothing more than a ghost had passed by and given them a shiver. Every stool was taken, so I leaned on the counter in a narrow space beside a plump Earther who was seeing how big a glass he could put down in one gulp to impress a group of finely dressed strangers. It wasn't sitting, but it at least provided my weary legs with a much-needed break.

The bartender was a young Earther woman, pretty and with her hair dyed purple. I ordered a whiskey and slapped down my Pervenio ID, linked directly to my personal credit account.

When she returned with my drink, she swiped my ID through a scanner and perused the information that popped up for a moment. She grinned and shook her head.

"First one's free today, Mr. Graves," she said before moving on to the next customer.

I wasn't going to complain. After spending a nice chunk of my reward for killing Yev Tavar on my hotel room, I wanted to make sure the credits I had would last me my whole unwanted vacation. They could be tough to come by, and even as a collector, I was prone to living job-to-job.

I lifted the cold, perspiring glass to my lips and took a swig. It was a foul bit of swill, no doubt as artificial as it was cheap. They always served the inexpensive stuff for the M-Day crowds. I reluctantly forced a mouthful down my gullet and placed it back on the bar, trying to ignore the pale reflection of myself that stared back at me from the glass. Sometimes I forgot how gray my hair was getting, or how there seemed to be a new wrinkle forming somewhere on my face every morning.

While I stood there, wondering where the years had gone, the space to my right was vacated and a slender man promptly squeezed in to order a water. I glanced over. There was no doubt he was an offworlder and not some recent immigrant to a Mars colony where getting some sun through the shielded domes could be even easier than it was on always-cloudy Earth. No, the man had the look of a Ringer born on Saturn's moon, Titan.

Like all Ringers, he was excessively tall and lean with knobby joints that appeared more delicate than they really were and a long face atop his lengthy neck, which was as white and veiny as a slate of polished marble. What really gave him away, however, was the sanitary mask pulled tight across his mouth and nose to go along with the rubbery gloves yanked halfway up his forearms. I'd been to Titan, so I knew its people wore all that protection to keep from getting sick around Earthers. For that reason, among others, it was exceedingly rare to see one on Earth's surface. None of his precautions seemed to be working very well either. The skin around his inflamed eyes was dark and saggy. Each grating breath he took sounded like a struggle.

Not wanting to get caught staring, I turned my attention to the view-screens behind the bar.

An advertisement interrupted the local newscast.

"Help preserve the human race!" a rousing male voice said as a recording panned across a post-apocalyptic scene. A burning tree sat on a hill overlooking a ruined skyline—a glorified reproduction of Earth after the Meteorite hit back in 2034. "Colonies throughout the solar system await your arrival, and Pervenio Corporation is proud to aid you in your transition. Help us add our domes to the crimson surface of Mars, or help with the harvesting of vital gases on the Ring. The fight to ensure our survival rests in your hands!"

The ad ended with the emblem of Pervenio Corp—a crimson helix wrapped around a crooked branch—projected over a crowd of people who were waving off a massive ship headed up into space. A small patch of text—which most people missed—popped up at the bottom of the screen, indicating all that couldn't be promised when someone decided to move offworld—most significantly, their safety or legitimate work.

For everyone who grew up on Earth, it was one of countless century-old ads put out by the USF or any of its sanctioned corporations encouraging the diffusion of the human race. After the Meteorite drowned half the planet and nearly wiped out humanity, that was the creed that drove the survivors. The idea was not to risk extinction by staying secluded on Earth.

I'd grown weary of the message by the time I could speak. To me, it was like listening to a song I'd heard so many times, that when it came on, I found myself mouthing the words without really enjoying or realizing it.

For the offworlder I'd assumed to be a Ringer beside me, the ad evoked a far different reaction. Even under his mask, I could see the twitch of resentment pulling at his lips, and the rage filling his bloodshot eyes.

It was easy to understand why. In A.D. 2031, when the colossal meteor somehow had its course altered and was discovered to be hurtling toward Earth, a small group of scientists under the leadership of a visionary named Darien Trass turned their attention to space instead of wasting time attempting to restore its old trajectory. Trass built an Ark for three thousand people and sent it to Titan, the orange moon of Saturn. He decided back then that it was the most promising celestial body in all of Sol for human expansion due to the resources offered by it as well as the ringed gas giant it orbited. The Ring, as it became called, had everything but breathable air and warmth.

Over time, the settlers of the Ring forgot about their old world, our world, as they focused on constructing their new one. Their initial ship grew into bigger and more advanced settlements across the surface of Titan. They began adapting to the low gravity and their sunless skies, growing taller, slimmer, and paler with each ensuing generation. They even grew accustomed to the cold. On the occasions a job took me way out there, I found the temperatures in the Ringer-inhabited lower wards of their colony blocks to be unbearable. They kept them at freezing, and for them, that was like summer.

It was sometime when I was still a child that our two peoples reconnected. Those who'd stayed behind on Earth as doomsday approached, and those who'd fled for colder pastures. At first, we tried to accept each other with open arms, but as more and more immigrants from Earth flooded into the Ring, they realized it wasn't only the Ringers' appearance that had changed. Being in sterile environments for so many years had crippled their immune systems, and we Earthers brought with us all the bacteria and diseases that no longer affected us.

Sickness on Titan prevailed. Entire colonies were crippled, allowing the physically stronger people from Earth to take control of every level of the Ringer infrastructure with ease. What had been a grand reunion quickly went sour. Earthers grew to resent the Ringers for Earth, and the Ringers never took too kindly to being assimilated into our culture or having their loved ones crammed into quarantine zones due to rampant illness.

Maybe it was the whiskey, but as I thought about how strange it really was to be seated next to a Ringer in the heart of New London, I found myself curious.

"Don't see many of your type out here for M-Day, offworlder," I said.

I didn't want to flat-out call him a Ringer yet, even though I was confident my assumption was correct. I knew better than most that people could be touchy about where they were from. It was possible he could merely be an exceptionally tall man from a proud Earther family unfortunate enough to have spent most of the last few generations buried deep within an asteroid mining colony. Could be that he was merely getting over an everyday cold and was bitter toward immigrants who could afford to go to a planet-sized moon instead of a floating rock on the edge of space.

He shot me a sidelong glare but didn't respond. Instead, he reached into his pocket and withdrew a g-stim with the markings of Venta Co on it, Pervenio's biggest rival. The injection contained a special concoction of chemicals and steroids that helped offworlders deal with Earth's gravity and not pass out from exhaustion. It was an older line, likely only purchasable on the black. The man stabbed it into his neck beneath his mask. His eyelids flickered as the chems coursed through his veins, then he stowed the pack. He took a sip of his water and looked back up toward the newscast.

A female correspondent came on screen, standing in front of a raucous mob somewhere else on Earth, discussing the M-Day festivities there. When she was done, another correspondent came on talking about somewhere else, and then another. It went on like that for minutes; long enough for me to need another drink.

The screen then cut to reporters stationed in colonies throughout the solar system. First, it showed the interior of one of the massive dome colonies on Mars, and then a view of the central atrium within a shiny colony block on Titan. There, the celebration didn't seem as jovial as everywhere else. The correspondent was jostled around while behind her, a throng made up of mostly long, pale faces hollered. A few punches were exchanged between a Ringer and a pink-skinned Earther before a gunshot rang out. The feed quickly cut away to the large galley of a construction ship orbiting the newly founded Europa Colony where the crowd appeared cheerful again.

When Titan went offscreen, the offworlder next to me grunted in a way that, through his mask, sounded like it may have been a chuckle.

"That's where I'm from, Earther," he said, confirming my thoughts. His voice was muffled slightly by his mask, but it sounded hoarse and weak, like an elderly man.

"So what brings you to our darling homeworld?" I asked. Inquisitiveness was a part of my job. Even on vacation, I had a difficult time turning it off.

"I thought I'd come visit an old friend before I die," the Ringer responded before he started to cough.

It was obvious he wasn't healthy, but I hadn't realized how bad until then. I could hear the built-up phlegm in his throat. Whether that was due to his offworlder lungs straining to deal with Earth's strong gravity or his apparent sickness was anybody's guess. At first glance, he didn't look like he could possibly be much older than forty. It could be hard to tell with Ringers, though. The low-g conditions on Titan gave them shallower wrinkles.

I took a tiny swig of my whiskey to cover for my immediate lack of a response. After swallowing it, I said, "I see. You're going to need a harder drink then, Ringer. Next one is on me."

He stared daggers in my direction, his ashen cheeks flushing with as much color as they possibly could. The glass he held rattled against the counter as his hand shook. "Titanborn," he growled before turning his attention back to the screen.

I wasn't sure what I'd said wrong, but again, I'd met enough people from places beyond Earth's gravity well to know that they were easily offended when it came to their titles. As I shrugged off his reaction, the newscast transitioned to a live feed located just outside New London. Everyone inside the Molten Crater hollered, "It's starting!" as they scrambled to get outside.

The M-Day anniversary address was about to begin, earlier than anticipated. I'd seen them more times than I cared to remember or admit. I thought about staying inside and watching on the small screen since I'd only just gotten my drink but quickly remembered that this year's Departure Ark had been designed by Pervenio Corp.

It seemed like ages ago they were selected for the second time in my life. Every fifth M-Day, the company that proposes the most promising design for a Generational Ark was commissioned by the USF Assembly to construct that vessel. Over the course of that period, anyone who was a registered citizen of Earth could be selected by a lottery to embark on a journey across the stars to spread humankind. For many Earthers, there was no greater honor than being chosen to propagate humanity. I was just curious to see the fruits of those poor miners on Undina who'd harvested so much of what was used to construct the grand vessel.

"Next time, then," I said to the Ringer as I tipped my glass in his direction. "Cheers."

I drained the rest of my whiskey before following the herd out. It burned and itched all the way down, but the relief it offered against the angry voices of the dead Undina miners reverberating in my head made it totally worth it.

When I reached the Molten Crater's exit, I glanced back over my shoulder. Everyone who wasn't passed out appeared to have cleared out. Even the bartender. Everyone except for the Ringer. He'd taken a seat on one of the vacated stools at the bar and remained alone, sipping on his glass of water, bloodshot eyes glued to the newscast.

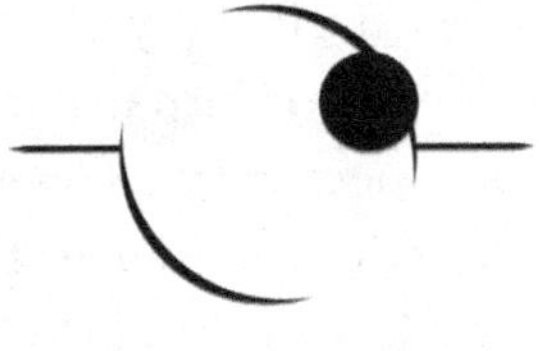

THREE

ONCE OUTSIDE, I didn't bother shoving my way to the edge of the raised walkway to get the best view. There was no way to miss the Departure if you were within the city, since New London was essentially converted into an enormous exhibition of the event. The countless ads strung along the maglev rail line and projected onto the glassy façades of buildings switched over to the USF feed live from the landing pad outside New London Spaceport. It was three kilometers or so away along the Euro-String, and only the richest citizens of Earth could get a spot there on M-Day.

None of the city's structures were exceptionally tall—Earthers had transitioned away from sprawling cities with skyscrapers to elongated cities on strings centuries ago for safety reasons—but they were tall enough for me to see fine over the bobbing heads of the augmenting crowd. As a trio of inter-atmospheric ships zipped noisily overhead, the myriad screens zoomed in on fifty men and women wearing dark-green tunics with badges on their chests consisting of eight small white dots along a line with a larger one in the center—The symbol of the United Sol Federation. Those fifty were the lauded members of the USF Assembly. The crowd broke into a frenzy of cheers as their supposed leaders came into view.

I couldn't help but roll my eyes at the sight of them. I recognized a few of their faces but never bothered to learn most of their names. I wondered if all the years traveling around Sol playing Mr. Fix-It for Pervenio Corp just made me cynical. The assembly may have been elected by registered citizens of Earth, but anyone with a real education knew they didn't have any legitimate power. Pervenio Corp, Red Wing Company, Venta Co—those were only a few of the more powerful space-faring corporations that directed the future of humankind.

I'd heard a retired, probably drunk, security officer explain it best during a rant while I was dragging a bounty into a holding cell many years ago. "If you compare us humans to a hand," he said, "then the USF is the palm. It holds everything together, but it doesn't move. The corporations are the fingers that plucked us out of a second Dark Age before reaching into the blackness of space as a personal 'screw you' to every god that's ever been prayed to. The assembly, Collector, is little more than the visible face of the corporatocracy, providing the illusion of control to billions of people who have none... folks like us."

In my opinion, truer words have never been spoken, and I've held them close to my heart ever since. I wish I could remember the fellow's name.

Once the noise started to die down a little, Talo Gavaren, the Speaker of the Assembly and the only name I actually did know, stepped forward to a podium and started doing what he did best. The haggard old man's buoyant voice filled the chasms of the packed city.

"People of Sol!" he began. "Today we must remember our ancestors. We must remember the billions of souls who lost their lives after the events of September 3, 2034. Three centuries ago, on that day, humanity was nearly wiped from the universe. But today, my people, I am here to tell you that we have never been stronger! Our continued existence, never more secure!"

The crowd went into a full-on frenzy. Shoulders bumped into me from every direction. Spray from raised drinks fell upon my head as if it were raining.

"We have spread out into Sol. From Earth to Saturn, and everywhere in between," Talo continued. "Right now, people on Luna are watching! People on Mars and Europa and Titan are watching! And now, for the tenth time since the founding of this federation, we will look even farther. My people, it is my great honor to introduce the man whose latest vision will allow us to reach beyond our lone star. One thousand of your brothers and sisters have been chosen to join that vision. They will bear the honor of carrying the flame of humanity, for centuries to come, to worlds unknown. My people, I give you Luxarn Pervenio!"

It was impossible to tell exactly what anybody was cheering for anymore. The clamor had been constant for the entire speech. Talo stepped down, and Luxarn Pervenio replaced him, surrounded on either side by guards in black-and-red armor with the logo of Pervenio Corp printed above their chests.

Luxarn was the wealthiest man in all of Sol. His corporation had been around since before the old governments of Earth dissolved into the USF. He had a stake in almost every major colonial effort in the solar system except Europa and had the largest slice of the Ring—which was undoubtedly the most profitable. Even though he was technically my employer, I'd never actually met him in person. Few had. My dealings went exclusively through the directors placed in charge of every city or colony throughout Sol, which Pervenio Corp administered. Sodervall most of all.

"Sol!" Luxarn pronounced, spreading out his arms triumphantly and laughing as though all the applause was meant for him. It may well have been. It was impossible to fathom how many in the raucous crowd worked under the umbrella of Pervenio Corp. Many probably didn't even realize it.

"I cannot express what an honor it was to have our esteemed assembly select our design for this year's Departure," he said. "Since that momentous occasion five years ago, we have worked tirelessly to construct the most advanced Ark in the history of humanity."

Luxarn rattled on about the many great feats of engineering his new creation contained. I missed all of it after the part where he said that once it reached max velocity, it would theoretically be able to reach the nearest star, Alpha Centauri, in approximately 128 years, even though it was headed to the Tau Ceti system farther away to avoid having the same destination of the last Ark, built by Venta Co. That may have sounded like an eternity to some, but I'd seen all the Departures in my lifetime. It was the lowest estimation I'd heard about an Ark's travel time by nearly fifty years.

It almost made the venture sound appealing enough for me to have wanted my name selected and my body frozen or however they sent the lucky winners, but only a small part. I wasn't sure how long I could go on without having the thrill of a new target to hunt down. Already being on vacation for a few days, including the shuttle ride from Undina to Earth, had my skin crawling. And I couldn't leave my daughter behind while I crossed the stars, wherever the hell she was in the solar system.

It'd been over a year since we'd even exchanged a message over Solnet—five or six since I'd seen her in person. We never saw eye-to-eye, but ever since her dying mother placed her at my feet and told me she was mine, Aria was the only true family I had, same as I was for her. After all, I hadn't spoken to my own clan-family since I'd become a collector as a still-young man. I always imagined one day I might sit down for a drink in some backwater bar, and by some chance, notice her across the room, all grown up.

"I give you *Hermes!*" Luxarn Pervenio finally announced, swiftly regaining my attention. His hands extended toward the sky.

The deafening howl of engines grew so loud that it would have drowned out the crowd if they hadn't already been rendered silent by his words. Merchants, drunks, beggars, and security officers alike stared up at the murky sky in anticipation. Soon after, the enormous ship sailed high above, right at the edge of the visible atmosphere, and cast a huge shadow over the entire city. It was the largest ship I'd ever seen, double the size of the one my lucky figurine was designed after, and that was saying something. The details were impossible to make out from so far away, but the thing was easily a kilometer in length and had an equally long, blue-hued stream of distortion trailing behind its twin impulse drives.

Awestruck applause started to build while the *Hermes* soared by. Without realizing it at first, even I began clapping softly. The ship weaved in and out of the layered clouds, too large to be obscured by any single one. If life existed on whatever planet it wound up on, I couldn't imagine what those creatures might think when that metallic mammoth pierced the sky. And even if the ship never actually reached another star, there was no denying it was one hell of a funereal send-off.

I was caught off guard when something caused the walkway to tremor so violently that I was thrown off my feet. Hot flames and shrapnel spit up into the air from the direction of the maglev rail station across the way. A portion of the blast tore through a USF security hover-car unlucky enough to have been flying overhead. Its engines sputtered, causing it to spin out of control and take a crash course straight toward the Molten Crater.

The crowd scattered, fleeing in every direction. The whiskey I'd guzzled had me feeling loose, but I was quickly able to gather my bearings. I jumped to my feet and fell in with them, but as I did, out of the corner of my eye, I noticed a young girl standing directly in the path of the hover-car. Terror froze her, and the sight caused me to stop as well. Her hair was curly and as red as the surface of Mars, like my daughter Aria's had been at her age. I glanced up at the glowing vehicle and then back at her before I cursed under my breath.

"Move, move, move!" I barked, whipping out my gun to get the panicked citizens to diverge faster as I took off toward the girl. I pushed more than a few of them out of my way. The hover-car grazed the top of my loose coat as I dove, pulling her down just in time.

The vehicle slammed into the Molten Crater's entrance. A dazzling display of fire and sparks erupted as its engine over-loaded immediately after, the force from the blast knocking me forward. My Ark figurine flew out of my pocket. I reached out for it just before my head slammed into the walkway. Everything went blurry, and for a moment, my mind took me back to the last time I was on Earth for a Departure...

Aria and I were in a Euro-String slum a short way east of New London. She was only eight years old, and since she was born on Mars, we were visiting Earth for the first time in her then-short life. More than anything, she wanted to see a Departure in person, and we had prime seats for the show. If we looked carefully enough, we could make out New London's low skyline of shimmering buildings through wisps of black smoke puffing up from a nearby industrial district on its outskirts.

A gunshot rang out. Aria stood, barely a meter tall, with my pulse-pistol clutched in her tiny hands. She gawked at the smoking barrel, and then across the dilapidated roof of the structure upon which we stood. An empty bottle rested on the parapet.

"You're getting close, girl," I said to her. I leaned down and gently repositioned her. "Remember to keep your eye down the sight. You may be small, but this gun is a work of art. There's barely any kickback."

Aria nodded. She pursed her lips, closed one eye, and took aim again. I held her elbow as she pulled the trigger, and this time, one of the bottles burst into a million pieces.

"Got it!" she cheered. She handed me the pistol and ran over as quickly as her tiny legs could carry her to see her work firsthand. She hopped up and down in triumph.

"Well done. Just like your old man!" I exclaimed, wearing a smile so wide they could've seen it from Saturn. "All right, let's try another."

I pulled a mostly empty bottle of whiskey out of my coat and chugged what was left. She giggled when I burped. Then I staggered over and set it down where the last one had been.

She ran over to me and frowned. "Can we go down there yet?" she whined. She pointed to the streets below where M-Day festivities raged. Earthers in colorful outfits crowded around the local Euro-String rail station, drinking and dancing as they watched the news-casts on large view-screens posted at every street corner.

She had the right idea. I wanted to go down too, but I was trying to remain inconspicuous. I'd been hired to take down a narcotics dealer stealing clients from local Pervenio medical facilities. He was on his way to a drop site in the apartment complex beneath my feet, attempting to use M-Day as cover. I was waiting for him. On any other day, gunshots on the roof might've chased him away, but it was so noisy on the streets that nobody would ever hear.

So, there I was, showing Aria her first M-Day Departure and getting a relatively simple assignment done so that I could make a few spare credits to spend on celebrations after she was asleep. Killing two birds and whatnot… I couldn't tell her that, of course.

I placed my hand on her shoulder and knelt to look her in her big, beautiful green eyes. "Doesn't look too bad, does it?" I said. "But I told you, it's too dangerous. You wouldn't want to lose me in that mob, now, would you?"

She shook her head vehemently.

"Exactly! Don't worry, we'll make a collector out of you yet. Then you can go wherever you want, whenever you want."

"With you, right?"

"Of course." I patted her before holding out the pistol for her to take. "Now let's see what you've got."

She reached out to grab it, but as she did, the crowd below erupted. A distant buffered sound quickly rose over the din. I peered through the lingering smog to see the outline of the Barsamin Ark Ship cruising high over New London. Aria dropped the gun when she noticed it. Her eyes looked like they were going to pop out of her head.

The Departure had begun. I'd already seen plenty of them by that point in my life, so it didn't take me much by surprise. Still, they were always a sight to behold. The tremendous Ark was designed by a company that was soon after absorbed by Pervenio. It was bulbous like a lozenge and had two bright engines, which from that angle looked like a pair of eyes wreathed in flame.

"Is that it?" she mouthed. She couldn't stop staring. "It's... so big."

"It has to be to fit one thousand lucky Earthers. The last one Venta Co built was even bigger, if you can imagine that."

"Where are they all going?"

"Who the hell knows? Probably one of the stars you saw on the way over from Mars. All I know is I'll be long gone before they get there." Aria broke from her trance for a moment and shot me an anxious look. "Not for many, many years," I reassured her.

She exhaled before looking back toward the Ark ship. I went to stand by her side, but as soon as I got there, my hand-terminal beeped. I'd tapped into some of the street-level surveillance feeds earlier on in the day to make my job easier, and as I glanced down at it, I saw that facial recognition had caught a glimpse of the man I was after.

"Aria," I said. "I have to take care of something. Do your dad a favor and wait up here until I get back."

"You're not going to watch?"

"I'll be back before it's over. Just going to pick us up something to eat and maybe a souvenir. You don't move from here, okay?"

She nodded, unable to avert her gaze from the ship.

"Good girl," I said. I rustled my hand through her soft auburn hair. "Remember, stay put. This is the best view."

I shoved my pistol in my holster and made my way over to the roof's emergency access hatch so I could quickly descend through the building. There was work to be done.

My eyelids sprang open. My ears rang from the hovercar exploding, but as I came to my senses, I felt something squirming against my chest. I peeled my aching body away and found the little girl I'd seen standing in front of the Molten Crater staring up at me. She breathed as heavily as I was, but at least she was alive. Maybe for a younger version of myself, it wouldn't have been so close.

Her lips trembled too much for her to speak, but she didn't have to. All I had to do was gaze into her bulging eyes as we lay there to know she was grateful. Apparently, her parents either didn't share the sentiment or didn't see what had happened because when they arrived, they ripped me off her. I handed her over without a fuss, but we didn't break eye contact until they ran her around a corner.

She really did look just like Aria had at her age.

I didn't think about that day on the rooftop much, but it was one of the first on the lengthy list of mistakes that drove her away from me. I'd left Aria alone there for hours until it was dark. She'd listened and stayed put, but her cheeks were wet with tears when I returned after a job well done and a few rounds at the nearest watering hole.

Luckily, I'd remembered my promise at the last second and purchased the same Barsamin Ark figurine I now carried with me from a street vendor downstairs right before returning to her. The moment she caught glimpse of the toy and all its minuscule details, her sadness washed away. She wore it on a necklace everywhere. Back then, she was easy.

I shook my head and buried the memory in the depths of my mind, then snatched the figurine off the ground before anyone trampled it.

I turned my attention to the spires of black smoke swirling up from the New London maglev rail station. There was nothing like the potential for work to keep me focused on the present. Whatever happened had the city in an uproar. Red lights flashed from countless security hover-cars and drones weaving between buildings. Sirens wailed so loudly they drowned out the screams of the terrified populace.

"So much for vacation," I said, sighing. I picked my pistol up and headed in that direction.

FOUR

WHEN I REACHED the site of the explosion, a large ring of crackling flame still bordered the blast's origin point. Fire repellent poured from security hover-cars, but a lot of work remained to be done.

The blast itself tore the place to hell. A portion of the platform was nothing but cinder. Luckily, the radius was small. Probably an improvised device. Someone didn't know what they were doing. Or maybe they did.

The corpses unfortunate enough to be in the center of the fiery circle were charred black, their clothing still smoking. More citizens right outside grasped at severed limbs and terrible wounds, screaming for help. That was the worst of the physical damage from the bomb, but it'd also caused the frightened populace of New London to descend into chaos.

As I closed in on the scene, I scanned the sullen faces of the USF soldiers attempting to establish order. They'd formed tight lines around the perimeter, and used shields and shock-batons to hold back swells of drunks and hobos. They struggled mightily, though that wasn't a surprise. The USF military rarely strayed from the larger cities on Earth, leaving the policing throughout Sol to private security forces. Nowhere on the planet was supposed to be more secure than New London.

"You can't be here!" a USF security commander shouted at me as I approached. I flashed my Pervenio badge, and the man instantly fell into a salute. "Sorry, sir," he said sheepishly.

"What happened?" I asked. It wasn't my job to help with security, but collectors from influential corporations like mine pretty much had free rein when it came to ordering around USF security teams. For good reason too. By the looks of it, most of them had never seen a dead body, let alone managed a minor riot. I even noticed one vomiting into an exhaust vent in an alley after trying to help someone with a missing arm.

I, on the other hand, was used to carnage. Thirty years as a collector. Thirty damn years being dispatched to solve problems everywhere imaginable. From the slum regions of Earth, where it wasn't uncommon to find bodies out on the streets half buried beneath snow, to the farthest colonies sprouting up in Sol. Those always had a healthy amount of violence. To me, cleaning up messes had become as easy as hauling cargo. It's not like I found joy in doing it, but I didn't get the sick feeling in my stomach the average person should get either. Sometimes I wondered if a part of my human programming was faulty, allowing me to have grown so numb to bloodshed. Good thing for me, I was never away from the job for long enough to dwell on it.

"Not sure," the commander answered. "I've never seen anything like this in New London." He was as nervous as his men. While he talked, he couldn't keep his gaze from wandering toward the rapidly swelling mob.

"I've seen much worse," I said. The affairs on Undina came to mind. I decided to change the subject before the thought wound up upsetting me. "We're lucky; barely a soul uses the rail station during M-Day. Thirty meters right or left, and the bomb, no matter how small, could've killed thousands." At first glance, I didn't count more than a few dozen who were unquestionably deceased.

"Maybe so, but with all these civilians hollering, we'll have a mess here for days." The commander turned toward a line of men and yelled, "Keep them back!"

Just then, a frantic citizen busted through the line, throwing one of the security officers to the ground and ripping the shock-baton from his hand. He screamed, "That's my wife!" over and over as he crossed the crime scene. Another officer attempted to restrain him but only got himself smashed across the face by the baton.

I groaned. These men were way out of their element. Slipping my pistol out of its holster, I took aim and shot the citizen right through the forearm. It was a clean shot. Shouldn't have caused any lasting damage. Even if it did, he'd get himself some nice meds and likely want to thank me for it later.

The weapon flew out of his hand as the man crumpled to the ground.

"Sir!" the startled commander yelled to me.

Ignoring him, I raised my gun and fired into the air as I approached the mob. Now I had their full attention. Even the security officers gawked at me.

"Next one that breaks the line will find themselves rotting in a cell on Pervenio station!" I barked.

The commander grabbed my arm and yanked me around. "Sir, you can't do that!" he protested, more fearful than stern. "This isn't your jurisdiction."

I lowered my weapon and leaned in so close to him our noses almost touched. "Take control of your city, Commander, or we'll have to. Remember that it was Mr. Pervenio's Departure that's been spoiled by all this." Truthfully, I couldn't have cared less about the Departure, but I knew a bomber loose in New

London meant potential work. I'd planned to take advantage of any opportunity to avoid my appointed vacation.

"Yes... yes, sir," he stammered.

I patted him on the shoulder and forced a grin. Then I swept my gaze across the gruesome scene once more to get a clearer picture. There really were few better places for the attack to have happened as far as avoiding casualties went. The New London Pervenio Hospital was directly across the street with lower-level access, even if it was through a sea of unruly New Londoners.

"Focus all your trucks and hover-cars on clearing a path to the hospital," I ordered. "Attend the injured. It isn't your job to figure out who's behind this; leave that to me."

The commander saluted again, then got to work. My stunt kept the mob at bay for the moment, but it wouldn't last long if he and his men didn't show some mettle. I could only hope I'd inspired them enough to know how far a little muscle could go in such situations.

Alone again, I pulled out my hand-terminal. The screen flickered. Damn explosion residue must have been interfering. The device seemed to be having a hard time locating a signal. I distanced myself and leaned against the side of a ground transport vehicle once I found a signal. USF medics struggled to lift a woman with a bloody stump left for a leg into it. She writhed and shrieked in agony. The terminal service dropped again, and the woman was a pain to watch, so I gave them a hand. After she was loaded up, I walked a little farther from the blast until the screen of the device returned to normal.

I scrolled through my contacts and selected Director Sodervall. My call was relayed to a satellite orbiting Earth and then started bouncing amongst the many laser communication relays spread throughout the solar system that made up the network otherwise known as Solnet. I won't pretend to understand how it all works, something about data encoded on light, but since he was all the way in the Ring, it took a few frustrating minutes to get through. The grainy image of his creased face popped up on the screen.

"Sir, can you hear me?" I asked. The response was incomprehensible, his voice saturated with static. I held it up to my ear and continued moving away from the blast until I was right on the edge of the mob, which was growing raucous again. "Sir?" I repeated.

"Graves, you're coming in clear now," Director Sodervall replied. It wasn't the best-quality connection I'd ever experienced, and there was a frustrating delay between each of our responses. Solnet was fast, and as a Pervenio Collector, I had access to the best relays, but he was posted on Pervenio Station orbiting Saturn, after all. It was a miracle we could even talk.

"Good," I replied. "The blast must be messing with reception."

"You're there already?" He sounded shocked. Like I said, it wasn't usually a collector's job to keep the peace.

"I was in the area. I've been getting tired of vacation anyway."

"Malcolm, you..." the director began before exhaling. I'm guessing he was hoping that after Undina, any collector besides me would've wound up right where he needed them. "How is it down there?"

"It could've been much worse, but these federation men clearly haven't seen anything like this before."

"They'll have to make do," he groused, a hint of bitterness bleeding into his tone. "We can't be expected to clean up all of their messes."

"Fine by me," I said, having to speak louder than I'd expected just to hear myself. The mob grew as boisterous as when I'd first arrived. I reached out and grabbed the first security officer I could find, pointed to his holstered pulse-rifle, and motioned for him to fire up into the air. He took my advice and things quieted back down.

"So do you have any leads on who's behind this, or are you planning to leave me off it?" I asked the director.

"I was thinking about it," he replied, wearing a smug grin. Of all the directors I'd ever dealt with, Sodervall and I actually got along best. It was why he'd become my usual handler. He had the dry, cynical humor that appealed to me. "Lucky for you, you're the most experienced operative we have stationed on Earth. M-Day is a big day for crimes offworld."

"Lucky me."

"Indeed. Unfortunately, we have no leads yet, but every major corporation with collectors near New London is already looking into this. They're desperate to prove our ineptitude, so you'll understand when I say that we need you to work quickly."

"I'll keep them far behind me." A medic rushed by, nearly knocking into me. He knelt by a citizen with skin so charred he barely looked human any longer.

"I hope you're rested, then." Director Sodervall paused for a brief moment and stared away from the screen. "Job's yours," he finally conceded. "Only you won't be doing it alone."

"Sir?"

"Mr. Pervenio has requested that whoever is assigned to this take on one of our promising young recruits straight out of the Cogent Initiative. I'm guessing you're familiar with the program?"

I'd heard a little. It was a program personally backed by Luxarn dedicated to providing Pervenio Corp with the most skilled and efficient agents in Sol. I won't say I wasn't flattered to be working with one of their prized, experimental trainees, but I'd always preferred working alone. Dragging Aria along with me everywhere I went before she ran off was the closest thing I ever had to having a real partner. A failed attempt at training her to be a collector had left a sour taste in my mouth, and me hesitant to ever consider taking on a new one.

"Sir, you know I work better alone," I said coolly.

"Sorry, Graves, but the orders come from above me. I haven't met your new partner—"

"Partner? Let's not get ahead of ourselves, huh?"

"If it makes you feel any better," Sodervall said, reclaiming control, "he has the highest scores in the initiative."

It didn't. I tried to keep calm, but nothing irritated me more than when company politics got in the way of my assignments. "Well, you tell Mr. Pervenio that this isn't the time for on-the-job training. Just let me do what I do best, and I'll take care of this."

"Like you did on Undina?" the director snapped. "Or did you forget that half the sector went dark because you were too slow."

I bit back my first response, still sore about what happened there, and now I couldn't help but think about it. I blamed Pervenio Corp for bad intel, but in my heart, I couldn't ignore the idea that maybe I was slipping. I'd made do with plenty less information over the years and gotten the job done cleanly. I couldn't let the director know any of that, however. My livelihood depended on it.

"But I got him, didn't I, sir?" I said through clenched teeth.

"I don't have time to argue right now, Graves." the director said. "If you're not willing to play nice, then I'll have to find someone who will, and you can continue enjoying your time off until I get you an assignment arresting some lowly thief somewhere cold. We old men need the rest, after all."

I pulled the hand-terminal away from my ear and cursed under my breath. After such a long time working together, he knew how to get to me. Neither of us wanted him to go searching for a freelance collector. Acting quickly was paramount. Only the collector who found the one responsible for the bombing would get paid. I intended for that to be me. Enduring a forced vacation until my credit account bled was a fate I couldn't stomach.

"Fine, dammit," I grumbled. "But if he gets in my way, I swear I'll leave him behind. We *old* men need the credits too. So what'll it be?"

Director Sodervall let out a sigh of relief. "I'm glad that's settled, then. Mr. Pervenio would prefer to have whoever ruined his Departure alive. One hundred thousand credits for you if he's breathing; half that if he's not."

"Split between me and this partner, you mean?"

"No. The Cogent's compensation is none of your concern."

"Tell Mr. Pervenio he'll have him alive," I promised without hesitation. The price had my pulse accelerating. It was the most I'd been offered for a target in more years than I could remember. Enough to curl up in a bottle for the next few years if I wanted to.

"Afterward, we'll discuss this partner thing," I added.

"I'm sure we will," Sodervall said. "You're to meet him at the USF security headquarters and proceed from there. Good luck, and try not to let anybody get killed this time." The call cut out before I could respond, but I decided it was in my best interest to ignore his last remark regardless.

A renewed sense of purpose stole over me and fueled my tired muscles. Even more than I cared about getting paid, I had no desire to become the aging collector quietly assigned to the least hazardous missions in Sol until the directors decided it was time for me to retire. I'd seen a few men go down that road, and I planned on going out under my own terms. After what had happened on Undina, I *needed* to catch the bomber. I needed to prove that I was still as valuable as any hungry young collector.

I immediately set off for the security headquarters, trying to reassure myself that having a partner might not be the worst thing. Ever since Aria left, flying alone through space from one end of settled Sol to the other, from job to job, had left me with a habit of spending most of my time stuck inside my own head.

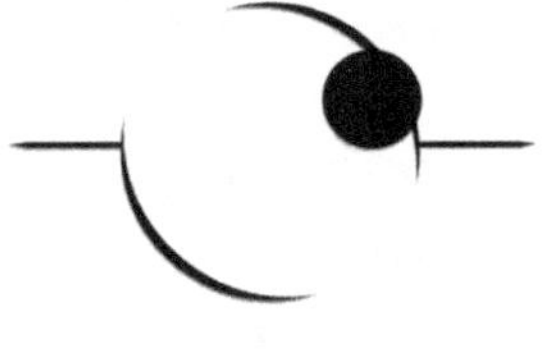

FIVE

The USF security headquarters was buzzing by the time I arrived. Drunk, incarcerated civilians packed every waiting room from end to end. It smelled like fresh vomit. Most had bloodied faces, and their lavish outfits were torn. It was difficult to make out any conversations with reporters on view-screens hanging from the ceilings chattering about the bombing... tireless talking heads debating what it meant for New London. I wondered the same.

A long line extended from the reception desk, which had an armed USF officer stationed on either side to keep the peace. Beyond the glass divider, which kept the rabble out of the headquarters' bullpen, calls from all over the Euro-String were coming in at an alarming rate. From what little I could hear, there were a lot of folks worried about family members who hadn't yet checked in. Every desk was staffed by an officer or secretary, and at least a hundred of them were arranged within the seemingly endless open room. I'd been in the headquarters plenty, but I'd never seen it so frantic. You knew it was bad when the room filled with drunks seemed to be the calmest.

"Would you stop staring at me with that thing?" one of the drunks slurred.

Guess I spoke too soon.

I edged toward the voice and saw the drunken civilian swing at a man in black. He missed spectacularly and was thrown backward. He would've bowled me over if I hadn't been paying enough attention to slide out of the way.

"You damn offworlders!" he snarled. He charged forward, but this time, the man in black deftly spun him around and into an arm-bar.

"It takes approximately twelve pounds of pressure to break the elbow of a human of your mass," the man in black stated calmly, his voice devoid of emotion.

"Let go of me!"

"I am currently applying eleven pounds," the man in black continued. "Please desist, or I will be forced to proceed."

Security officers shoved their way toward the scuffle to put an end to it, but they froze when they noticed who the man in black was. By that time, I'd gotten close enough to notice as well. Apparently, I'd stumbled upon who could only be my new partner.

He wore a formfitting black boiler suit with a nano-fiber inlay—something utilized more commonly beneath armor on offworld colonies. Whereas I kept mine concealed by my coat, a Pervenio badge was pinned proudly on his chest. His dark-brown hair was cut short, though his pale complexion contrasted so harshly, it looked black. He wasn't as pasty as a Ringer, but he had the skin of someone who'd spent almost his entire life on the inside of an asteroid. What really caught my eye, however, was the advanced-looking apparatus attached to the right side of his head. It encapsulated a glowing yellow lens positioned over his right eye—a scanner of some sort. His other eye was bare, but it was entirely white and stagnant, a shallow scar running across it from his left temple to the bridge of his hooked nose.

"Just let go!" the drunken man squealed.

My partner did as requested, pushing the drunkard away, leaving him to shuffle off in shame while clutching his injured arm. I took a step closer, but as soon as I did, my partner spun around with soldierly precision. His eye-lens angled itself to observe me from head to toe, as if completely independent of his stationary head. When it was done, he stood at attention and saluted.

"Greetings, Malcolm Graves," he said. "I've been waiting for you."

"Put that down," I replied and extended my hand to shake his. I tried my best not to stare at his blind eye. "They didn't give me your name."

"Zhaff," my new partner responded. His eye-lens tilted to view my hand, but he didn't grasp it. After a few awkward seconds, I pulled it back.

"That's it? Zhaff?" He said nothing, his lips remaining in a straight line. I shrugged and said, "Whatever you say. C'mon, we're going to look over the surveillance footage from earlier."

Zhaff nodded and followed close behind as I moved deeper into the headquarters. His posture was perfect, making me a little self-conscious. Each of his steps had a level of rigor that seemed as unnatural to me as his eye-lens was. I flashed my badge to the receptionist, and she opened up the sealed entrance of the bullpen so we could enter. New London had an insanely intricate surveillance monitoring of the city. Supposed safest place in the whole system, remember? I planned to see what we could find out from the feed before we made our first move. There were likely other collectors waiting for just such an opportunity, but Pervenio paid good money to allow us first access.

While we walked, I studied Zhaff out of the corner of my eye, trying to get a better sense of him. What I observed sent a shiver up my spine. He was taller than me, and judging by his physique, probably stronger too, but he was too young to grow a proper beard. He looked like he was still in his late teens.

I'd heard of the Cogent Initiative, but it was a fairly recent and clandestine program, so I'd never seen any of the recruits. I had no idea they were started so early—years younger even than I'd been when I set out on the path to becoming a collector. From what I knew, Pervenio Corp was taking people with certain traits and talents, and training them to be as deadly and decisive as the androids from fiction. Rumor had it they were even psychic, but people with some knowledge of the program claimed they were merely exceptionally attuned to reading people's faces and body language.

"Most people I know come with two names. But you're not just anybody, are you? Where'd the corporation drag you out of?" I asked as we traversed the headquarters. It bustled with activity. Countless officers fielded calls, running back and forth to deal with situations resulting from either the blast or what had followed it.

"That is classified," Zhaff replied.

"Look," I said, struggling to keep my cool. "I've worked alone most of my life. They saddled me with you, and I have a hard time trusting a man with my life if he won't even tell me where he's from."

"My orders are to work under your direction for the remainder of this assignment. If that is not an adequate arrangement, I can speak with the directors and request that they find another collector to replace you with."

"To replace *me* with?" I stopped in front of the surveillance center, grabbed Zhaff by the collar, and drew him close. "You know how long I've been working for Pervenio, kid?"

"Exactly thirty years, two hundred and eleven days," he said, not appearing fazed by my aggression in the slightest. "I have been fully briefed on your experience."

I released him and backed away slowly. I wasn't sure what I was expecting, but everything about Zhaff made me uneasy. That response didn't help. It had me wondering who was really in control. I knew the Cogent Initiative was valuable to Pervenio Corp, but I was beginning to grasp that I might've underestimated its importance. With so much at risk, I resolved to continue playing the good soldier for the time being.

"Just try to keep out of my way," I bristled.

Zhaff fixed his collar. "I look forward to learning from your experience."

"Great," I grunted as I stepped into the surveillance center. "Have me running a damn daycare for their freaks," I mumbled under my breath.

Inside, a curved array of view-screens displayed camera feeds from every corner of New London. Streets, inside buildings, outside buildings—everywhere. Those, plus all the scanners posted throughout the city, made it hard to believe someone had managed to sneak a handcrafted bomb into the heart of occupied Sol. It was a bold move, but it was only a matter of time. Every time some new precautionary measure was rolled out, someone somewhere found a way around it. That was simply the way of things.

Three members of USF security sat in front of the surveillance array. The one in the center wheeled around in his chair as Zhaff and I approached. He was as hungover-looking as I would've been if my day hadn't been interrupted. Struggling not to stare at the peculiar-looking Cogent seemed to sober him up a bit, however.

"We're not seeing anything, Collector," the security officer said jadedly. "Looked over the recordings a hundred times already. There are just too many people."

"You try heat-mapping yet?" I asked.

"Twice now. Too active. I can't pinpoint when anything out of the ordinary might've been set down."

Zhaff stepped forward. His eye-lens panned across the screens. "Numerous explosive devices wouldn't show up on a thermal scan, Malcolm Graves," he said. "Would you care for me to list them all?" Every word left his lips with immaculate enunciation, but his voice was completely flat. It was as if his speech were being dictated to him by someone at a computer far away before being fed out through his mouth.

I turned to him, expecting him to be kidding. Zhaff's face remained staid. "For all our sakes, please don't," I said. "With enough time at the site, forensics will ID the type of bomb used. I was there, and it looked like the work of something homemade. I don't give a damn about that, though. All I care about is who did it."

"Again, there are too many people," the security officer exhaled.

"Due to the explosion's proximity to the maglev rail station, I would estimate that between ten and fifteen thousand individuals passed nearby the general location throughout the day," Zhaff posited. "It would take me roughly sixty-eight hours to track each of their paths, excluding time required for sleep."

I thought about questioning whether a freak like him even needed sleep, but I took a measured breath instead before responding. "And what if the bomb was placed there days ago? I don't have that long."

I moved over to a view-screen that showed an aerial view of the area before the blast. Once there, I swiped my hand across the display and set it to play. Even at half-speed, it would've taken forever to trace anyone through the undulating tapestry of people and their colorful M-Day attire. Zhaff might've been able to do it without going insane, but there were thousands of citizens coming and going, and I didn't feel like leaving anything in the hands of my peculiar new partner. I fast-forwarded the recording until the moment the blinding explosion went off.

"Who would do something like this on today of all days?" the security officer asked.

"Many religious factions oppose humanity's expansion into the solar system," Zhaff answered matter-of-factly.

"They can be fanatical all right, but they aren't crazy enough to do something so brazen on the surface of Earth," I countered. "It goes against half of what they preach."

"There are numerous other dissident factions in Sol. Or it is possible a corporation in direct competition with Pervenio could be attempting to spoil their Departure."

I'd already considered all of what he said on my way over to the security headquarters. I couldn't place why, but none of it seemed right. "Doubt it," I said. "We're all the people of Earth today."

I set the feed to replay and leaned in close. A short time before the explosion, a shadow quickly passed across the lower half of the screen. The surveillance camera was positioned somewhere above the rail line, so there was no doubt the shadow belonged to a passing train.

"Are the trains usually running during the Departure?" I questioned the security officer. "All these years and I've never noticed."

He took a break from nervously tapping his index finger against his desk to reply: "That Euro-String line mostly hauls freight, so it never stops running, even on M-Day. The parting time you're seeing is one fifty-three p.m."

"The explosion went off precisely ten minutes and fourteen seconds later," Zhaff said.

"Lucky them for leaving on time," I said. "Are there passenger cars attached to it?"

"A few at the front..." The security officer sighed. He was clearly tired of answering questions he thought were pointless. "Look, sir. I've already checked on the few passengers who were registered as boarding that train. Their IDs and retinal scans checked out—all Earthborn citizens probably hurrying to beat the crowd after getting a glimpse of the Departure. Lucky bastards just made it out of there."

He was lucky I was distracted by Zhaff; otherwise, I would've reminded him who he was talking to. "I'm sure you have, but I'd like to see them," I said evenly. "Do you have a camera on that platform?"

The security officer withheld another groan as he typed something into his console and sent the feed to the view-screen in front of me. I rotated the image to get the best possible view of both the retinal and body scanners located in front of the entrance to the passenger cars. Then I rewound to the moment before the doors were opened and set it to play.

A handful of pedestrians made their way through the security checkpoint toward the departing train. No one seemed out of the ordinary. All the guards posted in the area stared at view-screens around the station while the Assembly gave their M-Day address.

"Malcolm Graves, there doesn't appear to be anything suspicious," Zhaff said as he stepped up beside me. His eye-lens was fixed on the screen, following every bit of motion.

I ignored him and continued to watch. It went on that way for a few boring minutes, but as I was beginning to grow frustrated, one of the passengers finally stood out. It was a man, hunched over and walking with a cane. The angle was too high to see his face, but a scarf covered his neck and mouth. The small part of his downturned face that was visible, however, had skin as white as paper.

I recognized the outfit minus the scarf, which must've been covering a sanitary mask. It belonged to the Ringer I'd sat next to earlier at the Molten Crater. Apparently, he hadn't been killed by the hover-car that crashed into it. He pretended to be an elderly Earther to hide his height as well as the fact that Earth-g added a funny lurch to his strides, as if a heavy weight were hanging from his neck.

"You said every passenger was a citizen of Earth, correct?" I questioned.

"According to the scanners," the security officer said.

"That man is not from Earth," Zhaff affirmed, without a shred of uncertainty in his voice. The Cogent didn't even need to recognize the Ringer's outfit to tell what he was, poor angle and all.

"No, and he's not an old man either," I continued. "At least, no older than I am. He's a Ringer. Anyone with eyes would have seen he wasn't from around here. Security at that station should be fired."

"There was a lot going on."

I drew a calming breath before I shouted at him. The USF was always too busy concentrating on expansion and developing a defensive missile matrix around Earth that could dispel another giant meteorite to train officers to handle a real situation. Until they got their heads out of their asses and started worrying about the right things—like angry offworlders—there was no point dwelling on it.

To Zhaff, I said, "I saw the Ringer at a bar before the M-Day address. When I left, he had his eyes glued on the newscast like he was waiting for something. I'm guessing he didn't stay there long after. Didn't get a glimpse of anything suspicious on him, but using a false identification right before a bomb goes off seems like a little more than a coincidence to me." I turned to the security officer. "Don't you think, Officer?"

The security officer's cheeks went red with embarrassment. He leaned over and squinted at the video feed. "But the retinal and ID scans come up clean," he protested. "Jack Fletcher, a retired factory worker from the outskirts of New London."

I glanced back at the recording. The Ringer's non-cane hand was closed into a fist, holding something as he approached the rail station's retinal scanners. Security was too busy watching the sky to pay much attention. Guy was smart. When the Ringer bent over to put his eye up to the machine, he used the closed hand to help lift his head, as if he were too old and weak to raise it without aid. Sick as he was, I hadn't found him to be that crippled in the Molten Crater. When the scan was complete, he simply limped into the maglev train's passenger car without any trouble and disappeared.

I shot a glance over to Zhaff. He nodded, confirming my unsettling assumption.

"Send a note to USF security to keep a lookout for Mr. Fletcher," I ordered. "And while you're at it, have a patrol sent to his residence. I have a feeling he won't be there, but wherever they find him, he'll be missing at least one eye."

The color drained from the security officer's cheeks. He swallowed hard and then started to draft a message.

I interrupted him. "Before you do that, where was the train headed? Can we have it stopped before it reaches its destination?"

Before the security officer could move, Zhaff rifled through some information on his console. Within a few seconds, he had an answer. "Express to Glazov station, Old Russia," he said. "It arrived there ten minutes ago."

"You should have had it stopped the moment that went off," I growled. "Hell, it never should have been running today."

"And deny Venta their scheduled shipment on board? I... everything checked out before dispatch. How were we supposed to know?"

I bit back anger. I wasn't sure why I expected USF security to be anything but incompetent. In our line of work, intelligent people went off to serve the true powers in Sol where the real action was. People on Earth assumed they were safe from anything but meteorites, until they weren't.

"Looks like we know where we're heading, then." I placed my hand on Zhaff's shoulder and grinned. His head instantly snapped around. His expression didn't change, but his eye-lens focused on my face as if it was searching for answers.

Once I removed my hand, Zhaff said, "We should wait to hear back about Mr. Fletcher from the patrol first."

"You're welcome to stay."

I set off toward the exit without looking back. It wouldn't be long before other collectors saw what Zhaff and I had, so there was no time to waste. After a short moment of hesitation, Zhaff followed, which made me feel a little better about the whole partner situation. He couldn't be further from Aria, but as far as I knew, Cogents were supposed to dutifully serve their superiors. Zhaff following me, despite his reservations, meant that at least for the moment, I was in charge.

With that realization and a solid lead to follow, I was feeling confident. If I chased down every offworlder who tried to falsify their identity to move freely around Earth, I would've been out of a job ages ago, but I'd seen the ire in the Ringer's face when the advertisement for migration to Titan came on. I don't believe in coincidences.

I stepped out of the surveillance center with a new bounce to my step. My mood came crashing back down when a familiar man waiting outside spun to face me. He was in his mid-thirties, wearing a fedora that looked like it belonged in ancient Earth. A few loose curls of wheat-blond hair wisped across his forehead as if he were perpetually posing for a picture.

"Malcolm Graves," he said, wearing a wry grin. He was Trevor Cross, a Venta Co collector. They'd been Pervenio's chief corporate rival in Sol since the Great Reunion with Titan. They were always after a stake in the Ring but recently had turned their attention to developing the moons of Jupiter in order to compete.

He and I had a similarly cold relationship. He'd only been a collector for around a decade, but there were very few people whose faces I wanted to punch more. It didn't help that he used a pistol that was an identical model to mine.

"Didn't think I'd see you here," Trevor continued. He positioned himself in my way so I'd be forced to shove him aside if I wanted to pass.

"Venta Co's still got you buying their groceries?" I replied. "Cute."

"Always with the jokes. Last I heard, you were on vacation. Figured you'd be spending it with that Ringer bitch of yours, not here. What was her name? Ry—something?"

"Not for years. Besides, somebody's got to find this bomber."

"Right, and that's you?" He snickered. "What're you going to use, your compass?"

I was struggling to keep my hands from curling into fists, when Zhaff tapped me on the arm. "Malcolm Graves," he said. "We are wasting time."

"Who the hell is this thing?" Trevor asked.

Before I could say anything, Zhaff stepped forward, Pervenio badge shining under the halogen lights of the security headquarters. "I am Malcolm Graves's assigned partner."

Trevor looked like he was going to burst out in laughter. "Wow. Never thought I'd see the day the great Malcolm Graves became a babysitter. They must really be pissed at you." He leaned in, his crooked smile so close to me I could wipe it off his face with one motion. "Or maybe they're just getting tired of watching your wrinkles get deeper."

My hand hovered over my pistol. I glared straight into his blue eyes, my blood boiling. A younger version of myself might not have been able to show such self-restraint. "Watch it, Cross, or I'll shove my pistol so far down your throat you'll be shitting bullets."

He backed away, still smirking. "That how they taught collectors to use them in your day, old man? I wouldn't want you to waste any lessons on me with your new partner right here."

I took a deep breath and allowed my hand to fall away from my holster. "You're lucky there's work to be done, or I'd give you one," I said as I shoved past him. Zhaff followed me wordlessly.

"I'm all ears, Graves!" he shouted as I walked away. "I'll tell you what: After I find the bomber, I'll use the credits to buy you a cane. You can teach your new pet a hell of a lot with that!"

I stopped and started to turn around, but when Zhaff walked by me, I decided against it. Causing more issues with Venta Co would only infuriate Director Sodervall more. That was the last thing I needed, so I swallowed my pride and continued on. Trevor had a problem with pushing people too far, and I had little doubt he'd get his one day.

"I'll beat you with it," I grumbled under my breath.

"What was that, Malcolm Graves?" Zhaff asked, completely calm.

"Next time, keep your mouth shut," I said to him. "Let's move."

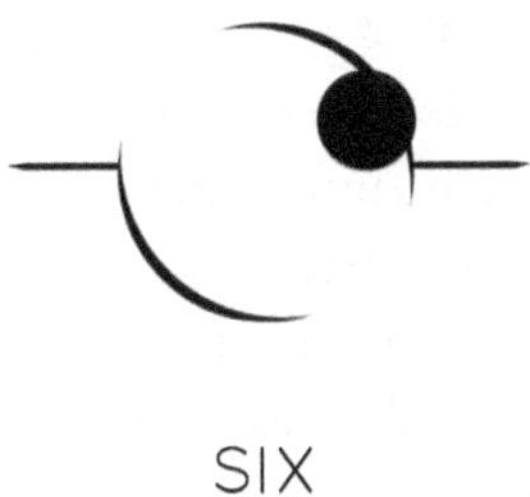

SIX

"I've never seen the streets this empty," I said to Zhaff. "On M-Day no less. What a shame."

Garbage from the day's festivities drifted aimlessly across the streets, and most of the outdoor activity came from USF patrols policing the city. Even the homeless were nowhere to be seen. Security hover-cars flitted high across the skyline, their bright spotlights sweeping across the ad-laden faces of buildings and plunging down dark alleys.

The New London rail station where Zhaff and I were headed was the only place that appeared busy with pedestrian foot traffic. Enhanced security had the inspection line stretching out past the entrance of the station. Citizens living beyond the city limits were desperately trying to get out of New London before anything else went wrong. A portion of the northern platform had, of course, been knocked out by the explosion, but all the others remained operational.

The nightlife in New London usually couldn't hold a torch to that of offworld colonies. Earthers, in general, were a conservative bunch. On most nights, you could barely spot anyone on the streets after midnight unless they were up to no good. M-Day was different. Revelry would rock the city, and lights would be shining until the sun rose the next morning; until stomachs were turning and eardrums were ringing. Presently, I could barely hear the soft beat of music emanating from indoor bars and clubs. Security made sure none of it spread outside.

"The celebrations continue inside," Zhaff responded. "It will be easier to monitor there."

"It's still strange to see," I said, glancing over at Zhaff. He stared forward, unaffected by the abnormal sight. "This is your first time here, isn't it?"

"That information is classified."

I couldn't help but chuckle, frustrating as his answer was. "Trust me, I can tell. Even *your* face wouldn't be so calm seeing it like this if it weren't."

"Are you sure taking the rail is the fastest way out east?" Zhaff asked after a brief silence.

"I'm sure," I said. "This new line of maglevs are two times faster than the best hover-car. Easy." I saw him reach for his hand-terminal like he was going to check my information. "Stop. Just trust me."

"Then, as I said earlier, we can request a Pervenio airship."

"Taking to the skies with all the craziness going on?" I said. "It'll take forever for one to scoop us up. They have better things to do securing the ports."

Zhaff checked his hand-terminal, and this time I allowed it. "By my estimation, we would arrive approximately three minutes earlier if we were retrieved with the next half-hour."

"And we'd alert the entire region to our presence. It's Old Russia; they might not even know there was a bombing. That gives us the upper hand. Besides, I messaged ahead, and Pervenio set our ride up for an express run. We'll beat any ship by a mile."

"If they do not cause any issues." He nodded toward a group of Church of Three Messiahs evangelists obstructing the entrance ramp to the rail station. They held up screens displaying only the word STAY and were dressed in layered robes with patterned tallits draped over their shoulders. The men wore headscarves and grew out beards out that dipped to the center of their chests. The woman covered half their faces with shawls. Each of them had a cross-shaped emblem tattooed down their forehead and across their brow.

"Right, it's your first time here," I said. "They're harmless. Just trust me and stay close." I slapped him on the shoulder. He stopped for a moment, stared at my hand, then continued on.

As we shoved through the crowd, an evangelist clutching the hefty tome of the Final Testament against his chest preached at us in an incensed whisper. It grew louder with every word, and the emptiness of the city made his voice echo.

"The ring of flame will swallow us all!" he shouted. "This is our punishment for trespassing in the realm of heaven! Repent, brothers. We must repent!" He didn't get a chance to say much more before a security hover-car positioned itself above.

"Disperse, now!" an officer blared through the vehicle's onboard speaker.

"So long as Earth remains, our feet are secure on her surface!" the evangelist hollered back. Then there was an earsplitting crack as the officer in the hover-car fired a pulse-rifle down at the feet of the protestors. They all fled except for their leader. At least until a second shot came inches from striking his head.

I didn't bother to watch the rest. I heard the pitter-patter of their bare feet slapping against the metal street as they scrambled. The lead preacher shouted, "You will burn!" again and again until his voice was a hoarse and distant echo.

"Soon as anything on Earth goes wrong, the fanatics come

out of the metalwork to lay blame," I said as Zhaff and I continued into the station. "Some people never learn."

"Judging by their beliefs, it does not appear they ever will," Zhaff responded.

"So you don't believe in any gods?" I asked. I knew the answer to that question the moment I met Zhaff, but I was curious to hear how a Cogent might respond. Curiosity... another side effect of my job I could never turn off.

"I have read all five thousand and ninety-two pages of the Final Testament and have seen nothing to justify any of its proclamations. Questions without answers are a waste of time."

"Amen," I joked. Zhaff didn't appear to get it.

We reached the platform for trains running to Glazov station. Those waiting in line to get onto passenger cars were scanned and patted down three times over. Extra effort too late, typical USF.

It would've taken an hour to reach the front if we were civilians, but that was another one of the perks of being a Pervenio collector. We presented our IDs and were led right onto the train bound for Glazov station. Like I told Zhaff, they'd reprogrammed it to dispatch immediately and expressly to Old Russia so we wouldn't waste any time.

I slumped down in a window seat as far from any other passengers as I could get and closed my eyes. Zhaff sat beside me.

"Do you, Malcolm Graves?" he asked as the train started up.

I looked at him, confused. "Do I what? And please, for the love of Earth, just Malcolm."

"Do you believe in any gods, Malcolm?"

For a moment, I thought about saying yes purely to push the Cogent, but I had plans to sleep through the hour-and-a-half trip to Glazov.

"No," I answered firmly.

I'd been to too many places beyond Earth, and seen too many horrible things in my life to have faith in some form of higher power watching over me. Plus, any god willing to drop a meteor on Earth didn't seem to me like a power worth praying to. The majority of humanity shared my opinion. Surviving the apocalypse compelled most people to forget about faith and cling instead to the tangible things that helped them survive, and to those with enough wealth and power to provide it all in our shattered world.

That was how the USF and its corporations came into being in the first place, but there were still factions of people who believed the Meteorite served as cosmic punishment for our transgressions. The preacher we'd passed belonged to the most prevalent of those groups—the Church of the Three Messiahs—which took the texts of what I'm told used to be Christianity, Judaism, and Islam, and blended them into what became known as the Final Testament. Maybe it all used to make sense, but the Meteorite jumbled everything from nations, to religions, to people's sense of things.

Somewhere along the line, the Three Messiahs' ancient teachings became a warning against traveling into space lest God complete the job he started with the Meteorite. It sounded silly to me, though I have to admit, I was envious of anyone who could have such unshakable faith in something beyond themselves.

"But I understand the appeal," I added.

"It is foolish to believe another meteor that size will strike Earth," Zhaff stated. "It was a scientific anomaly that will likely not occur again for many millions of years, if it ever does. At the current rate of human expansion, a similar instance in the future would barely dent the population."

"You know what I believe in? Getting sleep whenever I have the chance. If you're going to be a collector, you might want to consider adopting that policy."

Before Zhaff could reply, I turned away, leaned my head against the window, and closed my eyes. I knew I wouldn't be able to fall asleep right away since my mind was churning, but I was tired of conversing with the Cogent. I already missed working alone.

Zhaff was right, though. The chances of another substantial meteor hitting Earth were minuscule, yet the fear of it happening again was all that drove us. Everything those who remained on Earth had done since recovering from the Meteorite was done under the creed that humanity's extinction was being made impossible. The expansion into Sol. The way the Earth's settlements were reconstructed. How Earthers reproduced. Even the train I sat on.

Cities once expanded endlessly in every direction and rose to scrape the clouds, but in my time, everyone on Earth lived along strings of conurbations that stretched for hundreds of kilometers but rarely exceeded a kilometer in width. Six tracks of high-speed maglev trains ran down their centers like spines and along them, nodes of residential, commercial, industrial, and agricultural infrastructure alternated. This way, the areas remained spread apart, but if one segment of a string were to be cut off from the rest, it could survive independently. Like an earthworm growing two heads after being sliced in half.

New London was the largest bulge in any string, but even it only spread to nearly two kilometers in width. It also housed the USF Assembly Building, which at fifty stories, was the tallest building on the planet that wasn't a half-sunken ruin from the last age. The city fell along the Euro-String—the longest of the strings—which ran from the center of the European continent to the heart of Old Russia. Being that the aftereffects from the Meteorite had drowned half of Earth's habitable land, and billions of people with it, settling along the middle ridges of continents was the best way to ensure that it didn't repeat.

Every policy I could think of made perfect sense by that line of thinking. It was the world I'd always known: one of a people locked in constant vigil. Earthers weren't even allowed to reproduce without clearance from doctors that the genes of the parents didn't have any chance of resulting in disease. Most of us grew up in clan-families that numbered into the hundreds, mine being a family located a few dozen kilometers outside New London. Matching candidates for parenthood would join together to reproduce in phases and stick together so that nobody was ever alone and in danger. Call me a romantic, but I had a hard time with being promised to my clan-sisters, even if it wasn't technically incest. My daughter was born off the grid after I left the clan-family behind, and I was proud of that.

The constant reminders of mass annihilation were the biggest reasons I could never bear to stay on Earth any longer than I had to. It usually took longer for them to wear on me, but the older I got, the more I preferred the blackness of Sol and all its mysteries. For if Zhaff was accurate about the chances of another colossal meteorite hitting, then almost every policy the USF decreed was as big of a waste as those of the Church of the Three Messiahs...

And we were all just as big of fools.

Longing for a drink to quiet my mind, I peered through my eyelashes to see if the train had gotten anywhere while I was lost in thought. I saw the profile of a factory on the edge of the New London Industrial Node. It sat like an island of steel amid the barren landscape—nothing green in sight.

Billows of black smoke rose from the stacks poking through

the top of the factory the train raced by. They were quickly absorbed by a layer of dark clouds hanging overhead.

Unlike everything else, apparently, Earth's sky was already too damaged to worry about.

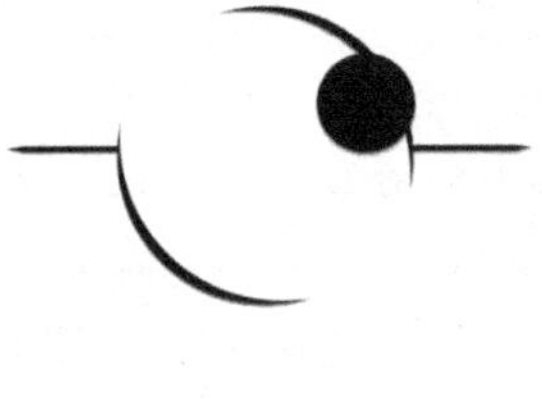

SEVEN

Somewhere along the ride, the soft vibrations of the maglev train lulled me into a deep sleep. I woke abruptly to a tap on my shoulder. Zhaff's face hovered above mine, the Cogent's head cocked to the side and his yellow eye-lens shimmering.

"We're here," he said.

I rubbed my face and followed him off the train. As we stepped outside, frigid air slid down my throat like a rope of knives. I decided to take smaller breaths from there on out before reaching into the pocket of my trench coat and pulling out a pair of gloves. Once they were on, I inspected my surroundings.

Glazov station, which was closer to a platform, was in the glacial heart of Old Russia—a slum that stretched for hundreds of linear kilometers in either direction along the Euro-String. The luster of New London was completely lost there. On either side of the rail, rusty metal shanties were crammed so tightly together it was hard to tell where one ended or another began. If not for the few bright ads and signs flickering along their corrugated surfaces, many displaying outdated products, it would have looked like ancient Marrakesh. A nearly empty grid of snow-covered streets connected all of them, and security consisted only of a pair of guards huddled up in a post on the train platform. It looked like they were playing cards and drinking. Hell, I couldn't blame them; it was freezing out, and I'd have killed for a few fingers of whiskey.

"We should head to the USF security post, see if they've heard any reports of a Ringer in the area," I said.

"Unnecessary," Zhaff quickly responded. His face was buried in his hand-terminal. "While you slept, I contacted every USF outpost in Old Russia. Surveillance in the area is scarce, but a camera spotted a man matching my description enter a hauler repair shop. I am presently uploading the location."

I tried not to let my wounded pride show. I knew Cogents were supposed to be efficient, but I had no idea *how* efficient. It was like after I'd told him how I set up an express ride to reach Old Russia, he had to outdo me.

"Well, hurry up, then," I grumbled.

While I waited, I moved beside a screen displaying an ad for a three-year-old line of heavy jackets designed by Venta Co. I had to admit, the thing wasn't terrible. At least it emitted some warmth.

I turned to Zhaff, wondering if the Cogent had intended not to bring a coat. He didn't seem affected by the temperature at all. I cupped my hands over my mouth and then looked up past the rail station's rippling canopy. It was snowing, and like most of Earth, the sky of Old Russia was congested with the usual mixture of dark clouds polluted both by centuries-old dust from the first M-Day and human-made toxins. Sometimes I wished that I'd known the blue and sunny skies of old. The omnipresent shroud was one of the many gifts bestowed upon Earth by the Meteorite.

The climate never fully recovered after it hit. Worldwide,

temperatures dropped, making it impossible to differentiate between seasons. Among the places that remained above water, New London was considered warm—and I couldn't remember the last time I'd gone outside without needing a winter coat. Compared with Old Russia, New London was a tropical paradise. Any farther north, and we may as well have been standing outside on Titan. An exaggeration for sure, being that the orange moon's surface was cold enough to turn a man into a popsicle in seconds, but at a certain point, I don't think it matters. Cold is cold, and I hated it.

"It is only six blocks east," Zhaff said finally.

"You're telling me he went through all the trouble of falsifying his identification only to clumsily be caught by one of the few surveillance cameras in Glazov?" I said. "Right around the corner from the rail station no less."

"It is likely he expected to be followed and is trying to confuse his pursuers."

"Maybe, but I'm not going to stand around here waiting until I'm a block of ice. We'll see what we find at the shop and go from there."

To my relief, Zhaff nodded and said, "I agree. Also, Malcolm, during our trip, the body of Jack Fletcher was discovered in the bathroom of the Molten Crater after they cleaned up what remained of the bar. It was missing an eye."

"Right under my damn nose," I said under my breath, making sure to turn my face away from Zhaff so he wouldn't see how embarrassed I most likely looked. Again, the notion that maybe the directors were right about me slipping popped into my head. I promptly shoved it out of mind. Arresting the first Ringer to ever bomb New London was too good an opportunity to allow doubt to get a hold on me.

"Finding Fletcher means that other collectors will be bearing down on us in no time now," I said. "I have no desire to watch someone else cash in. We better not waste any more time. Let's go."

We marched down one of the bleak cross streets of the slums, my long duster kicking up the accumulated white powder. The sound of electronic music echoed on either side of us, through thin metal walls and windows plastered with glowing advertisements. I could hear boisterous laughter and people hollering from inside in the Russo-English lingo typical of the area. As in New London, most of the M-Day celebrations in Old Russia had been forced indoors, though, for them, it was due to the unrelenting cold and not a bomb.

A few bearded Earthers lounged against the walls outside, but that was all. They accompanied the countless bottles rolling lazily across the metal-paved walkways. One bumped into my foot, and I knelt to pick it up. It was empty, a layer of frost built up around the nozzle.

"You'd think it'd be easier to get a drink today," I groused.

"It is not wise to ingest alcohol, Malcolm," Zhaff said.

"Now, or ever?"

"Both."

I chuckled, and before I could think of some sage piece of advice about how after so many years on the job it was the best thing for you, Zhaff turned with soldierly precision and headed left down a narrow alley.

"This way," he instructed.

A group of emaciated Earthers with scraggly beards stood clustered around a grille that spit up billows of hot steam. They wore heavy coats that would've been enough to keep them warm on their own if they weren't so worn down.

"*Zdravstvuj,* friends," one of them croaked as we approached.

Their sullen eyes watched us nervously, and I knew why. One look at us and they knew exactly why we'd come: There was a collection to be made. It was an expression I'd recognize no matter what colony I was on, although at least on Earth, people mostly stayed quiet and kept their distance so they didn't get hurt. Once Zhaff and I passed, I heard them let out a collective sigh, relieved to know that one of them wasn't the target.

"They saw something," Zhaff stated.

"How do you know?" I asked.

"I had a USF warning sent out to all citizens in the area to keep a lookout for any elderly men braving the cold."

"Of course, you did…"

"One of them displayed signs of guilt, as if he has seen one."

"You can go back and ask them if you'd like," I said, "but people way out here don't tend to talk to collectors."

"It is irrelevant. He can no longer help us."

Zhaff again stopped suddenly and turned to face a rusty door sunk into the corrugated metal backside of a structure beside an overflowing dumpster. It belonged to the hauler repair shop we were looking for. The door was slightly ajar, rattling as the cold air breezed through. I quickly positioned myself at the corner and pulled out my pistol. Zhaff did the same.

"They don't leave their doors open either," I said. With my left hand, I removed Aria's Ark figurine and gave it a kiss for good luck, like I always did before I got the feeling a job was about to get hairy.

"What is that?" Zhaff asked.

"Nothing," I lied, stuffing it back into my pocket. I slipped my heavy boot between the door and the jamb, pushing the door open just enough to edge in with my pistol aimed. Zhaff stayed right on my heels.

We rushed into an open space filled with inactive machine belts and broken-down vehicles. The only sound came from a newscast on the view-screen by the front desk that was left on. A report about the bombing in New London played, the news finally making its way to the forlorn slums of Old Russia. The garage door adjacent to the view-screen was wide open, flakes of snow wafting in.

I ducked behind the frame of a deconstructed hauler and signaled Zhaff to take cover by a workbench up ahead. As soon as I moved to follow him, a bullet glanced off the chassis, the sparks shooting out directly in front of my eyes. I fired off a frantic shot and dove, slamming into the workbench and landing beside Zhaff.

"You never should have come here!" a man yelled. It was without question the Ringer from the Molten Crater. His voice was hoarse from coughing.

"You are in violation of four federation laws," Zhaff responded as calmly as ever. "Lay down your weapon."

"Come and take it, mud stompers!"

The noisy engine of a hauler facing the open garage door turned over. Images of Undina flashed through my mind until I peered around the corner of the table to see the Ringer's pale arm sticking out the window. He had a pre-Meteorite, powder-based revolver aimed at us—a slug-chucker, we called them. I pulled my head back behind cover when he continued firing in our direction. I counted five more shots, and then it clicked. That was when he hit the gas.

Zhaff and I simultaneously sprang up to return fire. Our pulse-pistols were quieter at the barrel, but they packed three times the punch. Bullets clanged loudly off metal parts and shattered the narrow glass window on the back of the hauler. One of us managed to nick the Ringer's forearm as his vehicle swerved out onto the streets. It caused him to shriek, but it wasn't enough to stop him. Soon after, he was out of view, and I was left shooting at nothing but snowflakes. Zhaff had stopped as soon as he knew he was wasting rounds.

"Damn!" I grunted and lowered my pistol once the sound of the hauler disappeared. "You hit?"

"No," Zhaff answered. He bent down to examine one of the bullet holes left behind by the Ringer's gun.

I realized instantly that if it was his first time on Earth, he'd probably never seen an ancient weapon like the one the Ringer had wielded.

"It's an old-fashioned revolver, pre-Meteorite," I said. "He probably found it in the owner's desk. Shopkeepers like them out in the slums. They're small, unregistered, and easy to hide from robbers... or security." Despite their age, they were also actually fairly cheap on the black market. The wealthy preferred their old-world relics to at least be attractive if they weren't going to be useful.

Zhaff's eye-lens angled in my direction and he nodded. It felt good to finally have something to teach him.

I gestured for him to get up, and we continued to investigate the room. I raised my gun as we did, making sure to check every corner. Zhaff had his holstered. He strolled along calmly, as though he already knew we wouldn't find anybody alive.

"Dead," he declared, right on cue. He pointed at something behind the front desk, and I skirted my way around a machine belt to see.

The remains of a man were slumped against the wall, his head cracked open like a melon. The pool of blood that had formed beneath him was frozen, with a sullied wrench resting in the center, right beside his outstretched hand. Signs of struggle were evident, with many of the items from on top of the desk carelessly strewn about. An open drawer revealed a pile of loose bullets that had been left behind in the Ringer's apparent rush. I got near enough to make sure nobody else was hiding behind the desk before finally stowing my gun.

"Poor bastard," I said. Upon closer inspection, I found that the dead man had a fairly youthful look to him. My guess was that he was an apprentice put to work while the shop's owner was out celebrating M-Day. That was when it hit me exactly how sloppy the Ringer really was. He had taken every precaution to get out of New London safely, but as soon as he disembarked the train at Glazov station, it was like he didn't care about being captured. Murder weapon lying out in the open. Getting spotted on camera right outside. None of it seemed right.

"It appears he is no longer disguised," Zhaff said.

I buried the unsettling feeling deep inside, hoping that Zhaff hadn't noticed, and then glanced up. The Cogent had already moved past finding a corpse and was crouched nearby, examining something on the floor. I would've been relieved to find someone else as numb to death as I was, if I hadn't already discovered how young Zhaff was.

Beneath his hand lay a cane wrapped by a tattered scarf, with a sprinkle of blood on the frayed end. Whether it belonged to the murdered apprentice or to Jack Fletcher's now frozen eyeball lying on top of it, I wasn't sure.

"The Ringer's death toll is starting to pile up," I said. "This other one probably startled him and got himself killed."

Zhaff got to his feet and approached the gaping garage door. He stared outside for a few moments before turning back to me. "His tracks continue toward the border of the Euro-String and into the wilderness."

"What the hell would he want out there?" I said.

"I don't know," he replied, using those words for the first time in our short partnership.

"So you're human after all."

I couldn't keep myself from smiling. Zhaff knelt by the spots of the Ringer's blood outside and placed a drop into a reader on his hand-terminal for analysis. I started perusing the shop to see if there were any haulers left in good condition. They weren't complicated. They were basic, land-based vehicles used to transport goods across distances too short to require the rail line.

"No DNA record on file," Zhaff said, precisely loud enough for me to hear him across the shop.

"An illegitimate Ringer who's never been to the doctor?" I replied. "I doubt that." I spotted a decent hauler in the corner. The belted wheels were a little off track, but it looked like it would run.

"Let's take this hauler after him and find out," I said. I strolled up next to the vehicle. It was apparently due for repairs because the physical key was left dangling right outside the ignition. "We'll call in USF security to clean up this mess on our way," I said, reaching into the vehicle and cranking the ignition a few times. The engine merely sputtered. "This thing—" I was cut off by a clank near the back door. Both Zhaff and I drew our guns and aimed, though I found myself worrying about how he was a hair faster and not who the intruder might be.

"Hold your fire!" whoever it was shouted.

A pair of hands rose up from behind a machine belt. I wasn't sure who they belonged to until I saw a pistol identical to my own held in one of them. I fired a shot five or so meters to the left of him on purpose. It made me feel better.

"Whoa, hold it!" Trevor Cross yelled. He popped up farther so we could see his face.

"Oh, sorry," I responded. "I couldn't tell it was you from here. Old eyes and all."

Trevor released a nervous laugh and shuffled toward us. He went to lower his arms, but Zhaff said, "Why are you here, Collector?"

"I heard shooting," Trevor said. "Thought it might be a lead."

"Holster your weapon at once," Zhaff ordered.

"All right, all right." Trevor lowered his weapon slowly and slid it into his side holster. "No need to get angry. We're all on the same side here."

I tapped Zhaff on the shoulder and whispered, "I'll handle this." Zhaff nodded, stowed his pistol, and lifted the hood of the hauler I'd selected to start tooling around with the engine.

I kept my gun aimed and my eye on Trevor. There was no way I was going to trust a Venta Co rat when we had a real lead to follow.

"So, you just happened to be out here?" I asked him. "You weren't trying to follow *us* for a lead, were you? You know how I feel about contract poaching."

Trevor shrugged. "Hey, we're all after the same person. I followed the trail same as you did."

"Right. So you figured out it's a Ringer, did you?"

His eyes went wide. He nodded, but I could tell he was as shocked as I was when I first saw the Ringer standing next to me in the Molten Crater. He was an awful liar.

"Why don't you go home, Cross?" I said. "This is no place for kids."

"Tell that to your—" He stopped when he noticed the split head of the shop attendant slumped against the wall.

"Like I said. The Ringer we're after has a flair for killing. I'm sure Venta has a crooked shop owner you could go after or a streetwalker who isn't paying dues. That sounds more your speed."

"Funny, Graves. But I'm not the one who let him get away." He gestured toward the hauler tracks and the spots of blood on the snowy street outside. Then he walked up next to me and wrapped his arm around my shoulder. "How about this: I help you find the Ringer and we split the reward?"

I grabbed his hand as tight as I could and removed it. "I'd rather the Ringer kill me."

"Don't be a fool. He went to the wilderness. You know how big that is? If we find him, I'll let you be the one to turn it in. Pervenio doesn't even have to know I helped."

Zhaff stopped working and slammed the hood of the hauler shut. "Locating the bomber is our priority, Malcolm. It is true he could provide assistance in the wilderness and benefit Pervenio relations with Venta Co. I will contact Director Sodervall to draft an arrangement."

"I was wrong about you." Trevor stepped past me toward Zhaff, who was busy sliding into the driver's seat of the hauler. "Listen to him, Graves. Think of the headlines, all of us working together in the name of justice."

Zhaff turned the ignition, and this time the engine clicked a few times and hummed to life. Of course he knew how to fix one. He could do everything, but nothing more expertly than foul my mood. Zhaff pulled out his hand-terminal and started typing.

"I thought I told you to keep your mouth shut next time," I said to Zhaff.

"I apologize, but I am unable to keep my mouth shut and also speak," Zhaff replied without looking up at me with his eye-lens. "Communication is critical for this mission."

Trevor snickered. "This guy gets better and better. What do you say, Graves?"

I shoved past him and climbed up into the hauler. "Move over; you're too young to drive," I said to Zhaff, not even thinking that it was probably true. For once, he did something without a fuss. I took my spot in the driver's seat and wrapped my hands around the wheel. Then I sighed. "All right, hop in," I said to Trevor.

He beamed. "I knew your brain wasn't too withered up," he said. "This'll be fun."

Trevor grabbed on to the side of the vehicle and started to

draw himself up into the cramped backseat when I hit the gas. The hauler zoomed forward, causing him to roll over the trunk. He squealed like a young boy as he hit the ground and rolled, even though I knew we weren't going fast enough for him to receive anything worse than a scrape.

"Malcolm!" he hollered behind us. "I'll kill you!" The echoes of his screams grew softer as we zoomed toward the edge of civilization. The only thing keeping me from bursting out in laughter was the cold air rushing against my face. Leave it to the rugged Earthers of Old Russia to build their haulers without tops.

"That was not advisable," Zhaff remarked, still unruffled as always.

"We're doing this alone," I replied. I reached over with one hand and ended his pending call to Director Sodervall. "The Ringer won't get away again."

Considering I had no clue what the Ringer was trying to do, Trevor's help would've made things easier. But I wasn't sharing the credit, and I definitely wasn't sharing credits, which Zhaff seemed to be okay with. I wasn't sure if Cogents even needed money, so it wasn't his choice to make. I was in charge.

There was no one for the Ringer to kill where we were going. It was time to put his spree to an end and put my failure on Undina behind me where it belonged.

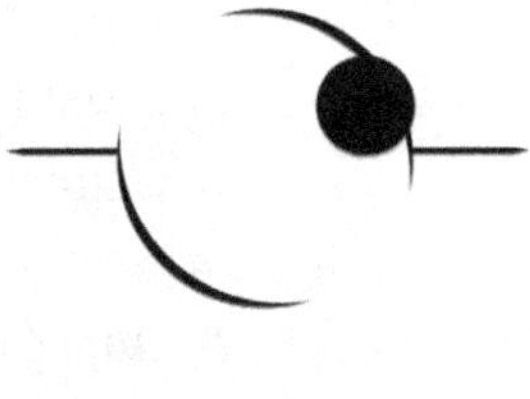

EIGHT

THERE WAS no wall to pass through when leaving the boundaries of the Euro-String, only a final row of shanties standing in a line, and then nothing. Civilization just stops, and the only thing beyond are ruins and wasteland. Most species of life on Earth weren't as fortunate as humanity when it came to surviving after the M-Day. Wild animals were nearly as rare as gold, and you'd have to search high and low to find naturally-growing foliage. Livestock, forests, crops—they were all grown in contained zones along the Strings.

I'd chased targets into the wilderness before. Most were dead by the time I found them, either frozen solid or starved to death. You could find shelter in the skeletons of ancient cities, but any supplies from the pre-Meteorite world had been used up a long time ago. The Ringer wouldn't last long if we weren't fast. I had no intention of letting the bastard die on his own; Pervenio wanted him alive, and I wanted that hundred grand.

Zhaff spotted the stolen hauler a couple dozen kilometers away, parked in a ditch at the edge of a frozen river that skirted an abandoned city and snaked toward the horizon in both directions. On the other side of the river, the city was trashed. Walls were missing, and rooftops caved in on most. It was a different sort of emptiness than what we had found in the slums, as if an entire culture had vanished suddenly and left behind only the bones to tell some distant civilization "we were here!" Pretty shitty legacy, if you ask me.

The first time I'd experienced the wilderness, a similar sight filled me with trepidation. It didn't affect me much anymore, but it was hard not to feel a slight sense of mourning.

We found the Ringer's hauler empty. No visible footsteps led in any direction, but we'd traveled so far from the Euro-String that the snow would have already covered any shallow tracks left behind by the light weight of a Ringer. If the frozen river had been tread upon, no cracks showed to inform us.

East of us, I saw the remnants of a bridge. Nothing was left of it except for the tarnished structural members around its landings and a few lonely metal columns poking up here and there through the ice. Still, I had to assume the Ringer crossed into the forsaken city somehow. There was nowhere else to go for shelter from the cold.

I switched off our hauler and hopped down. Taking my first step after sitting in the cold for so long reminded me that I wasn't as young as I used to be. My legs were stiff.

"He must have crossed here on foot," I said, stretching out my leg and tapping the ice a few times with my boot. It felt solid as bedrock, as if the river had been frozen for centuries. Probably had.

"The ice is more than a meter thick," Zhaff clarified. "It would take at least four men of your mass to break through it by walking."

"Thick enough to drive this piece of junk across?"

He crouched and studied the ice with his eye-lens for a few seconds. "Doubtful," he said. "The hauler would be unable to traverse the debris-covered streets in the settlement regardless."

"All right, then we'll have to follow him on foot. With the head start he's had, we'll be lucky if we ever find him in there."

Zhaff stepped toward the river and turned his head slowly from side to side, surveying the length of the urban area. "Without more than two of us, it will take too long," he decided. I couldn't tell if he was taking a shot at me for leaving Trevor behind. "The dense portion of this settlement covers approximately eight hundred hectares," he continued. "I will message Pervenio Corp to send airships to sweep the area." Zhaff began typing into his hand-terminal, but I held out my arm.

"Hold off on that," I ordered, remembering that, as far as I knew, I was in charge and Zhaff had to listen. "We'll cross here and split up to cover as much ground as we can. If we can't find any sign of him by nightfall, then I'll let you make the call. It'll save them money."

I knew that we, or at least I, would be paid handsomely for finding the Ringer's location, but I was still determined to bring the culprit back myself. Even if the carelessness of the mechanic's murder had me feeling uneasy, it wasn't enough to sway me from that desire. Getting a short break from Zhaff wouldn't hurt either.

"It is unwise to separate," Zhaff advised. "We have no knowledge of the suspect's training."

"He's a Ringer," I scoffed. "Here, in Earth's gravity, he'll be about as strong as a child compared with us. Plus, I saw him. He looked sick enough to topple over at any moment without even needing the help of our planet. He emptied his gun at us earlier and didn't have time to grab bullets, so I think either one of us could take him."

"He remains strong enough to rupture that mechanic's skull."

I bit my lip. "Who knows how many swings it took."

"I have been instructed to follow your lead, Malcolm. This

is, however, the third instance since our meeting when my recommendation has been disregarded. I will be taking note of all such occasions in my task report. Would you still like to proceed?"

I thought about calling him a mindless drone and a freak, but I held my tongue. "Affirmative, and I'd love to see that report when we're done here too."

"You are not authorized."

"All your skills and you still can't sense sarcasm." I sighed and shook my head. "You take the east side. I'll take the west."

"Agreed. If you do locate the Ringer first, do not engage him without contacting me."

"Will do."

I exaggerated a point toward my hand-terminal before walking cautiously out onto the river. Every subsequent step helped me to gain a little more confidence in the safety of the ice.

"What did I do to deserve this?" I grumbled under my breath once Zhaff was out of earshot.

I readjusted my duster so I could breathe into the inside of my collar and avoid the frigid air. Then I reached down to my belt, grabbed my spotter goggles, and set them to thermal imaging. When I pulled them down over my eyes, I saw nothing but darkness.

Hours passed. It was rare on Earth that the sky was clear enough to see the sun as anything but a dull glow. It wasn't at the moment, but I could tell it would be setting soon. My legs were getting sore, and my cheeks felt like they were ready to crack open from the cold. Since Zhaff and I split up, I'd neither heard back from him nor found the Ringer myself.

So much rubble and ice invaded the streets of the decrepit settlement that it was hard to traverse it quickly. Like many bodies of water after the Meteorite hit, the river had apparently flooded and was frozen soon after. The ice devastated everything it touched as it expanded. Treasure hunters dedicated their lives to digging through the ice to find artifacts from the old world, but mostly, all they discovered were the rusty chassis of ancient vehicles. I could see pieces of some popping up here and there like tiny islands of metal. It was as if every pre-Meteorite human alive had one of their own. I couldn't imagine that was safe.

It was hard to use landmarks to track my path when so much looked the same. Signs at intersections were completely tarnished and unreadable as well, so when I was forced to cut through gutted buildings, it was impossible to know if I was going in circles without constantly double-checking the regional scans on my hand-terminal.

I climbed up the half-collapsed stairs of what looked like an apartment building and looked out through a cavernous hole in the wall of the second floor. There was nothing out there but more rubble. I rubbed my hands together to regain some warmth before continuing on. Even with my gloves on, my fingers were numb. I decided I'd give it ten more minutes alone before I gave in and allowed Zhaff to call in the airships.

I shimmied out through the hole and searched for a way to get a little higher on the building since the stairs inside were nowhere to be found. A sagging balcony jutted out from the building one story up. A piece of wall snapped off under the weight of my foot, but I was able to use what little feeling I had left in my fingers to heave myself onto it. Once there, I listlessly lowered my spotters over my eyes, expecting to see nothing but darkness for the hundredth time. I swept my gaze from side to side, and again there was nothing. But right before I removed them, I noticed the tiny red blip of a heat signature on the edge of my vision.

I would've grinned if my face weren't so numb. I clambered down from my perch as fast as I could without killing myself. When I reached the streets, I whipped out my pulse-pistol and headed in the direction of the thermal signature.

Once I got closer, I began monitoring my steps, making sure they were light enough not to crunch the layer of ice that seemed to be everywhere. I arrived at a break in a cluster of buildings. A small, broken-down shack sat at the bank of a narrow tributary stemming from the river. It had no roof, and most of its stone walls had crumbled away to reveal a bare interior. Beyond it, barren land extended through a haze until a faded range of mountains sliced up in the distance through the thick veil of clouds.

I crouched behind a wall overlooking the shack and checked my spotters again. The heat signature was somewhere on the other side. I lifted my hand-terminal to my mouth and set it to contact Zhaff.

"I think I've located the Ringer," I whispered boastfully. Finding him may have been a stroke of luck, but for all Zhaff's supposedly extraordinary abilities, to me, there was no substitute for real experience. I wanted to make sure my partner was aware of that.

Zhaff's response came immediately. "It will be easier to capture him alive if there are two of us. I will be able to reach your position in precisely eight minutes and seventeen seconds." He didn't even need to pause to calculate the number.

"Fine, but if he starts moving, I won't be able to wait. He'll spot me following."

I ended the call before I could receive a reply. Then I peered at the ruined structure again, this time without my spotters on, and tried to locate the Ringer with my own eyes through the cracks. I couldn't.

Exhaling slowly, I turned my attention to my pulse-pistol, analyzing it to make sure everything was in working order. That went on for about a minute before I elected to ignore Zhaff's warning. I could take him down alone. He was only a weak Ringer, after all. I didn't need a partner. Plus, remaining still was making me shiver even more than I had been.

I readied my gun and approached the shack with furtive steps. I wanted to keep the element of surprise on my side just in case the Ringer had managed to snag a few extra bullets back at the hauler shop.

"Don't move, Ringer!" I shouted once I poked around the corner of the shack with my pulse- pistol aimed. "Or I'll blow a hole in you so large you'll freeze from the inside out."

The Ringer sat out in front of the shack, against a pile of stones that looked like they used to belong to one of its walls. His head turned toward me, but unlike most of the targets I'd ever tracked down, he didn't ignore the warning and attempt to run. He barely even moved. In fact, the worry seemed to drain from his face once he realized who the man barking at him was, and he returned to gazing out toward the faraway mountains.

The first thing I noticed about him was that he wasn't wearing his mask or gloves. They were lying on the ground next to him beside the empty old-world revolver. The next thing was that he was dressed in nothing but a thin boiler suit. The sleeves were shorter than Zhaff's and revealed stringy arms so white that they seemed to glow under the waning sunlight. A deep gash ran across his left bicep where either me or Zhaff shot him, the blood around it frozen. He didn't appear cold in the slightest. I was struggling to keep my teeth from chattering as I spoke, yet the Ringer didn't even have goosebumps.

"By Trass, I knew someone would track me down eventually, but that was faster than I expected," the Ringer said calmly before succumbing to a fit of coughing. His sickly eyes were even redder than when I met him, like two almond-shaped rubies. Every time he exhaled, it sounded like a broken-down air recycler. If the g-pill I saw him take back at the Molten Crater was the last he had, his lungs were probably verging on collapse from enduring Earth's gravity. "Impressive for a mud stomper," he continued after he gathered his breath. "Shame it had to be you, though."

"I don't know about that," I said as I advanced on him. "There are some of us who only prefer one aspect of alive or dead, no matter what the reward is. Especially for offworlders who blow up innocents. Lucky for you, I'm just trying to make a living."

"None of you are innocent," he stated categorically, retaining his calm façade despite the harshness of his words. "So what now, Collector?"

I was surprised the Ringer made no effort to deny his part in the bombing. Fugitives were rarely so compliant. Because of that, it took longer than intended for me to come up with a response. When I finally did, I decided to lie.

"It's up to you," I said. "Pervenio airships are already on their way to retrieve us."

"So it's that simple here on Earth?" he replied. "Offer a man chains and expect him to lock them on himself before following quietly?"

"Again, it's up to you." I kept my gun aimed steady as I moved behind him until I was close enough to reach out and touch him. "Make this easy on me, and I'll call them off. We'll take the train back instead; just us. Unless you'd rather start the interrogation right away. Trust me, the people who want you won't be as cordial as I am after what you did."

"Not so pleasant when foreigners come and murder your

people, is it?" the Ringer asked scathingly, his mask of composure finally beginning to slip away. The same rage I'd seen brewing in his sickly eyes back in New London returned in full force.

"You offworlders and your messages. If your flair for dramatics didn't keep me employed, I might find it irritating." I pressed the barrel of my pistol against the back of the Ringer's head. "Now c'mon, get up. Don't make this harder on yourself."

"As you wish."

The Ringer rose. I went to grab his wrists with my gun-free hand so I could cuff them with a band of collector-issued fiber-wire, but as I did, he whipped around with catlike fluidity and snatched the pistol out of my grip, and before I even knew what had happened, I stared down its barrel at a loaded chamber.

The Ringer panted from low g exertion, but somehow, he still managed to hold the firearm perfectly steady. His gloveless hand wasn't shivering the slightest bit. Not from the bite in the air or the wound on his arm. "I can feel your fear, Collector," he said, his gravelly voice sounding suddenly empowered.

I was stunned. Maybe I was just getting old, or my grip was weakened by the cold, but all I could think about was how I'd never seen an offworlder move so swiftly under Earth-g conditions. The man had clearly been proficiently trained.

"You don't want to do this," I said, trying to remain as poised as possible in the face of death. My survival instincts kicked in. Words came pouring from my mouth. "My partner will be here any minute. And if you escape him too, then the other collectors won't stop coming after you. How long do you think you can hide out here before you die of whatever sicknesses ail you? Not long enough to starve, I'd wager."

"I'm not hiding," the Ringer said.

I racked my mind to come up with anything that might buy me a few more moments. Zhaff had to be close, as much as it stung my pride to know he'd been right that I should've waited. "Most others won't hesitate to shoot you down on sight simply to save themselves the hassle. I'll tell my superiors you cooperated, Ringer. I'll make sure they treat you fairly. Get you the medicine you need."

"And what of the rest of my people?" the Ringer snapped. "When I left Titan, my wife was withering away to bones in one of Titan's quarantines. My son lives in fear of being sent to that place every day. Of being infected by your kind!"

Projecting his voice so loudly caused him to begin coughing again; this time, even more violently. When it was over with and he removed his hand from his mouth, I noticed a bloodstain on his palm. I tried not to let it show, but I could feel my usually steady heartbeat hasten as I realized I was standing in the sights of a man with nothing to lose.

"I can look into getting her treatment if you comply," I said. "I give you my word, Ringer... *Titanborn*." I remembered from our first meeting that he preferred that term over the more widely used *Ringer*.

"You can't promise me that," the Ringer said. By then, he'd noticed the blood on his hand as well. His gaze lingered on it for a second before he looked toward the sky. He breathed in deeply, thoroughly enjoying the chill that came with it. "It's so like Titan out here, minus the ruins. Beautiful. You mud stompers are so consumed with leaving that you don't even realize what you have."

Knowing I wasn't going to be able to talk my way out of this, I waited for an opening to appear so I could try to get my pistol back. Somehow, even as he reminisced, the Ringer's aim didn't waver.

"I'll never see my son grow into a man," he said. "I'll never feel the soft touch of my wife's lips again. Never see the silhouette of the Ring beyond the shroud..." A tear rolled out from his eye, freezing halfway down his cheek. He then stared me straight in the face. "Don't you see, Earther? I've been dying ever since I came to this world, and I won't suffer it any way but free."

The Ringer appeared more tranquil than angry. His finger grew more comfortable against the pistol's trigger. I swallowed hard, getting ready to pounce and make my last stand, when suddenly, someone shouted.

"Drop the weapon, fugitive!"

Our heads snapped toward the origin of the voice. Zhaff's silhouette appeared, standing between a pair of tall ruins, the yellow lens over his eye glinting. He was lining up a shot.

When I turned back to the Ringer, his lips lifted into a frail smile. "I'll have to take you up on that drink some other time," he whispered. "From ice to ashes."

I realized what was about to happen and lunged out, but for the second time in too short a period, I was too slow. The Ringer turned the pistol around on himself and squeezed the trigger. The forsaken city at our backs caused the gunshot to echo as if artillery had fired. His body collapsed in a bloody heap at my feet.

NINE

A BREEZE WHISKED AWAY the smoke hanging in the air from where the Ringer had fired my pistol. Purely out of reflex, I fell to the ground and reached for his throat to check for a pulse. I knew there was no way to survive a pulse-pistol round to the head from such close range. A gruesome, fist-sized hole was blown through the side of his skull, and his ghastly eyes stared toward the murky sky without blinking.

Zhaff arrived beside me in what seemed like an instant; his grim, emotionless façade aimed in my direction. "I told you to wait," he said, his always-flinty voice bearing only the slightest indication of the irritation his words conveyed.

I got to my feet, straightened my duster, and mustered the brazenness of a veteran collector. "He spotted me first," I said. "I didn't have a choice. I had him right where I wanted before you showed up and spooked him."

Zhaff's eye-lens zoomed in on my face. He was so close that I could see all its components and apertures working tirelessly behind the glossy yellow surface. "You're lying," he stated.

"What about you? You had the shot while he was still

aiming at me. If we're going to be partners, you damn well better take it next time!"

"He was preferred alive." Zhaff pointed to a fresh bullet hole etched in the frozen dirt only a meter away. I hadn't noticed it earlier. "He turned the pistol on himself precisely as I fired a disarming shot at his hand."

I looked back to the spot where I'd seen Zhaff aiming from. It was fifty meters away at least. "That's a long way to be shooting at such a small target with my life on the line."

"I would not have missed," Zhaff responded with unnerving certainty. "He is worth little to Pervenio dead."

"We get paid either way, dammit!" Saying those words out loud helped me remember that the Ringer was worth less to me dead as well.

I clenched my jaw. I knew I'd messed up. I wouldn't have survived so long as a collector if I couldn't recognize that. And I knew Zhaff could read it all over my face, but I wasn't going to give the Cogent the satisfaction of hearing it. Missing out on double the credits by a fraction of a second had me irked enough as it was. Coming up short on another mission made me sick to my stomach.

I bent down next to the body and got to work prying its cold, locked fingers off my pistol's grip. When I finally got it free and lifted it, the sky was already so dark it was hard to tell how bloody it was. I scraped the barrel against the rigid ground to clean it off as best as I could.

"What did you say to him to make him shoot himself?" Zhaff asked, breaking the silence.

I glanced up at him. I couldn't tell if he was trying to be funny or not, if he was even capable of that.

"What did I say to him?" I said. "Trust me, this is the first time I've ever seen this. I've hunted men and women from every background you can imagine. New immigrants, old immigrants, rich and poor. Hell, I've even tracked down some crazed preachers of the Three Messiahs. I've seen them look into the end of this gun and be ready to abandon everything they ever believed in just for a few more hopeless breaths. Given the same chance as this Ringer, none of them would've spared my life, let alone pulled the trigger on themselves."

"It is likely he had information about the bombing and didn't want to risk interrogation," Zhaff said.

"And let me guess. You would've gotten it out of him if we captured him alive?" I tried and failed not to allow my irritation to infiltrate my tone.

"It is a distinct possibility. I have had extensive training in extracting information—"

I cut him off. "Trust me, any man willing to do that wasn't going to get anything pried out of him. Not even by you. It's archaic, suicide. You'd think after a meteorite almost wiped us all out that a man wouldn't be so quick to take his own life." The sentiments of the USF were spewing right out of my mouth before I was able to contain them.

"His people did not experience the Meteorite."

My brow furrowed. I couldn't say anything in response to that bit of truth. Still, as I stared down at the body again, I couldn't help but wonder what it'd be like to be willing to die for something real, something more than credits. I could picture the Ringer's face right before the shot went off in my mind. He didn't hesitate at all. Pure conviction, and for what, I wasn't sure. It didn't make any sense to me.

"I have already contacted Pervenio airships for retrieval," Zhaff said. "They will be here as soon as possible."

"I don't suppose you'll tell them this couldn't be avoided?" I asked, suddenly not feeling very much like I was in control. Once the directors found out about how I botched the capture of a potential lead, I'd no doubt be sent back on mandatory vacation, or worse. Forced retirement seemed just as likely a scenario.

Zhaff didn't answer. I watched him kneel to further evaluate the corpse. He lifted the Ringer's head and looked through the gaping wound in the side of it. Even while doing something so undignified, each of his motions was executed with unbelievable deftness. His movements were so rote, it was as if he'd done it a hundred times, even though I knew he was only recently out of training.

It finally dawned on me. Zhaff was young, precise, loyal, driven by an unyielding sense of logic, and he likely didn't even require payment outside of his meals. All I was really doing out in the middle of the wilderness was helping to groom my own replacement.

The notion sent a chill up my spine so palpable I had to sit. We had a wait ahead of us while the Pervenio airships were en route. I left Zhaff to whatever it was he was doing and headed into the ruined shack nearby to take advantage of what little shelter it could provide.

HALF AN HOUR PASSED WITH ME UNSUCCESSFULLY TRYING to keep warm. The shack's crumbled walls were enough to block the wind, but the full coming of night was making the air even colder. It got so dark out that I couldn't even see my own hands, which would've been fine if I was able to sleep. The only light came from outside, from the faint glow of Zhaff's hand-terminal as the Cogent continued to analyze the Ringer's likely frozen-solid body.

As our wait extended to an hour, I started contemplating what I might be capable of doing after retirement. I had a few ideas what old collectors out of a job did until their inevitable deaths. Most of us never made it that far, and those I knew who did led secluded lives.

I could open up a restaurant on Mars, maybe, if I knew anything about cooking. Or maybe I could get a gig training security officers on burgeoning Europa. Corporations were always searching for men with field experience to help on new colonies, and that seemed to fit my wheelhouse. Though I had a feeling I'd wind up like the Ringer lying outside if I was forced to live the rest of my life doing that.

None of it had the appeal of hunting marks as they fled throughout Sol, bounties on their heads. The only possibility I sincerely entertained was spending my twilight years tracking down my daughter to see if I could even get a few words out of her in person before the end. That, at least, seemed like something as challenging as being a collector.

My hand absentmindedly fell to my pocket and Aria's toy. I flipped it between my fingers. For whatever reason, watching the Ringer blow his own brains out caused her to stick in my head. It could've been because I actually felt a tiny bit of pity for him after he'd brought up how he lost his own child. More likely, what had happened merely reminded me of another mission I'd screwed up back when Aria was the closest thing I had to a partner.

It was six years ago, and we were back on her homeworld, Mars. I'd asked for her help with a mission, and she reluctantly agreed. It was the last time she ever did...

I SIDLED AROUND A CORNER, PISTOL DRAWN. I WAS SURROUNDED BY TOTAL darkness, and I had my barrel-fixed light off so I wouldn't draw attention. My spotters rested on the top of my head. No heat signatures were in sight, so they wouldn't accomplish much covering my eyes. The darkness didn't bother me. The smell of the sewer I was in was horrid enough, so seeing what I was standing in might've been enough to make me gag anyway.

My hand grazed the moist, ribbed wall beside me so I could keep my bearings as I trudged forward. My feet sloshed through half a meter's worth of shit and who knows what else. If I didn't know any better, I'd have thought I was traipsing through the innards of a giant.

They were the waste trenches beneath Mars's oldest colony, New Beijing, tracing dark webs beneath a tiny terraformed portion of the planet covered by a dome. Garbage, excrement, used water—they carried everything unwanted out of the colony and dumped it all in rocky trenches exposed on the planet's surface.

I'd spent a larger portion of my life down in the sewers beneath Mars's many domed colonies than I cared to admit. Most of them were extensive enough to serve as perfect hideouts for the home-less, prostitutes, and fugitives. It was inside them where I'd met Aria's mother years back, and where she herself was born. Most people didn't delve as deeply into them as I was then, but Elios Sevari, the offworlder I was after, was clearly desperate to stay hidden.

He'd stolen valuables from a Pervenio merchant stationed in another Martian city and fled to New Beijing. The Red Planet was split among many corporations, and while New Beijing was run by Venta Co, it was hard to escape the influence of my employers. Still, I was on rival turf, so I couldn't take the man down on the surface where I'd be seen.

Elios stayed holed up somewhere in the sewers, only ever surfacing to find fences through which he could gradually sell all his stolen items. That was where my daughter came in. Aria was a perfect choice for the role of a black-market trader. By that time, she was a beautiful young woman, with fiery hair as red as the planet she was from, and skin as fair as milk. Offworlders were easily drawn to one another, so I knew it wouldn't be hard for her to catch Elios's eye. She only agreed to help after I promised her that she was just trying to catch him in the act of breaking the law and that nobody would get hurt.

I'd sent her into an underground cantina in New Beijing to earn his trust. After meeting Elios, however, she went missing with him for the better part of two weeks, only making contact once over Solnet to send me the merchandise she'd falsely purchased from him. I was confident that I'd taught her well enough how to survive and deceive, but I won't say I wasn't nervous for her life. So I'd taken things into my own hands and followed her trail into the old waste trenches to help her bring Elios down.

I rounded another corner and heard talking up ahead. I stopped, crouched, and glanced at my hand-terminal, taking care that no light would escape from the screen. A red blip on my radar displayed the location of a tracking program I'd planted in the Ark Ship figurine on Aria's necklace when she'd gotten older and tougher to keep track of. She didn't know it was there, but it was just in case things ever went wrong and her true identity was discovered.

I stopped and decided to finally pull my spotters over my eyes. I made sure to keep my gaze straight ahead, and after a short, malodorous walk through sludge, I found a cluster of heat signatures, Aria's among them. I breathed a sigh of relief. She was alive.

I shuffled forward, the current of the muck covering the sound of my movement. I got close enough to distinguish the other heat signatures. There was Aria, the fugitive, Elios, as well as a child—a young boy—on the landing of a service station that popped up from the slosh.

"Elios Sevari, you are wanted by Pervenio Corporation for robbery in the first degree," I announced. All their heads snapped toward me. Elios scrambled to the child and held out his arms to block him.

"Run!" Elios hollered to the boy. Tiny feet splashed through the sewers away from us. The boy couldn't move fast with the muck rising to his slender waist.

"*Come peacefully, and you will spend the next five years in a cell aboard Pervenio station. Resist, and the punishment is death,*" I warned.

Elios slowly knelt in surrender, but as he did, Aria stepped in front of him. She switched on the light of her hand-terminal and illuminated the sewers. I lifted my spotters to see her plainly.

"*Stop, Dad!*" *Aria yelled.* "*I won't let you take him!*"

"*Dad?*" *Elios asked.*

"*Just pretend you never found him,*" *she continued.* "*I already gave you what he stole, and he'll return the credits. He doesn't deserve this after... after everything.*"

"*Dad...*" *Elios repeated.*

He was behind Aria, but he crawled over toward a pile of bowls still full of some manner of leftover lumpy soup. In the light, I truly saw him for the first time. His left arm was a mangled stump beneath the hollow sleeve of his boiler suit, and that side of his face was also mottled with shiny scars that stretched all the way up to his receded hairline.

"*I'm begging you,*" *Aria pleaded.* "*Just let him go.*"

"*You know I can't do that, girl,*" *I said.* "*He doesn't have to get hurt anymore today, though.*"

"*You liar!*" *Elios spat at Aria. His voice spoke of heartbreak and betrayal.* "*A collector all along.*" *He glared at Aria with disgust. He bent down, and as he did, I noticed the pulse-pistol lying beneath the rim of one of the bowls.*

"*Liar!*" *he screamed as he tightened his only hand around the grip. Before he could move any further, I buried a bullet in his chest.*

The gun flew from Elios's hand and got lost beneath the muck. Aria dove to catch him but was too late. He slammed against the ground, and she was left cradling his limp body in her arms. Elios tried to speak, but all that came out was a glob of blood before the life fled his eyes.

When the child heard the gunshot, he stopped running, turned around, and shrieked. He hadn't been able to get far. "Papa?" he asked, voice shaking. He was skinnier than even offworlders ought to be.

Aria gazed up at me, tears running down her muddied cheeks. Her lips were quivering.

I stared, unable to lower my weapon. I'd never seen her look so shattered, and it didn't take me long to realize that the reason they were so deep in the sewers was that she hadn't intended for me to find them. She'd pretended to buy the goods from him and squared the debt, hoping that I wouldn't follow, but I did. I always got my man, no matter the cost.

"Why, Dad?" she whimpered. "He was only trying to keep them fed."

"He went for the gun—"

"You weren't supposed to find us!" she snapped. "He had no other choice! An accident in the water plant crippled him, and Pervenio wouldn't let him work anymore. Oh, Elios." She squeezed his head against her chest. As she did, his son got close enough to see his father covered in blood and began to sob uncontrollably.

"I didn't know," I said. "But he was going to hurt you." I was being honest. It's not a collector's job to ask questions. I did what was asked of me and made a good living doing it. That was probably why Pervenio had kept me on for so long.

"I deserved it..."

She stared down into Elios's glassy eyes, and then placed her lips against his, blood and all. I could hear her whispering to him. The sight of her like that made me feel sick. Who knew what lies he'd spewed to win her affections.

I waited there for a few minutes as the three of them wept, not sure what to do. Eventually, the foul stench got the better of me. "Aria," I said, "we've got to go."

She wrapped her arms around his limp body and squeezed. "I'm not leaving him."

"Yes, you are. If Venta Co finds out we were operating here, there'll be hell to pay."

I reached out to soothe her, but she pulled away. "I'm not leaving him!" she shouted. She started to cry into Elios's chest, and I placed my arm on her shoulder. That time, she didn't fight it.

"Aria, it's not easy what we do, but it's necessary," I said. "Say your goodbyes, and then we have to get rid of him."

She slowly rose to her feet without looking back at me. "You do it, then," she said, voice dripping with rancor. "Just another offworlder to you, right?"

"No, a thief and an attempted murderer," I answered, trying not to let her tone make me lose my temper. I knelt by the body and took out my hand-terminal.

"Yup, just another offworlder." She sloshed over to Elios's son, head bowed. When she reached him, she turned him around and held him in her embrace. "It's going to be okay," she whispered. "Look at me, and it'll all be okay."

I waved my hand-terminal in front of Elios's eyes to get a positive retinal ID and stored a bit of blood. Then I took a picture of his body, ensuring that I captured the bullet hole in his chest. Without his corpse, I needed something to present to Pervenio to get paid.

When I was done, I shoved him off the maintenance platform with my boot. He toppled into the muck with a splash, and then the slow current carried him along.

"Let's go," I ordered.

I walked back in the other direction, but when I didn't hear any footsteps behind me, I paused and glanced back over my shoulder. The child continued to cry, but Aria watched in silence as Elios's remains drifted into the darkness, never to be found again...

ARIA DIDN'T STICK AROUND FOR LONG AFTER THAT DAY. She stayed behind on Mars to find honest work, and I set off to continue doing what I did best alone. Until Zhaff was forced on me, at least. We'd exchange the occasional message over Solnet, but it'd been a year since the last time she responded, and the only words she wrote back were NOT ON MARS ANYMORE. It was clear she didn't want to be found, and this time, she wouldn't make it easy for me. As far as I knew, she could be anywhere in Sol.

Sometimes I thought about asking Pervenio Corp to track her down so I'd know she was all right, but I didn't have the spare credits, and there was no reason to tell them about her existence now. Considering her streetwalking mother dumped her at my feet, Aria was an unsanctioned, illegal child born from parents who weren't cleared for mating by the USF. People like her were considered illegitimates. My position probably could have kept me out of a cell if anyone found out, but I kept her a secret regardless. Director Sodervall would've never approved of me dragging her with me on assignments and winding up distracted. After deciding to keep her, my plan had always been to train her so well that when I did reveal her existence, he'd have no problem with us remaining partners.

I sighed. There was no worrying about that anymore. Illegitimates could get around the world they were born on with relative ease, but traveling between planets was difficult without a "real" identity. Apparently, I'd taught Aria enough for her to figure out how to get off Mars and travel throughout Sol without needing one. It was hard not to feel at least the slightest bit of pride about that.

I pulled out my hand-terminal and swiped the screen until I reached Aria's contact information. I just wanted to see her picture. I'd taken it right before I first sent her to see Elios. She was looking back at me with the spunky smile on her face that she always wore when she was happy. Her pretty red hair was tossed haphazardly over her shoulder. She never did care much about how it looked. Her necklace and the Ark Ship pendant, which I now carried with me, hung proudly over her shirt. She had no clue I'd used it back then to track her until one day when she ripped it off, threw it at me, and vanished.

I typed another message into my hand-terminal that I knew she wouldn't answer. It was all I could do. I took my time, making sure my numb fingers were striking the correct keys.

ARIA... I HOPE YOU'RE OKAY. I DON'T KNOW IF YOU HEARD, BUT THERE WAS A BOMBING IN NEW LONDON BY AN OFFWORLDER. IT CUT THE M-DAY ADDRESS SHORT, SO I HOPE SECURITY ISN'T TOO TIGHT WHEREVER YOU ARE.

I'M OUT IN THE WILDERNESS ON EARTH, NOT A STAR IN SIGHT. IF I DON'T FREEZE TO DEATH OUT HERE, I SHOULD BE BRINGING IN A NICE HAUL FOR FINDING THE BOMBER.

"Malcolm, they're approaching," Zhaff said, poking his head around the structure of the ruin.

I'd been so invested in choosing the right words that I didn't even hear him approaching. The hand-terminal slipped from my hands and hit the frozen dirt.

"Dammit, Zhaff!" I yelled. "Can't you see I'm busy?"

"You said to inform you when they were close."

"I..." I groaned. "I'm coming." My heart raced until he turned and walked away. I wasn't prepared to let him in on the existence of my daughter. I groped at the ground and found my hand-terminal. It was pure luck the thing hadn't broken.

I lifted it up and reread what I'd already written. As I did, the hum of anti-grav engines greeted my ears from outside. The emptiness of the derelict city made it resonate so loudly, I could feel my ribs vibrate. I wiped off the screen of my hand-terminal and then finished the message with the first words that popped into my freezing head.

I MIGHT NOT GET A CHANCE TONIGHT, SO HAVE A DRINK ON M-DAY FOR ME... DAD.

I took a deep breath, stared at the screen for a moment longer, and sent the message off to the Solnet laser relays before I could second-guess myself.

A bright spotlight shone down from the descending airship as I stepped outside, allowing me to make out its silhouette. It was a standard inter-atmosphere Pervenio carrier with broad red wings that housed rolling 360-degree anti-grav engines on the underside. It had the look of a stingray I'd seen a picture of in a pre-Meteorite museum, minus the tail.

A unit of Pervenio security officers hurried down the aft ramp once the landing gear touched down. They kept their pulse-rifles aimed while they spread out and secured the landing zone, as if there were anything to fear out in the wilderness. Pervenio officers never miss an opportunity to show off how well trained they are.

Zhaff saluted them as they approached. I thought about it but settled on a nod. My arms were getting too stiff for me to be willing to muster the energy for anyone other than Luxarn Pervenio himself strolling down the ramp.

"The body is over here," Zhaff said.

The officers quickly pulled out a shrink bag and got to stuffing the body in. Once they were finished, they carried it onto the ship.

"You two coming?" the leader of the unit asked.

"Don't have to ask me twice," I responded, relieved. I beat Zhaff to the ramp and wasted no time climbing up. Warm air washed over me from an exhaust vent and started to thaw my aching joints.

I crossed the cabin to an empty seat and pulled down my restraints. Zhaff sat in the spot next to me, his eye-lens poring over his hand-terminal. Once the ship took off, he turned to me and said, unemotionally, "We've been requested to travel to Titan."

I stared at him, dumbfounded. I'd been expecting the next message from the Pervenio directors to concern my failure, but he'd definitely said *we*.

"Titan?" I asked. "But we've already caught the Ringer here." I yanked out my own hand-terminal and checked for a message from Director Sodervall. There was none. Nothing from Aria yet either... as usual.

"Further examination of the blast site in New London has determined it was accompanied by a directional EMP burst with a limited range," Zhaff said.

"Makes sense," I said. "My hand-terminal acted a little extra screwy around the area shortly after."

"The EMP was used to provide cover while a small group of Ringers infiltrated the nearby Pervenio hospital."

"The explosion was a diversion. So our suicidal friend back there really did want to be caught." Suddenly, the sloppiness of the Ringer we chased out into the middle of nowhere wasn't so peculiar. We did precisely what he wanted. Hell, he'd probably plopped down next to me in the Molten Crater on purpose, knowing I was a collector and would be put on his trail.

Zhaff nodded. "It appears so. Supplies and documents crucial to the operations of Pervenio Corp were stolen from the hospital during the blackout. USF security has locked down all grounded ships on Earth without special clearance for investigation; however, it was likely too late. The stolen property is small in scale and would have been easy to smuggle through private transportation anywhere outside New London if that was the intent of the Ringers."

"So Pervenio wants us on Titan for, what, to try and head them off?" I said, desperate not to show the sudden sense of inadequacy that stole over me from missing so many clues.

"Yes, immediately," he said. "We are to depart for the Ring from Luna Station, locate the smuggled supplies, and apprehend whoever was behind this attack."

"Sounds simple enough."

"I have also been instructed to inform you that the successful completion of this task will result in payment equal to that of your reward for eliminating the bomber. This ship is returning us to New London. We will subsequently be provided passage on a passenger liner departing Luna tomorrow and meet with Director Sodervall at Pervenio station orbiting Saturn."

I leaned back in my chair. "Perfect. I'm getting tired of Earth anyway. Guess I can put aside my plans for Europa for now."

Zhaff's eye-lens focused on me like he was trying to figure out what I was talking about. I stifled a grin and closed my eyes. I wasn't exactly sure what was going on or why only Zhaff had been contacted, but I couldn't afford to care. This was one more chance. It almost didn't even matter what the pay was going to be. That was just a bonus that would make up for the fifty thousand credits I'd lost when the Ringer blew his own brains out. Even if I had to work with Zhaff again, and be on the freezing moon of Titan, I wasn't about to complain.

I'd been there on more than a few occasions in my lifetime, considering my primary handler served in the Ring, so I knew how frosty the locals could be. They went out of their way to make assignments trickier. Unlike immigrants in other colonies—who were mostly recently displaced Earthers with no affinity with the place they'd come to live—the Ringers of Titan weren't really immigrants at all. Not anymore at least. With gas-harvesting efforts on Saturn continuing to flourish, new immigrants flocked from Earth every year, forcing the Ringers to work for lower pay just to gain employment. The generations of people dating back three centuries who'd grown up there didn't take kindly to that. The Ring was their home.

For all those reasons and more, I didn't even think to ask about what specifically the Ringers had stolen. It was irrelevant. Collectors got our hands dirty so our employers didn't have to, and in doing so, we helped preserve the relative peace Sol had enjoyed since the Meteorite struck. That was my job. Concerns about retirement could wait.

IT WAS AFTER MIDNIGHT WHEN WE FINALLY ARRIVED BACK in New London. Just in time to enjoy the better parts of M-day. Security still patrolled the streets along the Euro-String rail station en masse, but I had no reason to stay on them with all the festivities moved inside. I invited Zhaff along but, as expected, he declined. Not that I minded. After the day we had, I needed some time away from him before I snapped. Instead, he disappeared to wherever it was Cogents stayed to finish his report. I only hoped it wouldn't reach the directors before I was safely aboard the transport to Titan, on my way to another assignment.

I headed into the first club I saw. It didn't matter how crowded it was with patrons and security officers at that point. Payment for bringing the Ringer bomber in dead had come through at some point before I arrived. It was half what it would've been had I listened to Zhaff and waited to confront him, but it was still enough for me to have no trouble enjoying that night and plenty of others.

I took a seat at the bar and ordered the strongest drink they had. Whatever it was, it felt like it was burning a hole in my belly as it went down. When I ordered a second, I noticed Trevor Cross sitting across from me. His head was sunken, his hat crooked, and he wore a sling on his arm. Seeing him helped me remember that fifty thousand credits were better than nothing. I'd gotten the job done. It wasn't the right way or the best way, but it was done.

I tipped my drink toward him and grinned. The booze had my eyelids feeling nice and heavy, so I probably added a little more insult to it than I should've, considering I was the reason for his sling. When he finally noticed me, he gritted his teeth, got up, and walked away.

A young woman wearing a tight, shimmering red dress promptly took his spot and must've thought my grin was intended for her. She smiled back and moved to sit at the stool next to me. My luck was improving. She had all the curves an Earther woman should have.

I wasn't too drunk to register—after a few minutes of conversation—that she was a working girl, but I didn't mind. Who was I to judge how anyone made their credits? I already had a room rented in the city anyway, and I planned on enjoying my last hours on Earth as much as I could.

Pretty girls from Earth used to throw themselves at me when I was young and handsome. They'd ask about what the rest of Sol was like or where I was coming from. I'd tell them stories about my most dangerous assignments, embellish a little, and enjoy a wonderful evening before running out on them the next morning. Collectors moved around too much to get attached easily, and I wasn't keen on winding up in a clan-family like my parents'.

I bought myself and the woman in red a round of the most expensive liquor in the place. Once my glass was filled, I raised it for a toast. "Let's enjoy the dying whimpers of another M-Day passed," I said.

"Another year," she replied, her ruby lips lifting into a smile.

I tapped the bottom of her glass with mine. "Another year."

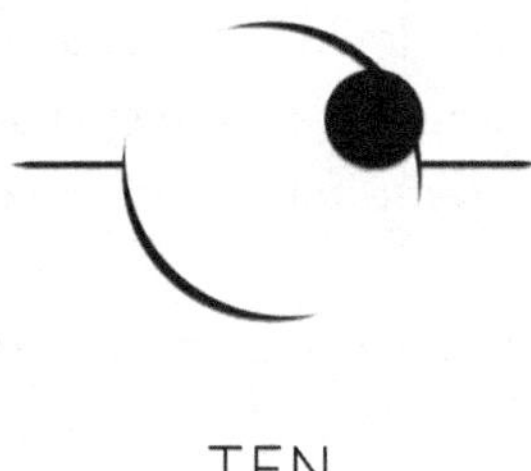

TEN

SOMEHOW, I managed to wake up the next morning just in time to catch the rail to New London Spaceport. After jostling through a healthy gathering of Three Messiah preachers spewing their usual lines about Armageddon, thanks to the Ringer attack, I met Zhaff at our gate. Running had me feeling nauseous. We were led onto a shuttle bound for the USF station on Luna.

The ionic impulse drives used in space didn't have the thrust to escape Earth's gravity well, so it took proper rockets to reach Luna. That helped the moon thrive as the largest ship-manufacturing plant in the entire solar system, where vessels of all types could come and go as they pleased thanks to its low g. Most sizable transport vessels were constructed there, including *Hermes* and a few other Ark ships that had been sent out into the great unknown through the decades.

Zhaff didn't say much during the twelve-or-so-hour ascension to Luna, and I was grateful for it. Weightlessness wasn't helping with my hangover, and neither were the few nearby passengers who were new to space travel and vomiting. I was worried if I opened my mouth for anything but breathing, I was going to join them. So I napped as much as I could, and when I couldn't, I stole glances out the viewport down at Earth, imagining how it might've looked when it comprised less brown and blue, and more green.

When we touched down on Luna, her meager force of gravity tugged on me and settled my stomach. We were quickly transferred to a tram bound for one of the station's larger, inter-Sol hangar bays.

Locals were hard at work in every area we passed. They were halfway toward looking like full-on offworlders, though their pasty skin was concealed by the layer of soot that came from working in the most factory-laden place in Sol. Even the largest asteroid colonies couldn't compare. Close to two million people lived on the moon at any given time, with shifts of worker-immigrants constantly rotating to and from Earth.

"How'd you sleep?" I asked, finally feeling healthy enough to speak.

"On my back," Zhaff said.

I was in no mood to offer a response to that. His devotion to logic was starting to seem like sarcasm after enough time with him, even though I figured it wasn't. I stayed quiet for a few moments, and then said, "So they find out more about that bomber?"

"Further scans couldn't locate a match for him in any database on Titan," Zhaff replied.

"Well, he didn't come from nowhere."

"According to you," he said, "he planned to be caught. It is possible whoever he is working with erased every trace of him ahead of time."

"Altering the recorded DNA of any relatives, deleting the genetic trail... It'd take more than your average hacker to do that."

"Or direct access to the mainframes on Pervenio Station,"

Zhaff countered. "There are thousands of inhabitants around the Ring working in medical labs, with sixty-seven percent having been born on Titan."

"Whatever they did, they made him a ghost," I said softly. I pictured the man's colorless face before the gunshot went off. It gave me goosebumps. The Ringer was willing to die for his cause without even needing a name of his own. No credits, no renown. Nothing.

"Pervenio will let us know if they discover anything further," Zhaff said as our tram slowed down.

"They won't find a thing."

It was years of experience speaking, but I didn't have a single doubt about it. I'd dealt with plenty of illegitimate offworlders trying not to be found. Hell, I'd fathered one. Very few of them had both the connections and killer-instinct to bomb Earth just to create a distraction. Whoever the nameless Ringer was working for or with, they were good, and I had a feeling we'd come face-to-face with them sooner rather than later if we kept on our path.

The tram came to a complete halt outside our departure bay, where the tremendous passenger liner scheduled to carry us to Titan was already waiting. The thing was easily half a kilometer long, and taller than most of the buildings down on Earth. The blocky hull was made up of a patchwork of shielded plates that guarded against radiation while crossing open space. When one was too tarnished or developed a breach, they simply tore it off and slapped a new one on, shinier than all the others surrounding it.

At least two hundred other Earther travelers were passing through security to get on. Many of them had large bags packed and wore the hopeful grins of immigrants about to set out on a fantastic new journey. I had no doubt most of them were either naïve or desperate enough to have seen one of the ads begging them to leave Earth and listened. As I looked around at all their faces, I couldn't help but pity them. Some of the men and women were attractive enough that I knew they could make a better living working the streets of Old Russia than on the Ring, wretched as that was. There were even children being dragged along by their parents. Future offworlders.

"They couldn't have chartered us something a little nicer?" I said to Zhaff. Not that I wasn't used to traveling on large passenger liners, but occasionally, Pervenio would set me up on private military ships. It seemed wrong to complain since they fronted all my traveling expenses and the hopeful immigrants in line around us had probably sold everything of value they owned to buy passage to Titan.

"The only other public ships scheduled to depart Luna Station today are heading to Mars," Zhaff replied. "The next one set to depart for Titan won't leave for another two weeks."

"What about private vessels?" I asked, remembering our current assignment. "One of the ships leaving this place might be hiding the supplies we're looking for."

Only the richest citizens of Sol could afford their own private vessels to carry them around the solar system on a whim. Those mostly belonged to corporations like Pervenio, which made Zhaff's earliest assumption that a rival might have helped with the bombing seem a little more probable.

"That is likely," Zhaff said, "though there are none listed as being dispatched to the Ring. Regardless, the USF's decree to increase the inspection of departing ships after the bombing would make smuggling near impossible."

"I doubt they'll find anything. Somebody is being awfully careful about covering their tracks and has a lot of credits to throw around to get people looking the other way."

"Agreed. However, Pervenio has asked for us to wait to

rattle the cages of any other organizations until we reach the Ring."

First, I wondered where Zhaff might have learned a phrase like *rattle the cages,* and then I sighed. "Politics, of course."

The decree made sense. Pervenio Corp had a stranglehold on the affairs of the Ring, and if another corporation was involved, it would be an easier place to extract information. Beyond the reach of USF security, things went smoother, and there were far fewer repercussions. Corporate politics always made things interesting. In Sol, wars over control were fought in the shadows with checkbooks, with barely a shot ever fired.

It took a few hours before the liner was prepped and every passenger was thoroughly inspected. There was no rushing a passenger liner the way we had the Euro-String rail. Zhaff and I kept our eyes peeled for anything suspicious while we waited, but trying to smuggle via a public vessel seemed bold, even for a group willing to bomb New London. Private transports were much less scrutinized.

"Right this way," a handsome young attendant greeted us once we eventually were permitted to board. He led us down the liner's spacious central corridor toward our sleep pods.

"Good thing they'll put us under for this trip," I said as I looked around at the many doe-eyed immigrants walking on either side of us. "Don't think I could take three months with this lot. You ever been on one of these?"

"Not this exact model," Zhaff replied.

"I meant an inter-Sol vessel this size. Or did Pervenio ship you around privately for your entire life?"

"That information is classified." I exhaled in frustration. "I have been on many vessels of this class, however, throughout my training," Zhaff elaborated before I could say anything clever. "It is a long opportunity for sleep." His blank façade didn't change, but the volume of his voice rose just enough for me to wonder if he was making an attempt at being humorous.

"Not sure if it counts," I said, smirking.

We were led into the port-side passenger hold where attendants pulled out our reserved, shelf-like sleep pods. They instructed us to place our belongings into the secure storage units underneath. I had my usual set of effects with me, which wasn't much. My duster, ID, lucky Ark Ship, hand-terminal, and belt complete with spotters, pulse-pistol, and a few other gadgets. The tiny duffel I'd packed and brought with me only had a few changes of clothing. Zhaff had even less. We stripped down to boiler suits and loaded into our respective pods.

I'd spent the majority of my life traveling back and forth across the vacuum, but I could never get used to the induced, dreamless slumbers that came with the trips. I would wake up months later, chunks of my life having fallen away in a flash. It was like time travel except for the part where my body felt the accruing years, and I'd wake up with another patch of gray hairs.

Sometimes by the time I arrived at a new destination across Sol, the difficulty of whatever assignment I was working on had escalated. Other times, the job had been completed by another company's collector weeks earlier, and there were no credits to be had. I hoped that wouldn't be the case for our continued mission, and since whoever was transporting the supplies couldn't move much faster than a passenger liner, it didn't seem likely. Heading off a smuggler between planets was rarely tough since the distance between them was so great. Finding out who was behind their actions—that was the hard part.

A chilly, gelatinous surface hugged my body and gave me a shiver as I lay in my pod. It quickly formed to every camber of my body, ensuring I would remain comfortable under the ship's initially high acceleration g-forces. An attendant hooked a few tubes with needles into my veins before a glass shield closed over me.

As I waited for the anesthetic chems to kick in, I wondered if Zhaff could even dream—and if so, what about. Probably a series of complex mathematical equations to solve for all of eternity. Or maybe a white, empty void. Before I could come up with any more ideas, I was completely under...

When my eyes next blinked open, the passenger liner slowed in its approach to Pervenio Station, Saturn. I yawned as the lid of my sleep pod popped open with a *snap hiss*. The trip felt short enough to have been a nap, but I knew around three months had passed.

I pulled myself out with ease since we were still in zero-g. That would change once we docked at the constantly rotating station where my muscles would be even weaker than usual from disuse. At the moment, however, I didn't mind letting the universe cradle me.

I floated there, gazing through a narrow viewport and out into space. Saturn took up the entire view. I couldn't see any stars, but I could see the glimmer of the planet's blade-like belt of rock and ice. Pervenio station floated right at its heart. The entire thing was built into Pan, a tiny shepherd moon causing a breach in the outermost Ring. Only roughly thirty-five kilometers across, it was a first-choice location for the wealthiest company in all of Sol to establish their headquarters in the Ring. From what I was told, Pervenio engineers utilized tremendous nuclear thrusters to instill the tiny moon with the fastest permanent spin any cosmic body had ever been given, at least at the time. It simulates an internal gravitational pull that's one-third the strength of Earth's, which doesn't sound like much, but is still more than even Titan can offer.

The countless craters dotting the surface were hollowed out, with tunnels crisscrossing the moon as if a great metal parasite had crawled inside and spread its limbs. Docking chutes jutted from the rocky outer surface like crooked fingers. No place in Sol received more ships on a monthly basis. Being located directly on the planet's Rings made dispatching ice haulers and gas harvesters extremely efficient.

The harvesters were especially lucrative. They worked tirelessly within Saturn's stormy atmosphere to siphon the valuable energy-efficient gases like helium-3 and deuterium that powered modern reactor cores and interplanetary impulse drives—the cornerstones of the emergent Sol-wide economy—needed. They were mostly automated these days, setting up balloons that sank into the clouds to be filled, monitored, then collected, but the fully manned harvesters could go deeper into the atmosphere, where the riches were in greater supply and where communication was impossible. People often said it was the most dangerous job in Sol, though I begged to differ.

The entire industry was part of what made the Ring so desirable and was the main reason other jealous corporations like Venta Co and the Red Wing Company set their sights on colonizing the moons of Jupiter. But even the largest of the gas giants in Sol didn't have those gases in abundance like its ringed cousin. Saturn was a relative gold mine, and while a handful of other companies had their own smaller stations orbiting Saturn, there was no question that Pervenio ran the Ring.

By the time Zhaff woke to join me, the liner was entering its hangar on Pervenio Station. Gravity pulled me back to the floor as the ship rotated to land on the inside face of the rotating moon's outer wall. It wasn't strong, but it didn't take long for my tired legs to start wobbling beneath my weight. The effects of the long trip even seemed to be impacting Zhaff. He still moved with the rigor of a well-oiled machine, of course, but I observed a slight lurch in his step. It was comforting, knowing there was something human about him, even if those signs wore off quickly.

We gathered our belongings without exchanging more than a simple nod and followed the crowd of weary immigrants off the ship. An older man, dressed in highly decorated black-and-red dress fatigues, awaited everyone directly inside the lofty hangar. A prim white beard hugged his sharp jawline, covering the jagged scar that sliced along the bottom. Director Sodervall in the flesh.

"Welcome to the Ring!" he announced to the crowd, clasping his hands together with apparent delight. "I am Director Sodervall, head of this station and your shepherd into this world. Both Pervenio Corp and the United Sol Federation thank you for your service! Humanity thanks you!"

He proceeded to give his usual speech to the immigrants. A lot of talk about starting fresh sprinkled over some lies about how grateful the locals would be for their presence. He had a knack for it as if he truly believed every word spewing from his mouth. After only a few sentences, I could see the travel-weary faces of the people he spoke to brighten with renewed excitement.

When he was done, a military escort led him and the immigrants off to physicians. I never had to go through the tedium of full immigration procedures, but I knew that the travelers would be extensively scrutinized before being fumigated, so they wouldn't risk infecting any Ringers with Earthborn illnesses. Only then would they be released into new living arrangements, whether those were in the major colonies of Titan or on one of the many other moons and stations orbiting Saturn that were run by Pervenio Corp.

In no time, Zhaff and I were the only new arrivals left in the hangar.

"You don't like him," Zhaff stated. His eye-lens was aimed toward the director as he led the immigrants toward their prospective fates.

I glanced up at the Cogent. I still found his ability to so accurately read my face unsettling, but I decided to ignore it. "I wouldn't say that. He's been my primary handler for far too many years, but you probably know that. We just haven't seen eye-to-eye lately."

"Because of me?"

"I wish it were that simple," I said, deciding not to be overly honest. Titan was a clean slate, a fresh start for me and my shiny new partner to catch a big fish. At least for as long as I could tolerate him. "Don't worry yourself about it. I know how to handle him."

Zhaff didn't have a response, and so we stood there quietly, waiting. Since he was the one who'd received our assignment to travel to Titan, I wasn't sure what our next step was.

"Malcolm Graves, I presume?" a man asked from behind.

Zhaff and I turned to see a Pervenio officer strolling toward us from the other end of the hangar. He had a tall frame, which meant he was probably born on the station, but a broad, Earther jaw. He faced me, but I could tell he was discerning Zhaff out of his peripherals and wondering what to make of the Cogent's strange appearance.

"The one and only," I joked. "Ready to get to work."

He wasn't amused. "Good. I'll lead you to your quarters, where you can recover from your journey."

"Lead away."

We followed the officer through a private decontamination chamber that washed away the stale, hospital-like smell of months in a sleep pod, and into a hall running parallel to the station's many hangar bays. A long, tall translucency ran along the floor at a downward angle, and beyond it, the icy rocks that made up Saturn's rings stretched out on a horizontal plane. Spotlights from a few working ice-hauler ships danced between them, and even farther away were the flickering lights of settlements on a dozen or so of the moons and stations that made up the vast archipelago of Saturn. Beyond that was a sea of starry blackness hankering to swallow it all.

When we reached a dormitory block, the officer stopped at a retinal scanner outside a sealed door. He placed his eye in front of it, causing the adjacent door to slide open. "Here you are, then," he said. "Director Sodervall will meet with you as soon as possible to brief you on the situation."

"Great," I lied. After what had happened on Undina and then Earth, I wasn't particularly looking forward to seeing him in person. He was a fair man, but only so long as his inferiors did what they were told and did it well.

The officer gestured toward the two beds on the opposite end of the room. A boiler suit was folded up on each of them. "Those are the newest line of weighted boiler suits. They'll help you acclimate to the low-g conditions both here and on Titan. You'll be able to move around more like you could on Earth when you're wearing them. Welcome to Pervenio station."

The guard gave Zhaff one more curious look-over before he marched back in the direction we came from. The room wasn't particularly spacious, but it was filled end-to-end with workout equipment, from things as ordinary as treadmills to some complex stretching apparatuses I'd never had the nerve to test. A large porthole built into the floor on the far side poked through the moon's rocky outer surface.

The only thing I cared about were the beds. I know I'd technically just slept for sixty days straight, but I threw on my new boiler suit and fell onto one as soon as the officer's footsteps died out. Drifting through space can take a hell of a toll on an older man's body.

"There is no time for rest," Zhaff said as he began examining each piece of exercise equipment.

"There's plenty of it," I replied. "No Ringer's getting off Titan now that Pervenio is on the lookout."

He turned around and set his eye-lens directly on me. "It is not them I am concerned about."

"Worry about yourself. Remember what I said about sleep? Unless you want me to get really grumpy, you'll let me get some."

I lay down flat and stretched my arms and legs as far as they could go. I'd traversed space too many times to let Zhaff tell me what I needed. Keeping my head on straight with proper rest was far more important than making sure my legs didn't get sore. I could fight through that. A few minutes after closing my eyes, the repetitious sound of Zhaff running on one of the treadmills lulled me into a deep slumber.

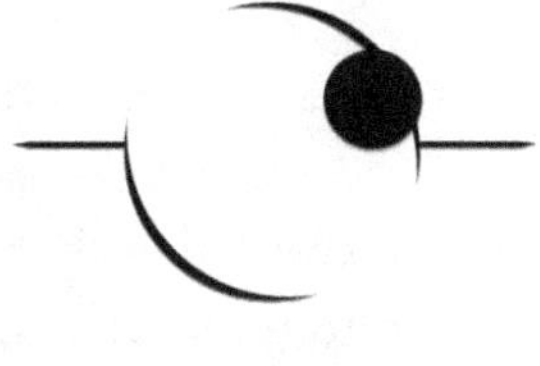

ELEVEN

Hours later, I woke completely refreshed. Like I've said, there's no substitute for real sleep. Zhaff remained on a treadmill, running with expectedly sublime form. His quiet breaths were measured, and there wasn't a bead of sweat anywhere on his face. He turned to me as I swung my legs off the mattress and stretched my arms.

"Good morning, Malcolm," he said the moment he noticed I was awake, continuing to run at full speed even as he spoke fluently. I'd never met a more efficient man in my life.

I exhaled and rubbed my eyes. "How long was I out?"

"Approximately five hours." He paused for a moment. "Now that you have rested, I would advise you to join me. It would be wise to train your body after so long a hibernation."

"Fine, fine."

I couldn't deny that he was right. Sleeping had my mind rejuvenated, but my legs still felt like marmalade after months in space. I lumbered toward a second treadmill. It was a decision I immediately regretted. Not only could I not keep up with his pace, but I started sweating after only a few minutes.

"Do you ever get tired?" I groaned, struggling not to stare at how effortless he made running seem.

"I do," Zhaff responded in his usual terse manner.

"*I do,*" I mocked. "How long have they been training you anyway?"

"Since I was two thousand, nine hundred and sixty-six days old."

I wasn't expecting an answer other than '*that is classified,*' so I found myself too startled to think of a response right away. I knew Zhaff was only around his late teens, but the emergence of the Cogent Initiative was a fairly recent occurrence. I couldn't imagine what a child version of him would have to say. The disturbing image of him growing up in a bio-tube popped into my head.

"You do have a family, right?" I finally asked.

"I have biological parents, if that is what you are implying," he replied.

"Yeah."

"I do. When my talents were discovered, I was taken from them to be trained in seclusion. Relationships would have been a distraction." He stepped off the treadmill and dropped into push-ups. His elbows bent to perfect ninety-degree angles.

"Tell me about it. So what are these talents? If we're going to be working together, I'd rather know something about the man who has my back other than the fact that you're a complete pain in my ass."

"Much of that information is classified."

As usual. I would've sighed, but there was no air left in my lungs from running. "Say whatever you can. They never told me much about the Initiative... or most of what they do, to be honest. I just want to know that you can't read minds."

"That is anatomically impossible at this stage of evolution. Recruits for the initiative are selected from children with heightened senses and intuition, among other abnormalities. I have heard us compared to savants, though that is not entirely accurate."

"So, basically, you're all brains, no guts."

"Considering all facets of human activity stem from the brain, yes," he said. "However, I was born with a low-functioning amygdala and a—"

"You're wasting your breath with that talk. I didn't pay much attention to science lectures when I was in school."

"Simplistically, while my intelligence quota is high, I am not proficient in what you would call social situations."

"No kidding?" I joked. His expression remained stagnant. "So, what, they slammed you into a solitary box and trained you to excel at the things you are good at?"

"It was not solitary."

The thought of being locked up was so unsettling to me that I nearly tripped. That was as close as I was going to get to a yes from him. Not sure what else to say, I decided to focus on my jogging and leave it at that.

"In your file, it said you belonged to the clan-family Amissum," Zhaff said, breaking the silence. "Why does your current surname not match theirs?"

"It did, a long time ago," I replied, shocking myself by answering so quickly. Nobody had cared enough to ask about my family in years, and I hadn't cared enough to tell anyone either. I'm not sure why I chose to open up then, but I did. I was probably just trying to distract myself from how much my body was aching, but I suppose I realized that if I wanted real answers about who Zhaff was, then I had to give some info about myself too. Like it or not, for the time being, we were partners, and I needed him to have my back.

"They were like most Earthers," I said. "Raising children in the safety of numbers, matching parents to avoid chronic diseases, you know the spiel. We lived a short train-ride outside New London. Two natural parents and a dozen others taking care of me and my fifty or so siblings. They were a nice bunch, factory workers mostly, I remember, but they were so happy with having the bare minimum. It never made any sense to me. I knew from the day I held a gun that I wasn't suited for a factory. Eventually, I couldn't take it and left. I got my own name when I became a collector for their protection and haven't heard from any of them since. Even if they did know or care where I am, they'd probably be too scared to talk to me, considering what I am. Can't say that I blame them."

"Safety is paramount," Zhaff said.

Hearing him echo the USF sentiments made me chuckle a bit, until I ran out of air. "I never really cared for having such a large family anyway," I said after taking a moment to catch my breath. "For being matched and sharing wives with the same last name even if we weren't blood. People call the Ringers primitive because they're still passionate about the whole monogamous-relationship thing, but it seems a hell of a lot simpler, even if it isn't as safe and efficient as my people like it. Anyway, I never got a chance to try that out before I accidentally planted a daughter in someone's belly—" I wished I could take back the words as soon as they left my lips.

Zhaff halted his routine and tilted his head in my direction. The change in his facial expression was almost negligible, but his one thin, dark eyebrow that wasn't covered by his eye-lens rose a hair, as if to indicate curiosity.

"You have created life?" he asked. "That was not listed in your file."

Years of keeping Aria a secret from my bosses and that one momentary slip, thanks to sleep-pod weariness, undid all of it. I'd only hid her so she could come with me on assignments rather than the directors sending her off to some clan-family so I could focus on the job or whatever they'd do. I wasn't the first collector to get a woman pregnant without USF clearance, after all, and I sure as hell doubted I'd be the last.

"It wouldn't be, but yes, I have," I said, deciding there was no point in trying to hide it anymore. Aria was gone, and Director Sodervall wasn't the type of man to chastise me all those years later when he, inevitably, found out about my illegitimate daughter from one of Zhaff's reports, especially considering the worst possible punishment he could muster was the Cogent already in front of me.

"I presume you are implying that you weren't merely a donor?" Zhaff asked.

"I think all men technically are," I snickered. "No. I was there when she was made, and for most of the years after."

"I do not understand. Where is your reproduction paperwork, then? And the selected partner?"

"She's illegitimate, Zhaff. Illegal. You can report me if you'd like, but it won't matter anymore."

"I am not an operative of the United Sol Federation. I would suggest you take up the issue with a Pervenio intermediary to the Assembly if you wish to report your crime and be punished accordingly."

I smirked. "I'll pass."

"Was your partner cleared?" Zhaff said after a brief pause. Only then did I notice that he'd stopped all exercise and sat on the floor, legs folded. I swear I'd never seen him so intrigued by anything, even if it didn't show much in his features.

"The mother? She was a streetwalker on Mars I favored in my younger days. Beautiful woman, with striking red hair..." My jogging slowed to a walk as she entered my thoughts.

We'd met during an extended assignment on Mars, in one of the many unused sewer systems re-outfitted as a brothel. She was well worth the price. I was never one to find anything more than pleasure in a woman's arms for a night or two, but we had a real connection. The next time I was on the Red Planet, I sought her out, and when I finally found her, she was dying from an infection from another client. She had an infant with her, claimed it was mine since she couldn't afford her fertility control when we met and dumped the girl at my feet. A black-market blood test proved she was right.

Looking back, I should've dropped Aria off somewhere suited for a baby and walked away. She would have had a better life. But, however she did it, Aria had me from the first moment I looked into her big, beautiful green eyes.

I shook the memory out of my head. I stood completely still on the treadmill now, staring blankly ahead.

"She died shortly after our daughter was born," I said to Zhaff. "More than two decades ago now. After that, I brought Aria—that's my daughter's name—along wherever Pervenio sent me. For a while, she'd help me when she could, but the older she grew, the less she approved of what my job entailed. Eventually, I got her involved in something that got her friend killed, and it was too much for her to stomach. She moved back to the Red Planet permanently, and we lost contact. Last I heard, she worked in a hospital there, helping the sick and dying."

Zhaff's lip twitched slightly after I finished, displaying a level of emotion I wasn't accustomed to seeing from him. Like he was allergic to anyone breaking the rules. His eye-lens remained fixated on me, but he didn't say a word. He just sat quietly until the silence made me break.

"Amazing that such a brilliant, caring girl could've come from an old wretch like me," I said, fingering the Ark Ship figu-rine in my pocket. "I only wish I realized earlier that making her was the only good thing I've ever done, though I don't suppose you'd understand that."

"I do understand," Zhaff replied immediately. "The propagation of human life is our greatest chance at progress."

It was the same jargon the USF had been spewing out ever since the Meteorite. The same shit that often dominated my own thoughts and made me itch when I stayed on Earth too long. She was my daughter, not just another body to help preserve the future.

"Do you ever think before you talk?" I grumbled.

"Always," Zhaff stated. He stood and started exercising again as if nothing had happened.

I should've known it would be a mistake opening up to him. It was difficult to be angry, considering how he could be, but I didn't lightly bring up Aria with others. Now he was one of the handful of people in the solar system I'd ever told about her, and probably the only one who'd remember.

I exhaled as I stepped off the treadmill and stared out through the room's viewport at the Ring. The station had rotated throughout the day, and I now had a view of the stormy upper atmosphere of Saturn, so tremendous that it eclipsed all of space. I wondered if maybe she was anywhere out there. At least because of Zhaff, and the mission report she would inevitably wind up in after we were done on Titan, her name might wind up Pervenio knowledge. Somebody might stumble upon her, so I'd know she was okay, provided she didn't change her name the way I had after I ran away.

"Malcolm?" someone outside the room said, drawing me out of my ruminations. It was followed by a knock at the door. I glanced at the sealed entrance but remained quiet. I had a feeling I knew who was outside and wasn't in the mood for any lectures. Zhaff didn't allow the calm to last.

"You may enter," Zhaff said as he stopped exercising.

The door slid open, and Director Sodervall stood in the entry.

"Malcolm Graves!" he proclaimed as he entered. I expected him to act far more cross after what had happened on Earth and Undina. Instead, he appeared grateful for my arrival. He rushed past Zhaff as if the Cogent wasn't even there, placed his wrinkled hand on my shoulder, and grinned. "Sorry to ruin your vacation with all this."

"Trust me, I don't mind." I returned the gesture. We were beyond the point of me having to address him as *sir* after every sentence.

"What has it been? Three, four years since I last saw you in person?"

"Something like that. I hear they call you the *Voice of the Ring* now. I can't believe they still have an old man like you in command here."

"Only until they find someone better," he joked. The smile he wore faded when Zhaff appeared beside him.

"I can relate. This is the partner you assigned me." I gestured toward the Cogent with both hands. "Zhaff. Fresh out of the Cogent Initiative."

Zhaff stepped forward with perfect posture and saluted. "Sir."

I could tell by the director's darkening features that he hadn't met a Cogent before. He saluted back halfheartedly before putting his arm around my shoulder. He turned me around and walked me as far away as the small room would allow. It was relieving to know that even he felt uncomfortable around Zhaff.

"A little young, don't you think?" Director Sodervall whispered into my ear. "Even for one of them."

I glimpsed back over my shoulder at Zhaff, who stood quietly in place with his eye-lens tracking us. I remembered how I'd noticed the same thing when we first met. His tall body moved with inhuman fluidity and precision, as if he were gliding effortlessly across a paper-thin sheet of ice with no fear of falling through. That was probably what made his age seem so bizarre. That or his taciturn face, which never showed any perceptible emotion.

I shrugged. "I figured you knew. Better to start them young, I guess."

"So I hear," Director Sodervall replied.

"Look, sir, about what happened on Earth, I—"

He shook his head and looked me straight in the eyes. "Forget it. We had no idea what we were up against at the time, but now we do. Focus on the job at hand." He turned back around so we were again facing Zhaff, though he continued to address only me directly. "You two need to build up your strength and plan your next move. You'll have access to all our shipping records, and whatever else you may need. I wish I could offer more help, but I don't have many officers or collectors to spare these days. Even fewer I trust with a job like this."

"I was wondering why they really sent us here all the way from Earth, especially after what happened. I've done business on Titan before, though. I should still recognize a few faces down there who may be able to help."

"Good. Ever since M-Day, we've been putting down protests and riots daily. Even after Luxarn announced he was planning to petition the USF Assembly for all offworlders, including native Ringers, to be permitted to take part in the Departure Lottery just to ease some tension. These damn Ringers are never pleased. If it were up to me, we'd send every single one of them off on an Ark ship toward some star and be done with it. Bastards were so eager to abandon Earth back in the day, after all."

"I'm sure Luxarn has considered it," I jested. The director shot me a glare that made me worry he was a little too comfortable with that idea. I hated offworlder drama as much as the next guy, but without them, I'd need to find a new line of work. "So I'm guessing you're expecting us to experience some trouble down on Titan when we land?" I asked, deciding to change the subject.

"Trouble? That's a gentle term for it. We extinguish new strains of dissidents here constantly, but there's a new group that won't go away. They call themselves the Children of Titan. Wear all white and paint orange circles on their chests like they're part of some ancient tribe. Hell, a month ago, they raided a terraforming research facility down on Titan. Blew the thing to pieces. Who knows why."

"They think Titan is their world," I responded, my conversation with the Ringer on Earth popping into my mind. "They don't want to change it."

"Indeed," he said, seeming rather disturbed by the notion.

"Any idea who's leading them?"

"Not a clue, but they seem to have great appeal amongst the locals, and with so many down there turning a blind eye, they have an uncanny knack for getting their operatives around our surveillance measures. We'd sweep all the colonies on Titan ourselves, but Luxarn wants us to keep our involvement relatively quiet so we don't rouse any more Ringers to their cause. If we march down into the lower wards in force, we may soon have a real revolution on our hands."

"Thank God for that. Keeps us employed." I nudged Zhaff, but he didn't seem to get the joke. He'd been paying close attention to everything the director was saying.

"Always looking on the bright side, Graves," Sodervall said. "You just worry about trying to find these smugglers. Mr. Pervenio has placed great importance on their apprehension."

I opened my mouth to respond, but as I did, a Pervenio officer came running into the rooms, out of breath. "Sir!" he said, saluting. "There's been an incident."

Director Sodervall waved him over listlessly, as if he was tired of hearing those words. When the officer whispered something into his ear, his eyes went wide with horror.

"Right now?" he questioned.

All the officer could manage was a nervous nod.

"I'll be there at once." He turned to me. "Your workout will have to wait, Graves. Follow me."

I regarded Zhaff. As always, he didn't appear perplexed, but the fact that he was also silent was enough for me to know that he, too, was unsure what was going on. I shrugged, and we followed the director and his guards out of the room.

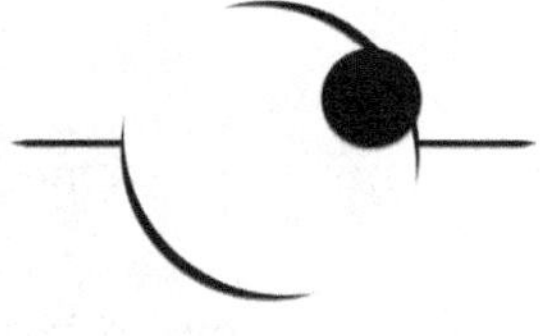

TWELVE

THE BUSTLING SECURITY headquarters on the other end of a tram through the core of the small moon made the one in New London look antiquated. The screens were larger, and many had holographic panes able to be touched and manipulated—the newest in televisual technology. There were also, of course, floor-embedded viewports, which currently displayed a stunning vista of Saturn's rings.

"This way, sir." The officer led us into Director Sodervall's private office. It was a sizable space filled with all manner of clutter. It was evident he was a very busy man with responsibilities extending well beyond keeping tabs on me. No wonder he didn't have time to bother with the Cogent Initiative.

The director keyed some commands into the console built into his desk, and then a large, holographic screen was projected in front of his viewport. He returned to my side. Zhaff was behind us, and I could feel his warm breath on my neck as he leaned in close.

"What's going on?" I asked the director.

"Just watch," he replied evenly.

He set the recording to play. The feed was grainy, but I

could distinguish what appeared to be some manner of soldier in heavy white armor standing in front of an airlock. An orange circle was inscribed over his or her chest plate, and the armor's visor was tinted enough to make it impossible to discern a face. The camera trembled a bit, which meant that there was likely someone on the other end holding it.

"The Children of Titan?" I questioned. Director Sodervall nodded with austerity.

Inside the airlock, at least a dozen Earthers banged on the glass of a circular porthole, screaming. A similar number of pale, long-faced Ringers were lined up in seats set on either side of the rebel soldier. They watched, though they didn't look like they approved of what was happening. Their eyes bulged with dread, and even though most of their mouths were covered by sanitary masks, I could tell by the way they drooped that many of their jaws were hanging open.

"We are descendants of those chosen by Trass—Titanborn," a voice deepened by some sort of distortion device said. It came from the soldier at the airlock. "We tire of being owned; of rotting in your q-zones as you suck our home dry. Retribution is coming. This is what happens to those who steal from *our* Ring. From ice to ashes."

Without warning, the armored soldier at the airlock pressed a button on its control panel, sentencing every Earther inside to death. The outer seal came open and, in seconds, the winds of Saturn reached in to yank them all out. Then the video went to static.

"That happened an hour ago on an old gas harvester named the *Piccolo*," Director Sodervall said irritably. "Somehow they've been able to broadcast that video all over this station."

The Ringer on Earth flashed through my mind, aiming my own pistol straight at me. I swallowed and pushed the memory away. The director didn't appear to notice.

Zhaff pulled out his hand-terminal and held it in front of us. In only a few seconds, he'd been able to pull up the video on the Rings Solnet network himself, as if testing whether the director's intelligence was correct. Disseminating something like that across the highly guarded Pervenio servers was no easy task. It meant these Children of Titan were as talented as they were bold and unpredictable.

"Do you have any idea where that ship currently is?" Zhaff asked before I could.

Without answering, Director Sodervall opened the door to his office and looked out on security headquarters. The panicked glare of every officer was fixated on him. "I won't ask again. I want the location of the *Piccolo*. Now!" he bellowed. The officers immediately lowered their heads and hammered away at their keyboards.

"You should also analyze the broadcast to discover how they were able to disseminate it on such a broad scale," Zhaff said.

"I know that, Cogent!" the director snapped. "My engineers have been on that for the last hour. We don't know how, but it originated on that harvester."

Without hesitating, Zhaff walked over to the director's personal computer and began typing. The sight came close to making me laugh, but I was able to hold it back, considering the current circumstances. The director didn't say anything, but he seemed to be more in shock than he had been while watching the recording.

Zhaff's eye-lens darted from side to side, incredible amounts of text scrolling across the reflection in the yellow glass. After half a minute, he stopped and looked up. "That is impossible," he stated. "According to your records, the *Piccolo* is far too dated to support a communications system capable of accomplishing this on its own, especially with the interference of Saturn's storms. It appears that the recording was somehow transmitted from the ship directly to this station, where your secure channels were used to post it publicly."

"How do you know all that?" the director questioned. He rushed over to see what Zhaff was looking at. I couldn't help but let a smile break onto my face despite the circumstances. It was nice to see Zhaff's abilities thrust into the face of somebody besides myself. Now Director Sodervall knew precisely what he'd signed me up for.

"He tends to surprise you," I said.

"That recording is now available on all local Solnet channels," Zhaff continued. "There will be no stopping it from being dispersed throughout the entirety of Sol unless everybody in the system disables their active devices."

"Skelly bastards!" Director Sodervall barked. "Mr. Pervenio is going to have my head for this. Can you trace how they were able to do it?"

Zhaff keyed a few more commands and scrolled through more information so quickly that Sodervall's eyes looked tired just from trying to keep up. "Not from here. I would need to see what was done on that ship."

"Then we'll have to get you onto it," Director Sodervall decided.

"Also, not possible," Zhaff said. "We are presently tasked with locating the smugglers behind the bombing on Earth. We must focus on our own assignment."

"I gave you the damn assignment!"

"I hate to disagree with you, Zhaff, but he's right," I broke in before Sodervall smacked him. "The Ringer I encountered on Earth used those same phrases before he killed himself: *Titanborn; From ice to ashes.* Call it a hunch, but I have a feeling the same people are behind both attacks."

Zhaff's eye-lens fixed itself on me. "Why did you not inform me about this earlier?"

I shrugged. "I didn't think it was important. Offworlders and their expressions. I've heard thousands over the years." I leveled a glare Sodervall's way. "And nobody told me the Children of Titan existed until today."

"It was need to know," Sodervall said. "But they're the right kind of bastards to be willing to bomb Earth on M-Day, all right. This could be another distraction to hide what they're really after."

"My thoughts exactly. Now we have a ship full of Ringers who saw what happened up close if they're still there. One of them might know something. It's our only lead, Zhaff. How many transport ships from the inner system are arriving on the Ring within the next week?"

Zhaff bent down and searched through the director's computer again. "Seventy-three," he specified. "It is possible, however unlikely, that they utilized a vessel faster than our passenger liner and arrived earlier."

"And the smugglers could be on any of them, assuming they're even coming here, or didn't pass their route through a dozen inner colonies to stay invisible. I say we follow this lead right now." I turned my gaze toward the director. "If thirty years as a collector has taught me anything, it's not to believe in coincidences."

"Sir!" an officer outside hollered. "We have a read on the *Piccolo*'s location. She's emerging from the upper atmosphere of Saturn now, heading directly for this station. We're getting intermittent messages from the surviving crew that the invaders have disappeared and that they're bringing the *Piccolo* back on their own accord."

"Well, it looks like you both won't have much choice," the director said. "They're coming right to you."

"They are lying," Zhaff decided. "Manned harvesters of that class have outdated nuclear-thermal engines with auxiliary ion thrusters to allow for travel within and out of Saturn's gravity well."

"English, Zhaff," I said.

Zhaff keyed a few more commands. "There is a nuclear reactor on board that is well past its recommended life expectancy and could be easily overloaded to damage this station," he said. "It cannot be allowed to reach us. According to you, the Children of Titan are renowned for utilizing violent, unpredictable measures. Lend us a ship, and we will intercept it." His tone wasn't any more authoritative than normal, but it held an acute sense of urgency that earned even the director's complete attention.

"I agree with Zhaff." I hated to say it out loud, but he was right. If both this attack and the one on Earth were connected, then the Children of Titan had used a bombing to divert our eyes from their true intentions. It was impossible to say what else they were willing to do.

The director exhaled and nodded slowly. "I'll prepare a strike team straightaway."

"Don't worry, sir, you know I've put down plenty of violent offworlders before," I said evenly. "We'll figure this out."

"I want to trust that, Malcolm, but let's try to keep this clean this time. We don't want another Undina situation."

I knew from the moment I saw him he wasn't going to let our conversation end without dredging up my recent failures in some way. I feigned a grin and bowed my head.

"With Zhaff at my side?" I said. "Never."

"For your sake, I hope not. Good luck, Graves." He patted me on the back before turning toward Zhaff, a distrusting glare plastered on his wrinkled face. "You too," he muttered. Zhaff saluted him, but Director Sodervall walked away toward his hectic officers without paying any attention.

THIRTEEN

A SMALL TRANSPORT vessel flew me, Zhaff, and a group of three Pervenio security officers toward the location of the *Piccolo*. All I could see through the cockpit's viewport was the starless black mass of Saturn as we headed straight for its dark side. Occasionally, tiny fragments of rock zipped by the cockpit's viewport, illuminated by the steady stream of light emitted from the ship's forward spotlights. Our path took us across the topside of the planet's inward rings, where they were at least relatively small and mostly ice. Still, the entire ship rattled every time one of them banged against the hull.

"Three minutes out!" the pilot shouted back into the holding bay. I could see a red blip nearing our position on his control console. There were no other visible ships anywhere in sight through the viewport. We were past all the ice haulers, and every working gas harvester operated within or just above Saturn's roiling atmosphere. Between the innermost rings and the planet itself, it was completely dead space.

"What happened on Undina?" Zhaff asked suddenly, breaking the silence. Nobody but the pilot had uttered a word since we left the station.

"What?" I asked, not sure if I was more surprised by the apparent randomness of the question or that he didn't already know.

"The mining colony of Undina. Director Sodervall told you to avoid a similar situation."

"I thought you reviewed my entire file?"

"I did," Zhaff clarified. "I studied the records of numerous eligible collectors to be paired with before I arrived on Earth, Malcolm. You were one of them."

Of course he had. He'd been thorough as always. A part of me wished he'd overlooked my name and saved me his presence, though that probably would've meant that Director Sodervall wouldn't have given me the New London bomber assignment. I'm not sure if I could've survived two weeks of vacation if he hadn't. I probably would have drunk myself into the bottom of a sewer out of boredom.

"I'm flattered," I said. "And Undina wasn't on it?"

"It was," Zhaff replied. "Based on the available report, the insurgents were disposed of successfully. Why would Director Sodervall want us to avoid that?"

"It was a joke. Forget about it."

"You are lying."

I sighed. I knew he wasn't going to drop it. "They were *disposed of successfully*," I said. "Just not as cleanly as the director would've liked. I didn't pull my trigger fast enough, and a lot of workers and guards died because of it. Don't worry; I won't be making that same mistake again. If these offworlders want to keep treating Sol like their playground, then I'm done trying to play nice."

"One minute!" the pilot updated us.

"One day, most of our species will be what you consider offworlders, Malcolm," Zhaff said. "Even the life you helped create was conceived offworld. It is our job to ensure the welfare of human expansion, no matter who commits the crimes that threaten it."

I wasn't sure what to say. I'd met many young collectors who claimed to feel the same way: that they did their work for more than a bounty. After a few years on the job, seeing the shit we see, there wasn't one of them who didn't forget about all that. When Zhaff said it, however, I knew it wasn't just something he told himself to feel better. He didn't even care about getting paid. There was nothing, no horror he could see, that would ever change his mind. I could respect that level of stubbornness.

"These days, we all feel like one and the same," I said. I patted his leg and nodded. "But all right, Zhaff. Let's make them pay, then. Helmets on!"

Zhaff nodded back, and we reached down, picked up our helmets from the rack beneath our seats, and placed them over our heads. The other officers on board did the same. We all wore Pervenio-issued, space-worthy armored suits with nano-fiber inlay that enhanced muscle performance. A gentle hiss as the helmet's seal formed around my neck, then I closed its visor. All I could hear was my own steady breathing.

"Coms check," I said. The com-link built into each suit connected our squad with one another and to Director Sodervall if he needed to make contact.

"I'm a go," each officer answered individually.

"I can hear you," Zhaff said last.

"The command deck is ruptured," the pilot announced, his voice now directly beside my ear. "You want to go in through the breach?"

"Negative," I said. "Take us to the cargo bay walls, and we'll cut in. If the command deck's exposed, whoever is on board might be expecting us to come through there."

"Roger that. I'm going to back up against it. Hold on to your seatbelts and prepare to breach."

My stomach jumped suddenly as the ship banked around hard. The force would've tossed me clear across the cabin, but restraints wrapped around my chest held me tight against my seat. I squeezed my eyes shut and ignored the pain pulling at my sides. A few seconds later, we straightened out, and all my innards did the same. I released a mouthful of air and set my restraints to release.

"I'm opening up," the pilot said. "Switch on oxygen."

I hit a button built into the wrist of my suit. I couldn't feel the change, but I knew the small amount of oxygen woven into the suit could be the difference between life and death out in the heart of space. This wasn't my first time breaching a rogue vessel.

The cabin depressurized, and then the rear hatch popped open. I used the hand bars along the ceiling to pull my weightless body toward the starless maw. Spotlights from the transport turned and shone their light ahead of me, revealing the hull of what I assumed was the *Piccolo*. A row of grated ducts stuck out from its sides like the keys of a piano, connected to tremendous pumps used to siphon gas out of Saturn's atmosphere and into vats inside to be refined and sorted. The plated hull had a discolored, yellow hue from being pounded by sulfur and ammonium crystals in Saturn's atmosphere. It looked like it was from a time before I was born—if that was possible—before the Earthers ever even reunited with the Ring. Director Sodervall wasn't exaggerating when he said the thing was old.

"Hold on," the pilot said.

Bow thrusters had us gradually reversing toward it. I grabbed hold of the ceiling as tightly as I could.

"Shit!" the pilot shouted.

The back of our ship slammed into it so hard that my tired arms gave out and I lost my grip. I flew forward, but before my helmet smashed into the side of the *Piccolo,* someone grasped the back of my suit and drew me back.

"Sorry, I came in too hot," the pilot said.

"I told you, you should have exercised," Zhaff said as he straightened me out.

His voice was flat as ever when he spoke, but it was actually the kind of remark I knew I might say in a similar situation. I hoped maybe I was rubbing off on him. All I could see through his visor and bulbous helmet was the yellow glare of his eye-lens. It made him look like some manner of ridiculous, mythical cyclops.

"That's what you're here for," I said. "Okay, boys. Light this thing up."

A short, ribbed tube extended from the back of the ship and formed a seal with the *Piccolo.* The process released a whistling sound so shrill it made me wince even through my helmet. When that finished, one of the officers floated forward with a fusion cutter in his hand. The blade of heat it emitted was so intense, it had to be powered by our transport's engines to operate. It took a hell of a lot of energy to cut through the dense hull of a gas harvester, no matter how old it was. They had to be built to withstand the tempestuous atmosphere of Saturn, and wind speeds during storms that could tear a man's limbs from their sockets.

Sparks flew out as the officer cut a wide circle. A chunk of the *Piccolo* came loose and was pushed inward, leaving behind an orange ring of smoldering, molten metal for us to pass through one at a time.

"How appropriate," I said under my breath as I stared at the opening, remembering the circle on the chest of the terrorist in that video.

"What was that, Malcolm?" Zhaff asked.

"Nothing. Weapons ready. Let's go."

The three officers pulled their weightless bodies through first, pulse-rifles at their hips. They used the chunk of the ship's hull as a shield in case an ambush was waiting for us. Zhaff went next, and I followed until all five of us floated somewhere in its cargo bay. The inside of the *Piccolo* was completely dark.

"Zhaff, oxygen levels?" I said.

He raised his hand-terminal and keyed a few commands. "Breathable."

I reached up, switched off my air supply, and drew my visor back. The warm, stale air was completely stagnant, which let me know that the air recyclers weren't functioning. Eventually, the oxygen would run out.

"Spotters on," I whispered, my voice now escaping my helmet. I lowered through the opening where my visor had been and switched them to thermal. The cargo bay remained completely empty of heat signatures.

"On," everyone but Zhaff replied. With his eye-lens, he didn't need spotters. To be honest, a part of me figured he could see through walls with the thing.

Zhaff tapped me on the shoulder and motioned forward. I nodded.

"Magnetize," I said, hitting a button on my suit next to my oxygen. My boots were slowly drawn to the metal floor. A minor magnetic force charged them, not enough to walk properly, but enough to keep me anchored after every extended step. It was similar to walking under the natural conditions of Luna, only the rest of my body still felt completely weightless.

The rest of the squad did the same, and we moved ahead through the cargo bay with long, bouncing strides. My pistol was raised, and the daunting quiet had me on edge. Other than our magnet-induced footsteps, the only sound filling the *Piccolo* was the gentle purring of its engines. Then I heard a clank.

"Shit!" one of the officers yelped.

"What is it?" I questioned.

Another officer switched on the flashlight built onto the barrel of his gun. A line of spherical harvesting tanks lined the walls. Thousands of liters of pressurized hydrogen and helium all around us, and more in smaller canisters to be transferred to cold storage. The officer had banged his forehead against the base of one tank, and it was still reverberating.

"Everyone, watch your step," I said. "We puncture one of those, and we'll all be cooked."

"We must reach the ship's command deck," Zhaff said. "Any rebel combatants or surviving members of the crew are wanted alive if possible."

"Good luck with that, freak," the officer who banged his head remarked. "I see one of these Ringer bastards, I'm putting them down."

I reached back and grabbed the officer by the shoulder. "We're here for information first," I growled. "One stray shot and this thing will go up in flames. Shoot to wound and only if you have to. Those are Director Sodervall's orders, so unless you want to take it up with him when we get back, you'll listen."

Regardless of how much Zhaff could irritate me, he was right, and I knew his report would reach the ears of Director Sodervall. I wasn't trying to screw up what was now my third opportunity to prove my worth in as many months. Plus, it didn't seem right that anybody but me could talk to my partner like that.

The officer grunted in response, but I could tell I'd gotten through to him and the others. They'd likely never heard my name—it wasn't part of a collector's duty to earn fame enough to be known—but they knew what I was. Any collector who'd served as long as I had held considerably more clout than an officer or guard. They'd probably never even had the opportunity to utter anything more to a director than the word *sir*.

"All right, Zhaff and I will head for the command deck," I said. "You three take the engine room. Gaining control of the ship is our highest priority. Remember, watch those trigger fingers. Com's open." The Pervenio officers went in the opposite direction at the first branch in the hall, leaving Zhaff and me to continue on our own. I turned to him. "You got the ship schematics?"

"Memorized," he said.

"Why am I not surprised? You lead, then."

Zhaff moved in front of me, and we started off down the dark passage. I decided after a few steps that my spotters weren't working for me. Waiting for heat signatures to pop up in a warren of winding corridors would only lead to me making mistakes. I preferred to see through own two eyes when I could.

"Screw this thing," I said as I removed the device and switched on the small flashlight fixed to the top of my pulse-pistol. "I'll leave the signatures to you. I'm going basic."

It might've revealed our positions, but our magnetized footsteps were the loudest sound in range, so it didn't matter much. With the flashlight, I could better see the condition of the ship. Much of the circuitry and systems were left exposed through the grated walls and floors. I noticed a spot of blood on one pipe from which hot steam poured through a narrow gash.

"I don't understand," I whispered. "Why switch everything off?"

"It is possible the broadcast utilized a great deal of energy," Zhaff answered.

"I guess so—" As the words left my lips, a male Ringer soared sideways across the hall ahead of us. "Freeze!" I barked.

"Don't shoot!" the Ringer whimpered. He grabbed hold of the wall and raised his free arm. It shook.

"Turn around slowly," Zhaff said.

As the man turned his head, I shone my light in his face. A

sanitary mask covered his mouth, but it was covered with blood as if he'd had his nose broken and his eyes were rife with terror. He held out his hands; they were empty.

"Please, I didn't do this," the Ringer said.

"Quiet!" I ordered. "Get on the ground now, and you won't be harmed."

He didn't hesitate. He extended his arms, grabbed hold of the grated floor, and pulled himself down, looking like quite a pro when it came to being detained. That was a common occurrence for Ringers from the lower wards on Titan, where learning how to steal food was a crucial part of staying alive.

"Cuff him," I told Zhaff.

Zhaff got behind him and held him down against the floor so he could bind his wrists with a band of fiber-wire. "Are there any militants remaining on board?" he questioned.

"I... I don't know," the Ringer stuttered. "They switched all the lights off and disappeared. I swear we didn't do anything!"

"He's telling the truth," Zhaff assured.

"Don't try to make a move," I said to the Ringer. He nodded vigorously, and Zhaff lifted off him. His weightless body started to drift upward, but without his hands, he would be completely useless at escaping.

I activated on my unit-wide com-link. "We've encountered our first member of the crew," I said. "He was unarmed."

"Us too," one of the officers responded in my ear. "He's alive," he added with a grumble.

I tapped Zhaff on the shoulder, and he continued forward. He turned left at the next branch in the corridor. My magnetized boots brushed across a large patch of blood splattered on the floor. It was still fresh enough to rub off on the soles.

"I guess not everyone got into that airlock alive," I whispered to Zhaff.

Zhaff stopped moving and knelt. He ran his gloved finger

through the grooves of what appeared to be bullet-induced dents on a nearby pipe. "Doubtful," he said. "The attackers used non-lethal rounds."

"How generous of them. So nobody got to miss out on their little show."

"It was a message," Zhaff clarified.

"Trust me, I know. I've seen plenty like it, though usually, they target officers or soldiers, not innocents."

"The harvesting of Saturn's gases is vital to expansion. Removing one ship, no matter how outdated, will cost Pervenio Corp greatly."

"Not to mention make Venta Co's efforts around Jupiter seem far safer to invest in," I realized. "Not just storms to worry about, but terrorists too. I'll give them this, these Children of Titan sure did their homework."

Something moved behind us. I whipped around quick enough to see someone's foot disappear around the corner. I went to follow it, but Zhaff grabbed my arm and shook his head. "Ignore it. That Ringer is unarmed. The command deck is close."

We walked until the corridor ended at a sealed door. The control console adjacent to it blinked red with the word ERROR.

"Locked," I groaned. "Naturally."

"One moment," Zhaff said.

He knelt in front of the console, drew his hand-terminal, and held it up to the screen. After a few seconds typing furiously to hack the controls, he turned back to me.

"Come," he indicated, taking my arm and leading me into an adjacent storage room.

"What's going on?" I asked.

"Raise your visor for breach and stow your firearm."

"What?"

Without answering, he sealed us into the room and signaled the command deck entry to open. Air in the corridor outside whistled as it rushed through the door, dragging loose parts and hanging wires out with it. I scrambled to close my helmet, and the moment I did, Zhaff opened the storage door and hauled me into the gale. It wasn't the initial burst of decompression, but it was enough to drag us into the command deck even with our magnetized boots on. With my arm in one hand, Zhaff grabbed hold of a console before we were sucked into space. Somehow, at the same time, he managed to seal the door behind us, halting the change in pressure and preserving the oxygen within the ship for the survivors. The vacuous conditions of space took hold.

"Next time, warn me when you're going to do something like that!" I rasped.

"I did," Zhaff replied.

"Be more specific, then."

I swung my feet around so that my magnetized boots would cling to the metal floor, then I studied the command deck. It had a dome-shaped viewport for a ceiling, but its structural members were splayed open, exposing it to space. As my gaze turned downward, I noticed that someone else held on to the floor, pinned beneath the ship's command console. Whoever it was, they were lucky they hadn't been flung out into the void.

"Don't move!" I shouted before realizing the Ringer couldn't hear me with my helmet sealed.

Zhaff pushed off the back wall and zoomed over my head. He perched on the captain's chair and aimed his gun down at the person. Whoever it was, they were also in a spacesuit, and their helmet turned slowly to see him. I shone my flashlight on the area as quickly as I could. Through the visor, I could see it was a young girl, probably in her late teens, with a pale Ringer face and hair so blonde it could've been silver. I was about to give Zhaff direction when I noticed she had something clutched in her hand.

"Hand!" I shouted into the com-link, not eager to experience a repeat of Undina.

Without hesitating, Zhaff grabbed the girl by the forearm and slammed it into the edge of a command console. The device, which appeared to be little more than an older model hand-terminal, floated out from her fingers. Zhaff promptly snatched it and placed it in his belt, then yanked her away from the command console, and pointed to the sealed entrance.

I turned around and drew myself toward it. Zhaff followed close behind with the girl in tow. We moved to the sides, then he set the door to open. Air gushed out, and the continuing change in pressure made it incredibly difficult to pull myself through, even with the augmented strength armored suit provided, but as I curled my legs to push off the floor and give myself a boost, I felt a strong thrust from Zhaff behind me. The door slammed shut behind us, and when I removed my visor, everything was quiet again. Zhaff tore off the girl's helmet and held his pistol against her forehead.

"What were you doing?" he questioned, his voice more elevated than I'd ever heard it. It was enough for me to know she would be in trouble if she lied.

All she could manage was to shriek in response and grasp for her injured arm. Her bulky suit made it difficult to tell, but judging by her expression, it was probably broken. She panted wildly, tears streaming down her pale cheeks. Her lips trembled.

"Tell me," Zhaff demanded.

Maybe it was because she was so young, but I actually felt bad for her. She didn't look like a terrorist at all. In fact, despite her face having many typical Ringer features, she was relatively short for one, and it made her look even more frail and harmless. She also wasn't wearing a sanitary mask like they usually did.

I placed my hand on Zhaff's shoulder and brushed him to the side. I knelt in front of her and gazed straight into her eyes.

"You'd better not irritate him," I whispered to her. "Just tell us what you were doing up here, and you'll be fine."

"Malcolm," Zhaff said. I glanced up at him, and he had her hand-terminal raised so that it faced me. The screen was completely white except for an orange circle in the center. "All of the data has been wiped except for this image."

The girl's eyes widened when she spotted the device. "I found that connected to the command console!" she said, her frantic breathing hardly able to keep pace with her words. "By Trass, I swear, I only found it when I got up here! I... I only wanted to see what they did."

Zhaff nodded to confirm her story, and I looked back at her. "I believe you," I said. "So the attackers came through the command deck. What happened to them?" I incidentally shook her shoulder a bit too hard, and she winced.

"They all left... I think," she moaned. "I... I was trying to switch the systems back on so we wouldn't run out of air, but I was locked out."

"Are you sure you did it correctly?"

"I am—was the navigator. I know how to run the ship. All of the power is being diverted to the engine's reactor using emergency overrides."

"Shit!" I cursed to myself. I switched on my com-link to message the rest of our squad. "Have you reached the engine room yet?"

"We're there now," one of the officers answered. "The Core's humming, but all the lights are off down here as well. Wait... we've got something. Argh—" His feed cut out.

"What is it? I repeat, what did you see?"

I heard gunfire erupt through the com-links of the other officers as they attempted to respond.

After a short period, theirs went silent as well.

"Zhaff, we've got to get down there now!" I shouted.

Zhaff started to run, but as he did, we were thrown back against the wall. A powerful force seized my body, enough to make me feel like my eyeballs were going to pop backward into my skull. The Ringer girl howled in pain. Without our suits on, it may have been enough to make us pass out.

It didn't take long for me to figure out what was happening. The *Piccolo* had begun to accelerate at a full burn, on a course set directly for Pervenio station. We stood on a four-hundred-ton projectile with a dated nuclear reactor powering its engine as well as unknown amounts of flammable gases that together could create an explosion as powerful as an atom bomb if it overloaded.

"We must go, Malcolm," Zhaff said loud enough so that I could hear him over the rattling of the ship's ducts and systems.

I looked down at the girl and said, "Don't move." She was crying, but she managed to nod.

I gritted my teeth. With the initial shock worn off, I was able to holster my gun and pull myself up by the ceiling so that I could get upright where my boots would work properly. Zhaff had accomplished that task far quicker.

We used whatever projections we could to pull ourselves forward. He made it look easier, and our suits helped, but there was no question that even his chiseled frame was struggling. For the moment, it didn't make me feel any better seeing him display signs of weakness. I couldn't help but wish I'd listened to him and exercised to get my muscles up to speed, but I think my unrelenting stubbornness was part of what helped me press on. I desperately didn't want him to get the last laugh... if he could laugh.

"Graves, what's going on?" Director Sodervall asked over the com-link with urgency. "Scanners have the *Piccolo* accelerating directly toward the station! Do not let that ship reach us or we will have to shoot it down!"

"We're working on it!" I grated. It was an effort just to speak. My lungs felt like they were being squeezed inside a vise. "How long until impact?"

The director went silent, and before he could find an answer, Zhaff had one. "Twenty minutes and thirty-six seconds," he stated.

"Yes... that," the director grumbled. "You have fifteen, Malcolm. If you can't find a way to stop it, you two better get your asses off that ship."

"We'll stop it," I said. "You just don't fire until you have no other choice." I had no idea how we were going to do that, but it seemed like the right thing to say to get back onto his good side. Especially if we succeeded.

"This way," Zhaff indicated.

We turned down a corridor, our bodies outstretched so we were holding on to the low ceiling with both hands and shuffling forward with our magnetized boots. We couldn't move very hastily, and the clock in my head told me we weren't going fast enough. The engine room was on the other end of the *Piccolo*.

My arms grew numb. My legs felt like they were back in the sewers of Mars, sloshing through a meter of shit. Zhaff built the distance between us with every reach, but I clenched my teeth and forced my body to keep pace. Maybe he could handle what was awaiting us on his own, but I wanted to be there. We were partners after all. I needed to prove he needed me if I planned on sticking around for longer than this mission.

I released the roar festering in my belly and pushed myself even faster. Zhaff glanced back, thinking I was injured, but I waved him to continue. I had been counting down in my head to try to ignore the pain, and by my calculations, we only had six minutes until Director Sodervall was going to give the order to blow the *Piccolo* into space dust.

We passed by another masked Ringer clinging to the wall, terrified. We ignored him. Zhaff clambered down a nearby stair-case beyond which the rumble of the engines grew louder. We were getting close.

I followed him, but when we reached the bottom, Zhaff held on to the ceiling, completely still. The reddish light leaking through the entrance to the engine room up ahead revealed the body of one of the Pervenio officers we'd arrived with. A grue-some cluster of bullet holes punctured the center of his chest, with a deepening stream of blood leaking out and pooling against the base of the stairs.

"Not using non-lethal rounds anymore, I guess," I wheezed.

"No," Zhaff stated. He, too, sounded slightly winded. He reached down and drew his pulse- pistol before continuing onward. I would've done the same, but I needed both arms just to fight the forces of acceleration and move.

A minute or so later, we found another officer lying through the engine room entry. His corpse lay longways and jammed the inner and outer seal, leaving both a quarter open. Zhaff pulled himself toward the man and checked for a pulse.

"Dead," he said.

He positioned himself on one side of the entrance, his body painted completely red by the light of the overloading core. When I finally caught up to him, I went to the other. That was when I finally decided to draw my pistol.

"Can you see anybody inside?" I asked.

"No," he said. "The core is causing interference."

I stared at him and saw that the countless systems behind the glass of his eye-lens were working hard to maintain focus. Then I noticed that his lips were twitching, even more than when he'd learned the truth about Aria. I wasn't sure what discomfort looked like for a Cogent, but I had to imagine that was it.

"We'll go in on three," I said. "Shoot to kill this time."

"Agreed," he said, and for the first time, I heard his voice affected by pain as well.

I counted down, then we snapped around the corner, guns raised, or at least mine was. Zhaff's pistol swayed back and forth like he was blind. The roar of the spherical engine core suspended in the center of the circular room was deafening. The pulsating light it emitted as it roiled made it impossible to see clearly. I took a step forward, and out of the corner of my eye, I picked up a shadow moving.

"Get down!" I yelled.

I was lucky I'd been holding on to the wall with one hand because I used it to throw myself at my partner and tackle him to the ground just before a barrage of bullets almost took off his head. His firearm flew out of his hand, and with our heads so near, I could hear the clicks of his eye-lens going haywire.

"The Ring will never be yours, mud stompers!" a man shouted. "We were chosen by Trass!"

"I'll take him!" I shouted. "Slow this thing down!" I yanked on the grated floor and sent myself soaring around the edge of the circular walkway wrapping around the core.

I could see the flash of the Ringer's rifle's muzzle as he attempted to track me. Bullets clanged off the walls, ceiling, and floor. If one of them struck the engine, we were all going to be barbecued. I felt a shot graze the top of the plating guarding my calf as I pushed off the wall and changed direction.

In my ear, Director Sodervall said, "Graves, you have thirty seconds or I'll have no choice but to shoot that rust-bucket down!"

"Just hold your damn fire!" I responded into the com-link.

I aimed my pulse-pistol toward the area where I thought the

Ringer was and unloaded the clip. He returned fire, but his shots veered off toward the ceiling until there were no more. My pistol clicked, and just as it did, the engine quieted. The *Piccolo* slowed down, and the pressure on my chest dwindled until it no longer hurt to breathe again. I remained puffing from exertion regardless.

The main halogen lights throughout the engine room blinked on, and I saw the Ringer in a tattered white boiler-suit—orange circle printed on his chest—lying on the floor around the bend of the spherical core. At least one of my shots had met its mark because there was a gash in the side of his neck with blood gushing out and spiraling across the room. He gurgled on it, but by the time I was able to drag my weightless body over to him, he was dead. His pulse-rifle drifted harmlessly away, and I grabbed it. It was nothing a Ringer should've been able to afford, but there were no markings on it, and the model number was removed. Purchased off the black.

"Reverse thrusters are activated, Director Sodervall," Zhaff announced through the com-link, sounding back to his normal self. "We're in control."

Director Sodervall breathed a sigh of relief. "That was too close," he replied. "Bring her in slowly, and we'll start cleaning this up."

I looked up and saw Zhaff on the other end of the room, holding on to the engine's manual override control console. He had his hand-terminal connected to it. Even impaired, he got the job done.

"You all right, Zhaff?" I asked, still panting.

He turned around to face me, expression blank as ever. "I am," he stated.

I imagined that was as close as I was going to get to a "thank you" for saving his life. Though, by slowing the *Piccolo,* he'd already made things even. That thought alone was enough to make me snicker. Either I was destined never to get an edge on him, or we were actually starting to make a decent team. The only thing I could be sure about was how glad I was not to have countless pounds of pressure towing on my tired body.

"Nice job," I said.

Back to working properly again, Zhaff's eye-lens angled toward the Ringer's body and focused. "And you, Malcolm," he replied.

I smiled wearily and nodded at him. He nodded back.

If I weren't weightless, I would've collapsed against the wall and taken a nap. Instead, I demagnetized my boots, closed my eyes, and allowed myself to enjoy weightlessness for what little time I could.

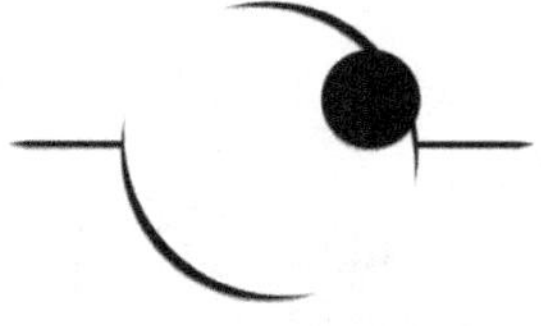

FOURTEEN

"I TOLD YOU, I don't know anything else," the girl we found on the command deck of the *Piccolo* said. Based on our records, her name was Cora, and she sat in one of Pervenio Station's cramped interrogation rooms. She'd already cried so much during our questioning that her cheeks were permanently stained. In her boiler suit, I could tell her forearm was fractured, but she still hadn't been permitted to receive medical attention.

"You're saying that a man around your age named Kale Drayton was behind this?" Zhaff asked. He sat across from her while I stood leaning against the door. We'd spoken with half of the twenty or so Ringer members of the crew recovered from the *Piccolo* by then, and many of them had brought up that same name. My and Zhaff's first legitimate interrogations together as partners. He wanted to start with her, but I insisted they let her get some rest so she could calm her nerves. My little act of generosity to try to loosen her up.

"No... I mean... I don't think so," she said. "But they seemed to know him."

"They?" I asked. I knew who she was talking about, but

keeping a suspect thinking was a trade secret. Of course, I couldn't look directly into her soul like Zhaff seemed to be able to do.

"The people who attacked us," she clarified, her gaze held on me. She'd spent most of the conversation doing that rather than staring into Zhaff's eye-lens. I couldn't say I blamed her. "They took him with them."

"Right. He was forcefully taken by three armored soldiers in white other than the one we found on the *Piccolo,* but only him. And you don't know why?"

She shook her head meekly.

"You're never going to get anywhere with these people unless you spill a little blood," Director Sodervall said into my ear. He had me on com-link for the interrogations, claiming that dealing with Ringers was his area of expertise.

I rolled my eyes before reaching up to switch off the device. I could picture him cursing me under his breath.

"Show her," I said to Zhaff.

He pulled out the hand-terminal we'd found her with on the *Piccolo* and placed it on the table in front of her. Her eyes bulged again upon the sight of it.

"What about that thing?" I asked. "Was that really the first time you saw it on the command deck?"

"I... I can't remember..." she stammered.

Zhaff turned his head toward me. I motioned for him to stay quiet before he said what I knew he was going to say. She wasn't a practiced criminal, and even *I* could tell she was holding back.

"C'mon, Cora," I said, strolling over to the table and leaning down beside her. She didn't look much like my daughter, but I hoped if I employed the same tone I used to while scolding Aria, then I might be able to get her to talk without needing to get violent. She seemed ready to break.

"If it were up to my partner here," I said, "there'd be officers snapping your fingers off until you told him what he wanted to know. Being that you're still alive, I'd say this can get a whole lot worse for you unless you start answering our questions truthfully."

Cora continued to stare at the device in silence. A heavy tear rolled down her cheek, and I could tell words were forming in her throat. "I saw it... with Kale," she said finally. She pointed at the side of the slim device, at a series of scratches along the edge. "It was his, I think."

"See how easy that was?" I asked.

"He wouldn't do something like this." She sniveled. "I swear it! In the name of Trass, I swear it."

I slammed my hands down on the table right in front of her and said, "Because of him, all of you on the *Piccolo* went hurtling toward Pervenio Station like a bomb. He was going to kill you!"

"It wasn't him!" She grasped my arm so abruptly that Zhaff jumped to his feet and had his hand wrapped around the grip of his pistol. "I know him. It wasn't him... It wasn't him."

I took a deep breath, peeled her fingers off me, and stepped away. Her broken arm made her wince. Zhaff released his weapon.

"I'm sure it wasn't." I waved toward the officer outside the door. "We're done with you for now. And would you get her arm looked at already?" He offered a halfhearted nod before grabbing her.

"It wasn't him!" she screamed repeatedly as the officer dragged her out, not stopping until she was well down the hall and thrown back into one of Pervenio Station's famous cells. They were three-by-three-meter rectangular boxes with blank surfaces on every side except for the floor, which popped through the exterior of the station. That surface was glass, and the thin barrier between breathable air and deadly vacuum was said to be an airlock that could be opened at any time if someone misbehaved. At least, that was what the prisoners were told. I'd never *actually* seen someone spaced through one of them.

"Malcolm, she knows more," Zhaff said.

"She's not going anywhere, even if she does," I replied. "Besides, it's nothing that will help us. Or can you not see it?"

"See what?" Zhaff asked.

I grinned. "You've never been with a girl, have you?"

"I have been beside many females."

"I mean *been* with one. Intimately. Or do they cut off your..." I gestured to his hips. "You know, when you enter the Initiative." It was a very real possibility based on everything I'd learned about him. The thought made my stomach turn over, and I felt the need to check my groin just to make sure everything was still there.

"They did not. However, as with all members of the Cogent Initiative, my ability to reproduce naturally has been impaired."

I could only imagine how Pervenio Corp went about that. Somehow, a vasectomy seemed too simple a solution.

"Well, there's more to it than just making kids," I said. "No wonder you are... how you are."

He didn't allow any irritation to show, but his eye-lens focused on my face as if it were looking through me. "Malcolm," he said, "I do not see how this is relevant to our investigation."

"Apparently, you weren't taught everything. Cora obviously has feelings for this Kale fellow. I'm sure we could get his life story out of her, but I bet it's like that of any other Ringer who's been pushed too far."

Zhaff considered what I said for a moment before stating, "I do not know if I agree with your assessment."

"Trust me." I placed my hand on his shoulder and sat him down. "After we're done here, I swear I'm going to take you out for a night with the best woman I can find in Sol and then you'll understand. We'd be wasting our time with Cora. She's no criminal. Please tell me you can see that at least."

"I will rely on your experience in the matter for now."

"My experience." I laughed. "So did you find out any more about Kale Drayton before she was called in?"

"Yes." Zhaff pulled down his own hand-terminal and quickly perused the screen. "Security says his name was listed on the manifest for the *Piccolo*. He is from the lower ward of Darien Colony, level B-2. Security shows him at the center of a riot in the Darien Upper Ward three days ago, before he departed for his harvesting shift."

"And they let him leave?"

"It does not appear that he partook."

"Sure."

"Security has already raided his hollow since we learned of his name from the captive named Desmond and found nothing. His only living relative is a mother who was contained in the Darien quarantine zone. Katrina Drayton."

"Dead?"

"Gone. After the raid on the *Piccolo*, she disappeared from the facility and cannot be located."

"Damn... so after all that, he's just another worthless lead."

"It appears to be. Director Sodervall has been informed about the situation, and he will initiate a Ring-wide search for both Draytons."

"I doubt they'll find anything. The Children of Titan somehow got her out of a secure q-zone. They're something else."

I sat on the table and rested my head on my hand. My neck was unbelievably sore from the *Piccolo*. Out of the corner of my eye, I noticed the bright-orange circle on the screen of Kale's hand-terminal.

"What about that thing?" I asked.

"The hand-terminal was altered to allow the communications systems of the *Piccolo* to penetrate the Pervenio network," Zhaff replied. "I have been unable to discover its other capabilities or trace its origin. The programming is beyond my proficiency, or is perhaps unbreakable now that it has been utilized."

"Beyond *you*?"

He didn't look ashamed as he nodded, but for whatever reason, I felt like he was.

"Damn these people. Why would they leave it behind for us to find, then? We know the one operative was left behind to give his life crashing the ship into the station. But the broadcast was already transmitted. Seems like too simple a mistake." The thought of another Ringer willing to commit suicide gave me a shudder. The director had the man's body scanned, and as with the bomber on Earth, there wasn't a single match in the database to tell us who it was.

"Perhaps the program needed more time to infiltrate Solnet?" Zhaff said. "I can spend more time analyzing it."

"Maybe. Or maybe they left it as if that damn orange circle were a middle finger. Like they knew even you wouldn't be able to crack it to find them."

I snatched the device and spun it around. Physically, it looked like any other Venta-distributed hand-terminal of the same model, but if Zhaff couldn't crack it, then the Children of Titan were even more skilled than I thought. He'd sliced into the *Piccolo's* engine controls in less than twenty seconds, after all. But it was our only lead. We were going to need to find someone to look at it who was even more talented with programming than Zhaff. Someone like...

"Rylah," I whispered.

"Sorry, Malcolm, I did not hear you clearly," Zhaff said.

"I have an old connection nearby. She goes by Rylah. Whether that's her real name or not, I'm not sure. The only thing I know for a fact is that she has the capability of sending out a recording like that if she wanted to. I've seen her hack into the Pervenio security mainframe on Darien like she was doing a children's puzzle. If something goes down in the Ring, she knows at least a little about it."

"And you believe it was her?"

"Nah. She never was one to play sides. Honestly, I'm not even sure whether she's a Ringer or not. Has that hybrid look like Cora. She's helped me out of a few jams before, though."

"I will have to know more about her before I agree or disagree."

I sighed. "She's an information broker holed up deep in the Darien lower ward on Titan. You mentioning that the Drayton kid was from there made me think of her. It'll be a steep price, but if anybody can find some digital breadcrumbs about who'd uploaded that recording, it's her. If we find that person, I have a feeling they'll know not only where the people who attacked the *Piccolo* disappeared to, but where our smugglers from Earth are."

Zhaff leaned in, his luminous eye-lens poring over my face. "Why do you seem hesitant?"

"I've been doing this for a long time, Zhaff. Rylah and I, we have a history."

"You do not trust her, then?"

"Trust has nothing to do with it."

Rylah didn't allow many people into her life unless they were willing to pay a hefty sum, but we'd been intimate more than a few times while I was stationed in the Ring years back. She had a thing for collectors, or so I was told. I just hoped she didn't take it personally that I'd lost touch with her.

I may not have been sure if she was a full-on Ringer or not, but I knew she'd lived on Titan long enough to have adapted many of their tendencies. They could be very sensitive about people they considered to be their *mates* leaving, although she hadn't made an effort to contact me either. The last time I'd heard from her also happened to be the last time I saw Aria, so I usually tried not to think about it if I didn't have to. But bringing Rylah's name up out loud caused the memory to come rushing back to me as clear as day...

I SAT ON THE EDGE OF MY MESSY BED IN A ROOM ON THE HIGHEST LEVEL of the Pervenio-run hotel in New Beijing, Mars. It was a fancy place with painted walls trimmed with burnished steel and faux wood, and a beautiful viewport looking out over the colony. The planet's thin atmosphere gave everything beyond it a reddish tint, even the other tall towers rising beneath New Beijing's four-kilometer-wide segmented dome enclosure. A few hover-cars darted by, hauling freight from one of the nearby vertical farms.

The shower ran in the bathroom where Aria washed off Elios's blood. She'd been drenched head-to-toe in it when we sneaked back in. I myself was covered in hardened muck and a stench so foul that I would've thrown up if I wasn't already so used to it. I held a half-drained bottle of liquor in my hand. I wasn't sure what kind because it was unmarked. I'd snatched it from a dealer on the way up and didn't really care what I was drinking so long as it dulled my mind. It had a relatively smooth taste, considering how little it cost.

"Trying to start a family without me, Mal?" a woman asked me, her voice sounding like it came from somewhere far away. "Who is he?"

I glanced down at the hand-terminal sitting on my lap, almost having forgotten that I'd made the call to Rylah, it'd taken so long to connect. She had skin as pale and smooth as the paper in ancient books, and lips colored bright red. As far as beautiful offworlders go, I'd say she was second to none.

"Who?" I asked.

"Right behind you," Rylah said.

I looked back over my shoulder and remembered that Elios Sevari's son slept on the other end of the bed. The sheets would never recover from the muck he was covered in. I'd allowed Aria to bring him up with her on the condition that she'd start looking for a nice clan-family to drop him with as soon as he was rested.

"Oh, him," I said. "That's the orphan from the assignment I messaged you about."

"I figured as much," Rylah said.

I took a healthy swig from my bottle of whiskey, placed it down, and then lifted the hand-terminal so Rylah could see me, but mostly so I could see her better.

We'd met on Titan during a recent mission when I was trying to locate a serial-killing Ringer with a knack for taking out Pervenio officers. She hacked into a few local monitors for me and found his location. We'd been close ever since. I wouldn't say I loved her, but she was the closest I think any woman had ever come to that in my life, even more than Aria's mom. Calling over Solnet when she was millions of kilometers away on Titan was a huge step for me. Plus, I needed a distraction.

"Hey you," I said. Sweet talk never was my strong suit.

"You look like hell," she answered.

"I feel like hell."

"How's Aria?"

I checked to make sure the water in the bathroom was still running and then replied, "She'll be okay, Ry. She's stronger than she looks."

Rylah grinned, and maybe it was the alcohol in my blood, but it was exactly what I needed to see. She had the kind of smile that could make a man forget everything he stood for. "Oh, trust me, I know that," she said. "I met her, remember? Still, it's not an easy thing sometimes to do one's job."

"I doubt it was for me at that age either." I shrugged. "I can't really remember."

"That probably doesn't help," she jested. She didn't point, but I could tell her gaze had shifted to look straight at the bottle pinned between my lap and my stomach.

I smirked as I lifted it to my lips and took another swig. Rylah rolled her eyes, but given how good our present connection was from my 5-star hotel room, she couldn't hide her snicker, subtle as it was.

"She'll come around," I decided. "She always does."

"Well, if she doesn't soon, you bring her to me, and I'll make sure to tell her about all her father's 'finer' qualities."

"I'll keep that in mind if I ever come back there. You know I can't stand the cold."

"You'll be back," she said, her trademark confidence oozing into her tone. "We'll make it warm enough for you together."

"Seeing you this clearly is going to make it hard to stay away."

"I'll be sure to start some trouble to get you back quickly, then."

"Fine by me. Just nothing too bad or I'll have to lock you up."

"Oh, I'll think of something." She put on a wicked grin for a moment, then her lips straightened. "Now go. Talk to her before you lose her and worry about me later."

I sighed. The shower had turned off anyway, so I knew I didn't have long before I'd have no choice.

"You're right," I said. "We'll talk soon, Ry." I wasn't sure if I should smile and nod or blow her a kiss, so I settled on something in the middle. I can only imagine how ridiculous I probably looked to her. I really never was very good with women beyond the first night.

Her expression told me that she was doing her damnedest not to laugh. "Bye, Mal. Don't keep me waiting here too long."

The sound of the door to the bathroom opening with a whoosh

stole my attention and caused me to miss how Rylah handled the farewell before the transmission cut out.

Aria walked out, wrapped in a plush towel as white as she was. Her skin was clean, but her lips continued to tremble as they had since the moment I shot Elios. Her Ark Ship pendant hung from her slender neck like always.

"Was that Rylah?" she asked, her voice brittle. She didn't even look at me when she spoke. Her eyes stared forward blankly, as if she had watched a gory scene from an old horror movie repeatedly until it made her numb.

"Yeah," I replied. "She gives her best."

"Good . . . I like her. For you, I mean." It was obvious she was just trying to make small talk to try to avoid the situation. I was perfectly fine with it. Aria had never known her mother, so she was constantly trying to push me to meet someone. Hell, the way she'd looked at Rylah the first time they met was half the reason I was willing to give the woman a real shot.

"Me too," I admitted.

Aria took a seat on a couch across the room. Her hand quaked as she used it to brace herself so she didn't fall. She stared out through the room's viewport, and we both sat there wordlessly until the silence made me itch.

"You feel any better?" I finally mustered the willpower to ask.

"No," she mumbled, still unable to look at me.

I raised my bottle to my lips and took another sip. "You will. These things happen."

"I won't," she snapped. This time, she stared daggers in my direction. And it wasn't merely the kind of look that every daughter gives her father when she's upset. Aria meant it.

I returned an icy glare. I knew I'd done what I had to under the circumstances. She had to know it too. If she'd told me what was really going on, maybe I wouldn't have pulled the trigger. Secrets always have their price.

"Are you going to hold this against me forever?" I asked. "Two weeks you disappeared with that man. Of course I thought something went wrong."

"Like it would have made any difference? I'm not a child anymore. I took care of the job my own way."

"Your way is dangerous. Fugitives will say anything to survive, Aria. You can't believe a word he said to you."

I could see tears beginning to well in the corner of her eyes again as she stared toward the floor. "We could've loved each other . . . I know it."

I pointed at her with the head of my bottle and then took another sip. "There's no room for that in the life of a collector. You've learned a valuable lesson."

"What about you and Rylah?" she snapped.

"That's different. She's not my target."

Aria remained silent at first. She turned her head and gazed back through the room's viewport, her whole body trembling as if she were ready to explode.

"I was only trying to protect you," I said before she could think of anything.

"That's all you've ever been trying to do," Aria said. "Ever since I was a girl."

Aria sprang to her feet. I heard the child on the bed roll over to see what was going on.

"You remember that Departure on Earth?" Aria went on. "When you left me alone on a roof for hours to keep me safe. I couldn't even see my hands it was so dark when you got back and gave me this." She ripped the necklace off her neck and held it up. "What's the point of being safe if you're alone?"

"Alone? I brought you with me everywhere. Do you know what would happen if Pervenio Corp found out about that?"

"I never asked you to."

"And I never had a choice. Not every collector has an illegitimate daughter handed off to him. Would you rather I left you with the USF in the hope they'd match you with some worthless clan-family? Girls your age dream about seeing the things you've seen—about walking down dark streets and knowing they can handle anything that comes at them."

She opened her mouth to respond and then stopped herself. I could see the roll of her throat as she swallowed hard. She fell back onto the couch and returned to gazing through the viewport. "And I thank you for that, but I'm done."

I was lifting the bottle when her words sank in. I froze. "What?" I said.

"I'm done," she repeated. Her voice may have sounded calm, but her eyes were glazed over and bloodshot. "You're right. I've spent my whole life traveling around Sol with you, and for what? I don't want to be a collector. I never have. I only wanted to make you happy."

I put down the bottle, got up, and walked over to her. I figured she was just acting impulsively because of what had happened. That she needed some time to cool down. I tried to place my hand on her slender shoulder, but she turned her whole body toward the window to avoid me.

"You do," I said. "Now get some sleep. When you wake up, I'll even help you find Elios's son a proper home, and we'll put all this behind us."

She turned her head toward me, and for the first time in my life, I saw in her face a girl who was completely shattered. The job had broken many before me, but I never thought it'd get to Aria. If I wasn't already drunk, the sight might've made my stomach churn.

"You'll put it behind you," she whispered sharply. "I won't. I can't. I'm not going to hold you back anymore."

"Aria—" I began. She silenced me.

"No, I'm done. This was my last mission either way. I sent an application to be a nurse at the new Venta Co hospital going up here before I ever met Elios. If they accept me, I'm taking the job. If not,

I'm going to keep looking. You won't have to worry about keeping me a secret anymore. I know how to get around off the grid."

My mouth fell open. I stumbled backward, unable to believe the words I was hearing. Venta Co had been Pervenio Corp's foremost rival since before I was born. I never cared about what'd caused it, but after years on one side of the enmity, I naturally found myself bitter toward the other.

"Venta?" I mouthed. "You don't just go behind my back, but right to our rival?"

For a moment, Aria's anger with me fell to the wayside, and she grew defensive. "I didn't go behind anything!" she said. "Pervenio doesn't have a hospital here on Mars. I'm trying to help the best that I can."

"No." I shook my head in disbelief. "No. I won't allow it. You're too damn good at this! A few more jobs and Director Sodervall won't be able to deny you're worth officially taking into training when I tell him all that you've done. You'll be set up for life."

She jumped back to her feet, and one of her arms accidentally slapped my pistol off the couch's end table. She glared straight into my eyes, her cheeks flushed with indignation. "Sure," she said, "as long as there are more of us offworlders to put down."

I was incensed, unable to control myself as I raised the back of my hand to smack her. I stopped before I actually did it, but it was too late. She'd seen the motion, and that was all she needed to see. She didn't even wince, as if she'd expected me to do it. She just pursed her lips, then took the Ark Ship figurine I'd given her so many years before, ripped it off her necklace, and snapped it in half. A few sparks flew out from the tracker I'd hidden in it.

"I figured out how you found me, by the way," she said, tossing the two halves at my feet. "Some collector you are."

"A least I know what it takes," I said.

"Yeah. You're such a hero."

She stormed by me and over to the bed. I didn't hear what she whispered to the terrified child who'd woken at some point during our argument, but she got him up and led him out of the room without looking back. She didn't even care that she wore nothing but a towel.

I didn't watch her leave either. I cleared my throat as I knelt to place my pistol back safely on the table. Then I shuffled back to the bed, snatched up my bottle of God knows what, and held it against my lips until it was empty...

I never did find out whether or not Aria got that job. I didn't have the stomach to ask during one of the few occasions we exchanged messages after that day, before even that stopped. It was hard to imagine her doing anything else except helping people, though. She always had a knack for it, even if I was too blind to realize it at the time.

The memory made my chest sting far more than any other ever could. A part of me always wished that I'd gone after her, but I was too damn proud. It was the last mistake I'd ever get a chance to make with her.

I suppose that was why I lost contact with Rylah afterward. I knew she'd always remind me of that day, and so did she. But it was time to get over it. We didn't have the best history, but I had little doubt I might be able to convince her to help for the right price. She was an information broker first and foremost. If it meant beating Zhaff to a lead, then it was worth finding out.

"Malcolm?" Zhaff said.

I realized that at some point while I was lost in thought, my hand found its way into my pocket and clutched the Ark Ship. I quickly pulled it out. Zhaff leaned in close and analyzed my face with his eye-lens. The bright overhead lights of the interrogation room drew my gaze to the mottled skin around the scar across the bridge of his nose.

"Sorry, what was that?" I asked.

"I said, if you have described her accurately, I agree that we should pursue her," Zhaff said. "It is a sound strategy. Otherwise, we must begin investigating every incoming ship and every hangar throughout the Ring after interrogating the rest of the *Piccolo's* crew."

"I'd rather eat a bullet. That's what Sodervall's staff is for." I exhaled slowly. "Fine, I'll contact Rylah. Hopefully, she hasn't changed too much over the years."

I took out my hand-terminal and searched for the last bit of contact information I'd used to communicate with Rylah. It'd been roughly six years, so I wasn't even sure it would work. I typed out a message anyway.

RY... I'M NOT SURE IF YOU STILL USE THIS LINE. SORRY IT'S BEEN SO LONG. I'VE RECOVERED A DEVICE I THINK YOU MIGHT BE INTERESTED IN LOOKING AT. I CAN BRING IT TO YOU ASAP. WE CAN DISCUSS PAYMENT LATER, BUT I PROMISE IT'LL BE WORTH YOUR WHILE... MAL

I stared at the screen for a few seconds, swallowed, and then hit send.

"There," I said. "Now we better get down to Titan so we don't keep her waiting if she answers."

"Agreed," Zhaff said. "I will request for Director Sodervall to prepare a shuttle for us as soon as possible."

I feigned a grin and nodded to him. Whether or not it was my own fault, the mission that had started all the way back in New London was dredging up pieces of my past I would've rather left buried. As I watched Zhaff stroll calmly out of the room, all I could hope for was that getting it done right would be worth the trouble.

We were only halfway back to our quarters when Rylah answered, and it became too late to turn back.

I'M INTERESTED. COME MEET ME, SAME PLACE WHERE WE USED TO. DON'T KEEP ME WAITING AGAIN... RYLAH

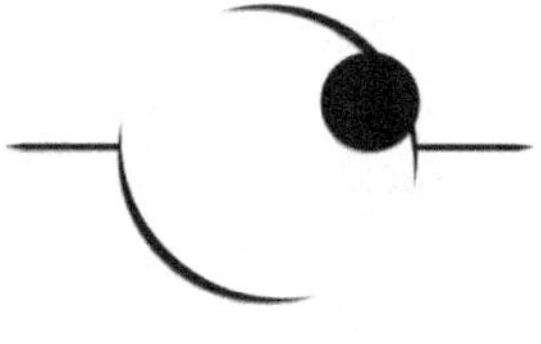

FIFTEEN

Following the *Piccolo* incident, it was going to take a few hours for Director Sodervall to prepare a ship down to Titan that wouldn't draw attention to us. When it came to meeting with Rylah, I wanted to avoid making a scene, especially after the Ring-wide address Director Sodervall decided to issue in response to the attack. I'd advised against it, but Pervenio officials had a knack for ignoring my advice.

"People of the Ring," he'd said. "By now you've all heard of the horrible fate which befell the *Piccolo* and its loyal Earther crew members. I speak to you now, not as your director, not as the Voice of the Ring, but as one human making a solemn promise to others. The terrorists behind this attack will pay for their crimes. They call themselves the Children of Titan, but we are the people of Titan. Together, we have all helped the Ring thrive! One cowardly act will never thwart all that we have accomplished.

"I am asking—begging for your help in bringing the man responsible for the unwarranted slaughter of twenty-one innocent members of the *Piccolo*'s crew to justice. He is Kale Drayton, an eighteen-year-old male from level B2 of the Darien

Lower Ward. We believe he was also behind a riot that took place not two days ago in the Darien Uppers and cost the lives of two veteran Security Officers. Consider him armed and extremely dangerous.

"But he is not alone. People in league with these terrorists can be anywhere. Working beside you. Living beside you. Any accurate report of suspicious behavior will be handsomely rewarded. Anyone who is able to provide information leading directly to the arrest of Kale Drayton will personally receive one hundred thousand credits from the account of Luxarn Pervenio. It is time for us to take back the Ring from lawlessness! Lastly, anyone caught replicating the symbol of the Children of Titan anywhere in Sol will be punished by the fullest extent of USF Colonial Law.

"Your safety, no matter where you or your parents were born, is our utmost concern. The fight to ensure our survival rests in all of our hands."

It didn't feel right putting the blame on some kid we couldn't find and probably never would, but as the Voice of the Ring, Sodervall made the final calls when it came to security, answering only to Luxarn Pervenio. All I could do was focus on my and Zhaff's task, and that meant preparing my mind to see Rylah again so we could find who was responsible for New London. If Kale really was behind the Children of Titan and everything else, we'd find out in due time. But my gut told me this was bigger than some kid. Director Sodervall's speech revealing the existence of the terror group would simply add to the tension on Titan once we arrived.

It didn't make our short break on the station waiting for a ship very exciting either. As essentially a base of operations for gas harvesting, Pervenio station had little in the way of amenities. There were a few places to get a drink near the docks, sure, but tired laborers weren't the best company, especially ones who were afraid the Ringer members of their crews were going to try to space them if they got the chance.

When shifts finally ended that evening, me and Zhaff were to be stuffed onto a public shuttle headed to Darien, Titan. Director Sodervall led us to the hangar early, a host of officers surrounding him. He wasn't planning on taking any chances with the populace he oversaw, it seemed, even on his own station.

"Here you are," Sodervall said as we stopped outside our shuttle's hangar. "Do what you have to, Graves, but try not to start a full-scale rebellion while you're down there. I've got enough of a mess to deal with already."

I smirked and shook his hand. "You know I never cause too much of a stir. We'll keep you in the loop."

"Good."

"And let us know if you get any more out of the harvester's crew."

The director pursed his lips. "I'll take good care of them. If the crew knows anything else about this Kale Drayton character or what happened, I'll get it out of them. Dealing with Ringers is what I get paid to do."

"Handsomely, I'll bet."

He chuckled. "Good luck, Graves." He turned and nodded firmly in Zhaff's direction. It was the most warmhearted acknowledgment he'd offered the Cogent since we'd arrived at the Ring. He even waited for Zhaff to salute before walking away.

Zhaff and I made our way into the hangar. My legs were starting to feel reinvigorated after the workout I'd gotten on the *Piccolo.* I decided I'd have to try to rub that in his face, when the Cogent glanced down at his hand-terminal and stopped.

"This way," he said. He yanked my arm and directed me back outside the hangar toward a tram line.

I shrugged him off me. "Hangar's right here," I said, confused.

"We are early. Luxarn Pervenio would like to meet with you before we go down. We will not be left behind."

The words came out of Zhaff's mouth as though he'd just spoken an ordinary sentence. My mouth fell open, and my throat went dry. That was a request I never thought I'd hear. "You're joking?" I asked.

"I am not. He arrived late last evening to oversee the efforts being taken to pacify the Ring."

"What could he possibly want with me?"

I naturally figured the worst. I figured Zhaff's report had finally made it to him, which had likely broken down our entire day on Earth piece by piece, stressing every point where I ignored his advice. Director Sodervall may have been content with moving on after the *Piccolo,* but Luxarn Pervenio was a completely different animal. In thirty years, I'd never even been within a hundred meters of him, though I couldn't recall having botched such a significant job, let alone two in a row if I counted Undina. My fears over forced retirement resurfaced.

"He did not inform me," Zhaff replied as again he reached out to pull me toward the tram.

I was too shocked to fight him. Zhaff specifically said *he,* and he was always specific about his words. That meant this time Luxarn had messaged him directly while my hand-terminal remained quiet. It seemed at every turn since our introduction, I'd completely underestimated the Cogent Initiative and what it meant to my employer.

We rode the tram a short distance across the station. I asked Zhaff what he thought Luxarn might want more times than I can remember, but he didn't offer any information. We arrived at a private suite of rooms all strung together by ample hallways with portions of the walls trimmed with real wood. Not the faux shit you see on most of the colonies throughout Sol either. The real thing. I could tell because it gave off a pleasant, earthy aroma that I'd only ever experienced in the Pervenio-owned tree farms back on Earth. Very few places existed in Sol that displayed authentic wood like it was meant for decoration.

Heavily armed Pervenio officers were posted everywhere, and there were dozens of adjacent hangars being used to test military equipment and various other technologies. Zhaff led me to a set of towering doors clad entirely with mahogany. Two officers stood outside, but they didn't say or do anything besides stare straight ahead.

A retinal scanner was built into one of the doors. Zhaff placed his eye-lens against it, and the doors swung open without delay.

"I will wait here," he said, stepping aside.

I took short, wary strides inside until the door sealed shut behind me. The inside of Luxarn Pervenio's office was much like the rest of his compound—pearly metals everywhere with even more wood trimming. There was even a wooden molding wrapping the ceiling that was hand- sculpted with the images of fruits and vines, some of which were long extinct. An assortment of old-world relics lined the walls, from faded paintings to marble statues that may have been missing limbs but remained remarkably life-like.

The opposite end of the room had a wide viewport extending along an angled portion of the floor. Through it floated Saturn, the planet's icy rings slashing like a sickle blade through the blackness. Luxarn sat at a desk fashioned out of mahogany, same as the door, back to me and facing the translucency.

"Do you realize how vast our solar system is?" he said. His smooth voice teemed with the eloquence of a man raised among the highest echelon of Earthers.

I assumed he was waiting for a response since he stopped speaking, but I was too much in disbelief of where I was standing to come up with anything snappy. I remained quiet until he continued speaking on his own.

"Trillions upon trillions of kilometers of dark, empty space and here we men are, longing to fill it all." He rotated his chair to face me. "Truly remarkable, isn't it, Mr. Graves?"

His face had a peculiar look, one that never showed on any of the hundreds of newscasts I'd seen him on. It wasn't instantly obvious like cheap cosmetic surgeries were, but there was an undeniable artificial quality to him. He had the bone structure of a middle-aged man, but stretched over the top of it was smooth, handsome skin that looked like it belonged to someone not beyond his mid-twenties. His combed brown hair didn't have even a touch of gray to it, and his hazel eyes still bore the insatiable hunger of youth. Despite all of that, I knew he was older than I was, considering that according to recordings, he was already a teenager when his father first sent crewed transports to Saturn before the Great Reunion.

"It is—" I froze. I wasn't even sure what to call him... Mr. Pervenio, or boss, or sir. He was the wealthiest man in all of Sol, and arguably the most powerful if one subscribed to the idea that the USF was merely a figurehead like I did. I settled on "Sir."

"There is no need to be coy, Mr. Graves," he replied. "I've heard tales about your sharp tongue. I wouldn't want you to restrain it on my account. Come, sit." He beckoned me to the chair opposite his. He was as stately in his gestures as Zhaff was robotic. Even the manner in which the loose sleeves of his exquisite crimson tunic drooped seemed intentional.

"How many stories?" I countered, not wanting to disappoint. I stepped forward and took a seat, though not without checking my peripheries to ensure we were completely alone. The situation was too unusual for me to feel at ease.

"Enough of them. I keep track of all my collectors. I have a great deal of respect for what you do for me."

"And yet, somehow, I have a hard time believing you've invited me here to congratulate me on a job well done."

"I suppose not," he said, amused. "Are you thirsty?"

"Always." If we were about to discuss retirement plans, I wasn't about to deny an opportunity to drink with Luxarn Pervenio, or anybody, to be honest. That was another lesson I'd have to teach Zhaff before I was booted out. Never turn down a free drink.

Luxarn looked away from me. "Bot, can you retrieve the barrel-aged whiskey, 2284 vintage?"

"Yes, sir," an automated voice with a highborn inflection responded.

Something zoomed by my head so quickly I ducked and nearly fell from my chair. When I looked up, I saw a metal sphere hovering near a counter built into the wall. Its tiny anti-grav boosters sounded like a vacuum and left behind a trail of distortion from its underside. Delicate appendages extended from all over its bulbous body. One lifted a bottle of whiskey with a tag I didn't recognize and poured it into two glasses being held by others.

"Remarkable prototype, isn't it?" Luxarn asked. "I haven't thought of a name yet, but one day, households throughout Sol will be able to own one of their own."

"A personal bartender," I said. "Not bad."

"'*The Pervenio Service Bot will help with all of your everyday needs,*'" he pronounced as if he were quoting somebody. "Or something like that. I pay a large sum for people to think of better slogans than me."

"I got into the wrong line of business."

The bot placed two orbs of ice into each glass before soaring back over to us. On the front side, or what I had to assume was it, was a large, circular, yellow-hued lens. The way it rotated and focused reminded me of Zhaff's eye-lens. As it grew nearer, I could distinguish all of the mobile panels of its metal shell, which likely concealed other useful arms. One probably had a screwdriver, and I had no question that one day another would wield a pistol. With humanity's focus on expansion, robotics was one field that had fallen by the wayside. It seemed I might live long enough to see Mr. Pervenio change that.

It stopped by the edge of the table, wavering a bit, and placed our glasses down harder than expected. The clank echoed. Luxarn's glass nearly spilled, but he was able to catch it.

"Still working out a few kinks," he groused before raising his drink. "This whiskey is from the year we made contact with the Ring. Most men wouldn't appreciate it. I'm sure you will."

I nodded and returned the gesture. Then we each took a swig without saying anything else. I preferred the bite of something cheaper to wake me up, but it went down smoother than any drink I'd ever had the pleasure of tasting.

I wiped my tingling lips and went to speak, then noticed the yellow glare of the bot. I was exhausted with the color. "Sir, would you mind?"

Luxarn swallowed a mouthful of whiskey and laughed. He patted his mouth with a folded napkin sitting on his desk. "Bot, please go and wait by the counter."

"Yes, sir." It hummed away, finally allowing me to focus.

"So why did you invite me here, sir?" I asked. "Zhaff and I are about to head down to Titan to catch the smugglers you're after."

"Straight to the point," Luxarn said. "I like that. You'd have made a shrewd businessman."

"I'll add it to my list of occupations to consider after I retire."

"Retire?" His brow furrowed. "I hope not yet. Especially not after what you and Zhaff were able to accomplish on the *Piccolo*. I remain in dire need of your services. You see, my father risked all his wealth backing the efforts to send colony transports to Saturn and reunite with our lost kin. Now Ringers like the one you encountered on Earth or saw on that horrific recording are threatening to shatter the fragile alliance I have spent half a century cultivating here."

I did my best to conceal my relief. I had a feeling I'd gained a bit of rope in my job security after the *Piccolo*, but it was still nice to hear it out loud. "To be honest, sir," I said, "after Zhaff's report about what happened on Earth, I never thought I'd be here."

"Yes. I saw every excruciating detail of that report. How is your new partner, by the way?"

"Excruciating." I downed my whiskey and set the glass on the table. "But he's good at what he does, and I can respect that."

Luxarn suppressed a chuckle. "Trust me, Cogents definitely have their uses, but Zhaff wouldn't have gotten anything out of that Ringer anyway. I doubt he knew any information other than where to place the bomb. According to Director Sodervall, dozens of the Ringers responsible for inciting recent riots on Titan have been detained, and none of them seem to have any reason other than distaste for people like you and me. Someone, somewhere, told them to do something awful, and they listened without asking who. These Children of Titan are a new sort of enemy. No structured leadership, and yet incredibly precise."

"Yeah, Zhaff and I have already gotten a taste of that. But we've got our assignment, sir, so what exactly are you asking?"

"I invited you here because I know you're not stupid. A bit

rash perhaps, but over three decades, you've only managed to serve my company loyally. As I said, I do pay attention. There's not a single collector I know of who's been on the job as long as you have without calling it quits or winding up dead. So either you're lucky or you're exceptionally good at what you do."

"A little bit of both if you ask me. More unlucky than not lately, it seems."

"Perhaps, but your recent failures have given you a greater glimpse at the kind of fanatics we're dealing with. That, and despite everything Zhaff noted about your inability to take his advice on Earth, he also informed me that you were the one who got a lead on the bomber and managed to save his life on the *Piccolo*."

"Did he?" I asked, completely shocked.

"He did. And even he missed the fact that the explosion in New London was merely a distraction, which is why you are here now. I've never seen him work well with anybody else."

"*Well* might be a bit of a stretch."

"Yet here we are." Luxarn paused and took the final sip of his drink. He lifted the empty glass in my direction. "Would you like another?"

I happily obliged. One word to the bot and it carried the bottle over and topped us off, fresh ice and all. The Ring had no lack of it.

"Zhaff is extremely important to Pervenio Corp," he continued, "so I'm hoping that after you successfully retrieve what was stolen along with those responsible, you will stay here and continue to work with him so that we can bring an end to these Children of Titan. Call it an extended assignment."

The request for a prolonged partnership wasn't the way I saw our conversation going. Naturally, I couldn't say no to him, even if the thought of countless more missions and months alongside Zhaff made me itch. There was no better person to have stuffing your pockets than Luxarn Pervenio. Director Sodervall's unexpectedly pleased reaction to seeing me on Pervenio station was beginning to make a little more sense. If I had the backing of Luxarn, then his only choice was to force a smile and act like my closest friend... though I couldn't explain his treatment of Zhaff.

"For how long?" I asked before I could stop myself and think of a gentler way to put it.

Luxarn's eyes narrowed, and for a moment, I saw the ravenous glare of the man who owned half of Sol. "As long as I require," he said sternly. "This is too crucial a time to display weaknesses. I have Venta Co and Red Wing Company breathing down my neck, trying to prove that Jupiter is as viable an option for gas harvesting as Saturn. After that horrid attack on the *Piccolo,* people may start listening to them. If we can't continue to work safely here, then immigrants might stop coming. I can't have that."

"No need to explain to me. I'll continue to work with the freak for as long as it takes, but only under one condition." I realized that I might have again been too bold. Luxarn's eyebrows lifted in astonishment. He definitely wasn't used to being spoken to in such a manner.

"And what is that?"

I took a deep breath. It was too late to back down. "I won't take orders from a kid. I want the same deal as on Earth. He can offer whatever advice he wants, but I'm in charge."

Luxarn's expression relaxed, as if he'd expected a different request. "Of course. Deferring to your experience will do him well. And know that you will be paid generously for looking after him. Twice the usual rates, considering he doesn't need credits."

"I had a feeling he didn't," I replied, withholding a grin. I wanted to say that if I'd known how beneficial screwing up a job would be, I would've done it more often, but I decided to hold my tongue. I didn't want to remind Luxarn of that after receiving such a promising offer. Instead, I tossed back the rest of my whiskey, stood, and saluted him. "Thank you, sir."

"No. Thank you, Mr. Graves."

As I turned to leave, he stopped me by clearing his throat.

"Oh," he began calmly, "and Zhaff may look young, but I would advise heeding his counsel when you can. That *freak* is my son."

I almost choked on air as I processed what he said. I stared back at Luxarn, who leaned forward with his fingers steepled on the top of his desk and his hard gaze boring through me. The spherical bot hovered beside him, all-too-familiar yellow lens aimed straight in my direction. I knew I probably should've kept walking, but the liquor in my belly convinced me to do otherwise.

"What are you saying?" I said. His words didn't leave much room for guessing, but I was caught off guard. As far as I knew, Luxarn Pervenio didn't have a legitimate heir to his empire yet.

Luxarn poured himself another glass of whiskey and drank the entire thing in a single gulp. He wiped his mouth with his hand this time. Then he said, "His mother was an offworlder from Mars without a name. I couldn't have an illegitimate smear my name, so I made sure he was kept a secret and left him in her care. That didn't mean I could help loving him, but he was always a troubled boy. He didn't speak for the first four years of his life... he just watched, waited.

"As he got older, others his age didn't take kindly to his silence, but he couldn't be bullied. He couldn't be rattled. My son would sit there and take the beatings until one day a boy went too far. Unable to get a rise out of Zhaff, he beat his face so bad that sight in his left eye was lost."

"I'm sorry, sir, but I—" I had to clear my throat to continue.

"I've seen him at work. No way would he have let some boy do that to him."

"Not the Zhaff you know now, no. That was when I decided to risk taking him in myself. My best doctors claimed he had a particular concoction of social disorders afflicting him, and said that he would always suffer from dissociation. My genes don't take kindly to being told something's impossible. I decided to think of a way he could make use of his peculiar talents; a way he could realize his worth to the future of humanity."

"The Cogent Initiative," I said.

"Yes. But I had no idea how proficient he would become. After only a few short years of focused training, he could outfight my finest soldiers despite his size, and outthink my finest agents. I quickly sought out others like him to give them all a purpose. The bastards discarded by the USF because they bore a chronic disease.

"They can never replace men like you, of course—those with instincts and passion for their work—so it was no accident I paired you two together. We reviewed many potential partners, and you were my top choice to guide him in our brutal world. Now here we are. Together, who knows what a force you two can become?" Luxarn wore the same dreamy-eyed look on his face he'd been wearing when I first walked in and found him staring out into space.

I was speechless. Of all the collectors he had throughout Sol, Luxarn Pervenio had selected me to work with his only son. It was just as hard to believe that as it was to believe a man like him could possibly have fathered an illegitimate child like I had. But he had no reason to lie. It seemed I had more in common with the wealthiest man in Sol than I'd ever imagined.

"I'm honored, sir, but why are you telling me all this now?" I asked. It was the first thing that popped into my head.

"Without knowing who he really is, you saved my son's life.

I know how difficult he can be. For that, you deserve to know what you're dealing with. Earth was one thing, but down on Titan, there may be dangers even he is not prepared for."

I swallowed hard. "And I'm grateful, but—"

He waved his hand to silence me. "Very few people know what I've just revealed to you. I trust that you will keep it our little secret. The USF would love any excuse to discredit my proposal to expand the Departure Lottery."

I forced a complacent smile, knowing full well that I didn't really have any other choice. "What's another secret?"

"I knew I could count on you." Luxarn clapped his hands and leaned back in his chair. "It's time you go to him, then. Good luck down there, Mr. Graves. Now that you know what he means to this company, I expect you will do everything in your power to get the job done by his side."

"Everything," I affirmed. I went to take a step away, and then another thought crossed my mind. "Does he know, sir?"

"Have you ever tried to withhold the truth from him?"

Luxarn put on a haughty grin that warned me not to dare press the matter any further. I didn't. I wasn't sure what else to say anyway. I smiled and nodded, and somehow managed to lift my suddenly very heavy-feeling legs so I could trudge out of the room.

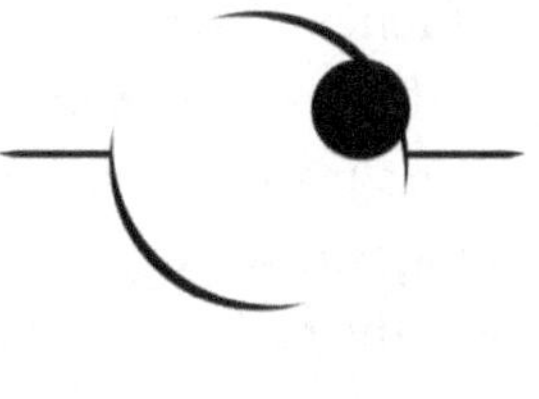

SIXTEEN

A HANDFUL of moons hovered outside the viewport of the small shuttle transporting Zhaff and me to Titan. They were big and small, far and near. Titan was the largest of them—a pale-orange orb dappled with pockets of shadow that gave it the appearance of a windswept skull. I found it fitting for a place where the locals were as icy as the temperature.

I peered over at Zhaff. He'd been staring at his hand-terminal the entire trip, his eye-lens rifling over information so rapidly, I wasn't sure how he retained any of it. After what Luxarn had told me, it was impossible to view him the same way. I'd spent months—albeit most of it in hibernation—not knowing I was directly beside royalty. Even Director Sodervall didn't appear to know, judging by the way he treated Zhaff. I wouldn't say I felt deceived because I knew that I was part of a very small group privy to the truth, but I honestly think I would've been happier having remained ignorant. Strong as Luxarn's whiskey was, the news was completely sobering.

The shuttle shook violently as we pierced Titan's thick, stormy atmosphere. Gravity kicked back in. It was only about one-seventh Earth g, but it was enough to feel a sinking sensation in my stomach.

"You are nervous," Zhaff said to me, noticing me grab my restraints and hold on tight.

It was simply out of reflex. There may have only been a thin layer of rattling glass and metal between me and a frozen tomb, but landing safely was the least of my concerns. It was obvious he could sense something was wrong, though. I just wasn't sure I wanted to let him know the real reason why.

"Anxious to get this over with is all," I said.

"You are lying," Zhaff replied. "You have been anxious ever since you stepped out of Luxarn Pervenio's office."

I sighed, realizing how right Luxarn was. It was foolish to try to hide anything from him. "To be honest, I never thought I'd be in the same room as the man, let alone have a conversation with him."

I paused and stared at Zhaff's scarred eye. I wanted to stop dancing around the issue, but it was hard to imagine he'd ever been a child, let alone beaten by one. Yet there his useless eye was, sitting like a cloudy white marble amongst a series of jagged scars. "What do you think of him?" I asked.

"We have exchanged many conversations," Zhaff replied. "He believes that every being has a purpose, whether small or crucial, toward ensuring the future of humanity. He has dedicated his life to the expansion and evolution of our species. It is a vision that must be supported."

"I know what he believes. I meant what do *you* think of him? Of Luxarn Pervenio, the man? The most powerful in all of Sol." I took a deep breath. It wasn't that I thought Luxarn was lying, but I decided I needed to hear the truth from Zhaff's mouth to believe it. "Your father..."

Zhaff's eye-lens snapped toward me and analyzed my face. He must have approved of what he saw because he returned to looking at his hand-terminal and responded with words other than *That is classified.* "I am surprised he told you," he said. "My feelings toward him are irrelevant. He gave me purpose, Malcolm. Without him, I would not exist. He helped create me, like you helped create your daughter."

My throat went dry. He left out the part where Luxarn and I both kept our illegitimate children secret for our own reasons and transformed them into weapons. Maybe Luxarn knew, and that was why he felt he could trust me with the secret.

As I stared at Zhaff's emotionless face, I couldn't help but wonder if Aria would've wound up the same if she'd stayed with me. As numb as a collector who for thirty years never once put down his gun.

"Just like that," I said.

"Are you not satisfied with my answer?" Zhaff replied.

I loosened my restraints and reached up to lay my hand upon his tall shoulder. "I'll tell you what, Zhaff. Let's just worry about catching these smugglers and bringing an end to all of this. Deal?"

Zhaff considered it for a moment and then nodded. "Agreed."

He didn't press the issue any further. I knew I couldn't allow myself to dwell on the thought and wind up distracted. No matter who he was, or why he was, there was work to be done. For obvious reasons, the fact that Luxarn had met with me personally had me yearning to get the job done, and done right.

I turned away from Zhaff and looked out the viewport beside my seat, barely able to see the tip of the shuttle's stubby wings. The dense air of Titan meant they didn't have to be long to help it balance in flight. After a few minutes, the ship stopped shaking, and we were safely through the upper atmosphere. The pilot brought us down near a factory complex built along the side of one of Titan's famous methane lakes, puffing out smoke.

There wasn't much else to look at with storm clouds rolling in from every direction. It was a desolate place, locked eternally at nearly two hundred degrees Celsius below freezing.

As we soared over a ridge of frozen rock, I tracked a cluster of thick pipes running out of the lake toward the half-buried colony block that constituted Darien. In the newer Earther colonies around Sol, people tried to construct every structure at a scale reminiscent of the ones on Earth. The first people to settle Titan had apparently forgotten the ruined, contemporary cities of their homeworld. It was at least a two-kilometer-long chunk of metal that rose thirty meters into the air, making it appear like a monolithic ziggurat. It only seemed taller because it was surrounded by flat, sandy plains, but the brunt of the block's pressurized, inhabitable area extended far underground. There were tiny gaps here and there for translucencies and hangar bays, but for the most part, they were completely enclosed by the double-layered metallic shell that held the unbreathable and freezing air at bay.

Darien had access to everything a self-sustaining internalized city could need. A constant stream of exhaust and smoke puffed out through vents along the top, mostly the result of underground factories and water purification plants that siphoned liquid out of Titan's subterranean ocean and made it potable. I could also make out the angled panels of glass and steel extending away from the base of the block, housing its extensive hydroponic farms. It was like a moat of green around a metal castle. During storms, the sand would whip around and mask it, but it was a welcome view of life in an otherwise lifeless setting. The only sign of human attendance was the occasional flit of trams shooting through tubes along the raised lines that ran off into the distance toward other colonies.

If my people had designed Darien, they surely would've considered the ridiculous danger of not spreading out for fear of stray asteroids, but Darien was already laid out by the Ringers at the time of the Great Reunion. It was the oldest settlement on Titan, said to be constructed three centuries ago out of parts from the original ship Darien Trass built to carry over the first settlers fleeing the Meteorite.

A tiny portion of the block's stark façade folded open as we approached, and the shuttle slipped into the revealed hangar. It was located in Darien's shiny upper ward, filled with all manner of shops, offices, dwellings, entertainment venues, and transportation hubs. Once inside, the ship was able to touch down more gently than a ship ever could on Earth. The low g made that easy, though with my weighted boiler suit on, my body felt as if it were back on my homeworld.

Zhaff, the workers filling the shuttle, and I filed out into the busy hangar. Security was on us immediately. It figured we would arrive in Darien right as many of the monthlong gas-harvesting shifts let out. They patted us down and checked identification, conveniently overlooking my and Zhaff's pistols once they realized who we were. They even snuck us false IDs that declared we were recent immigrant workers from the damaged Undina mining facility just in case we needed them—compliments of Director Sodervall.

Despite our treatment, I got an immediate taste for how much worse Titan had gotten since I was last there. Pervenio security officers were everywhere, and they wore thick lines of tension on their faces. Their eyes darted back and forth, tirelessly scrutinizing every weary passenger, and if someone's skin was even a shade too white, they were checked over three times. Decontamination chambers stood at every entrance, but even they seemed to be less about keeping out diseases and more an excuse for another layer of security. People stepped in and stripped down until there was nowhere to hide anything.

We waited until the hangar was completely clear, and then, as we went to leave, I stopped at the security post.

"What are you doing, Malcolm?" Zhaff asked.

"I hope you don't think we're going down into the lower ward with all of this," I replied, gesturing to my clothes, pistol, and other equipment. "We're going to have to blend in. Like everyday harvester workers. Rylah won't let anyone near her dressed like us. Hand-terminals only in case we need to make contact."

No matter what we wore, anyone next to an obvious Earther like me would be in danger where we were going. A problem for another time.

I removed my duster as well as all my effects—Aria's Ark figurine included—and handed them to a security officer. Losing any of it to a greedy Ringer down below wouldn't end well.

I took off my shirt as well since it bore a Pervenio badge. I may as well have been wearing a target. That left me in only the unmarked weighted boiler suit we'd been provided when we arrived at the station.

Zhaff scrutinized my face for a moment. "I will defer to your judgment. You are the one acquainted with the information broker." It wasn't necessarily a gesture of trust, but at least I was getting better at convincing him to see things my way. It was beginning to feel like a genuine partnership.

Zhaff already wore only his weighted boiler suit, so the only change to his outfit he had to make was removing the badge he wore proudly on his chest.

"No Earther going down there for leisure would be permitted to wear a gun either," I explained. I unfastened my pistol's holster from my belt and paused to look it over. I loved my gun as much as any man could, and I could count on one hand the amount of times I'd let it out of my sight while on duty. It usually ended poorly, but I was still alive. It had to be done.

"C'mon, you too," I said as I finally mustered the courage to place it down.

He pulled out his firearm and silently looked it over. "Malcolm, I have been instructed on the current dangers of this settlement."

"Trust me. It's better we leave them here than have them confiscated down there. I know these kinds of people."

He nodded and relinquished it.

At that, we both stood weaponless, in relatively unassuming clothing, with nothing but our hand-terminals, which looked like any others as long as nobody scrolled through our contacts and found a name like Sodervall. But they couldn't without our thumbprints. The hacked terminal we'd retrieved on the *Piccolo* was tucked securely into the side of my boot.

I was about to signal Zhaff to move, when I regarded his face. If my jacket was a target, the device covering his eye was a bulls-eye. The thing had *valuable* written all over it, and I knew we wouldn't get far in the lower ward without a thousand Ringers trying to rip it off him to sell on the black. It wasn't like Earth where people were careful most of the time, and I wanted to keep the risk as low as possible.

"That lens. Can you remove it?" I asked. In all honesty, I had no idea whether it was attached directly to his brain or if there was even a human eye beneath, considering what I'd learned about his useless exposed one.

"I am able to, but it is calibrated to enhance my ability to see, aim, and analyze."

"Well, you're going to have to try to work without it. That thing will earn us way too much attention."

Zhaff froze for a moment before nodding that he understood. "Agreed," he said. He reached up and undid the latches built around the device, each one digging into his flesh. It took him about a minute to remove the apparatus, and underneath it, his skin was raw and chapped. The eye it revealed looked to be healthy. It was hazel, just like his father's.

As stagnant as his face always was, his working eye was the opposite. It darted from side to side, investigating everything around him. I couldn't help but stare. For the first time, he didn't look like some strange cyborg out of a story. He looked like a young man with a troubled past. I hoped that he was just as capable without the augmentations the lens provided as he was with them.

"I was instructed never to lose it," he said as he held it up to his face. I noticed the barest signs of sadness ripple across his face, as if he'd never been apart from it. It was a new look for him.

"They'll take care of it," I assured. I gestured toward the team in the security post. "Anything happens to any of this and Director Sodervall will have you on cleaning duty for a year," I said to them. They each swallowed nervously before hurrying over to gather our belongings.

I guided Zhaff toward the decontamination chamber leading out of the hangar. "Now, we're both a little too tan these days to go down to the lowers empty-handed," I said. "I hope you have credits on you."

"As usual, I am tapped into the Pervenio military account," he said.

"Of course you are." I smirked. For a moment, I'd forgotten who he was. "All right, she's waiting for us on level B5 of the lower wards in a club called the Foundry. Let's hurry there before she changes her mind."

He nodded, and we stepped forward to pass through the decontamination chamber separately. I went first and was forced to strip down like meat out to market. Electrostatic cleaners made my hair stand up and tickled my skin. I hated being exposed like that. When the process was complete and I was pronounced clean, I put my boiler-suit back on so fast I nearly ripped a sleeve. Zhaff followed soon after.

Unlike the colony block's bleak exterior, the upper ward was bright and airy. Rectangular towers ascended through the tall space on a wide grid, supporting the ceiling of the enclosure like grand columns. Each had shops and market-stands a ground-level, and above that were divided into spacious Earther apartments until they reached the ceiling. Verdant gardens hung in glassy containers between them to serve the luxurious residences on the highest level, glimmering like floating green crystals.

Life was everywhere, unlike on the surface of this rock. Thousands, both Ringer and Earthers, returned from work shifts. It was easy to tell them apart—Earthers and Ringers. Besides their pinkish faces, many Earthers had the credits to afford at least a decent weighted suit. Ringers, on the other hand, wore sanitary masks and gloves and moved with the hitched hop-step typical of walking in low gravity. I always found it kind of funny-looking when placed beside a normal stride.

As we left the docks and plunged into a marketplace that stretched across four of the tremendous columns, my eyes were besieged by countless colorful ads. They lined the sleek walls and shone above every shop stand. Even Zhaff had to pause for a minute to allow his exposed eye to adjust. The ones closest to the docks advertised for a burgeoning market of luxury cruisers that apparently sailed around within the inner atmosphere of Saturn, where the gravitational pull was remarkably similar to Earth's. Extravagant vacations like that made it easy to understand why Ringers resented my kind.

The farther in we got, the more dizzying it became, with all the promotional announcements struggling to broadcast above both the din of the crowd and the shouting shopkeepers.

"Blankets! Warm enough to keep you alive on the surface!" one hollered.

"Missing your family back home on Earth? Connect with them over Solnet through a brand- new hand-terminal!" yelled another.

"Weighted suits! Thin as a leaf!"

After ten minutes of walking, the end-of-shift crowd began to dissipate. Mostly Pervenio officers and Earthers were left behind. The latter were busy either shopping for the latest in high fashion or searching for the perfect entertainment venue to start off their nights. The only Ringers I could spot by then wore worker's clothing and were doing whatever it took to keep the upper ward looking like a sterling testament to human ingenuity. From sweeping the floors of all the restaurants, bars, and shops to scrubbing the glass and walls throughout the block until everything sparkled; they did all the things Earthers didn't want to.

In my experience, most Ringers strayed from the upper ward as much as they could. They preferred staying down in the parts of Darien that were buried beneath the surface of Titan, where the lights were dimmer, the stench fouler, and the dangers to their health less pronounced. They never got to see any sunlight, in contrast with the upper ward where areas were cut with long translucencies revealing the copper glow of Titan's sky.

It'd been years, so nothing looked overly familiar until I spotted the towering statue of Darien Trass—the man who'd first sent ships to the Ring before the Meteorite hit Earth—rising through the upper ward's central atrium. The walkways wrapping him were lined with generous planters displaying all sorts of colorful flora that apparently once thrived outside on pre-Meteorite Earth.

With all the mentions of him lately, I couldn't help but stare at the monument. It had to have been retouched since the Ringers first erected it back when the upper ward belonged to them because the face looked remarkably similar to Luxarn Pervenio's. I never noticed until now that I'd seen him up close. No coincidences.

A short walk from there and we neared the main lift, which sank through the crust of Titan to the levels of the lower ward where Ringers lived. A pair of Pervenio officers rushed past us and almost bowled me and Zhaff over.

"You, halt!" one of them demanded and raised his pulse-rifle.

A group of children nearby scattered as fast as they could, threading their way into the marketplace's crowd. They were definitely Ringers, and as I watched the officers pursue them, I wasn't completely sure whether or not they would've opened fire had there not been other Earther pedestrians in the way.

I looked back to what the children were fleeing from. Three-quarters of an orange circle was painted over an advertisement for a tanning salon that would help immigrants retain their skin tone. They hadn't been able to finish the circle before they were seen. A mob of Earther civilians had formed around it. They all looked frightened.

"They've even got children doing their work," I said to Zhaff.

Zhaff didn't respond. His single eye was fixed on the scene as we passed. In return, suspicious stares from the Earthers gathered by the symbol barraged him. I may have been used to his appearance, but I could understand their concern. The way he looked. The way he walked. I decided to grab his arm and pick up our pace. It appeared we weren't destined to feel comfortable on any level of Darien.

We were able to reach the main lift without further complications, but once there, we found a very small percentage of

Earthers to be taking the plunge with us. I'd been to Darien before, so I knew the upper ward was fine for my kind if you were simply looking to wade through crowds shopping, eating food, and having a drink. But the lower ward was the place to go if you really wanted to unwind—as long I didn't wear a Pervenio badge and had credits to spend. At least, it was the last time I'd been there.

Director Sodervall was right. Things were worse here, but I had a feeling Zhaff and I were about to find out just how much.

SEVENTEEN

WHEN THE DOORS of the Darien central lift slid open, it felt like we'd been transported to a completely different world. The lower wards of most colony blocks on Titan had been around since before the Earthers had made contact with Saturn, yet remained untouched. Pervenio Corp was considerably less interested in keeping the nether regions of their Titan settlements shiny and presentable.

While the upper ward was bright and airy, down here, the network of squat tunnels branching off from the cavernous node surrounding the lift made it feel like a labyrinth. The shit beneath the sheen. Much of the walls were exposed to rock and covered in pipes and ducts, and the portions that were lined by panels of serrated metal were rusting. Luckily, the lights on the ceilings were dim enough to make that difficult to notice. The walls were dotted with circular hatches for small, cave-like apartments the locals called hollows.

The change in the air, too, was tangible. The lower wards on Titan were kept around freezing, just how Ringers liked it. I immediately regretted not bringing my duster. Also, in contrast with the fresh air above, the wards reeked of salt from water treatment plants and soldered metal from factories. They were sprinkled all throughout the lowers, at the end of every tunnel—everything Pervenio profited from but preferred to keep buried. Noisy air recyclers too old for their own good didn't help.

As Zhaff and I walked, it was easy to notice how the tides had shifted. Pervenio security teams were sparse, all of them posted within guarded booths positioned at the decon-chambers surrounding the lift that we were forced to pass through. Lanky Ringers were everywhere with their alabaster skin and sanitary masks. It wasn't as crowded with them as the upper ward was with Earthers, but Darien sank deep into Titan, and the lower ward had many levels. Last I read, roughly three million people lived within Titan's numerous colony blocks, and three-quarters of them were Ringers with ancestry dating back to the first settlers. They may have been weaker physically, had fewer weapons, and been focused on trying to buy their sick relatives medicine, but I understood Luxarn's fear of letting a faction of dissidents spark their animosity. Being stronger doesn't count for much when you have three angry rebels jumping on your back.

Beggars roamed freely. It was hard to tell who was starving and who wasn't since Ringers were all so bony compared to me. I wagered on most of them. Any job an Earther wanted, they got first choice, which left a large portion of lower ward residents without legitimate employment.

Pale, strung-out salt sniffers observed everything from the deep shadows of tunnels, their gazes locked on me instead of Zhaff. Some of them were snorting foundry salts; most had a crazed look in their eyes, as if they were waiting for an excuse to kill something. They didn't bother us, but as we continued on, I couldn't shake the suspicion that another, more menacing group watched from out of sight.

In fact, everyone kept their distance. On Mars, it was hard

to walk anywhere in the seedy sections of the cities without being hounded by streetwalkers. Doing whatever it took to survive wasn't frowned upon among offworlders as it was back on Earth. But on Titan, sex workers had become a scourge; the lowest of the low. They'd helped spread disease more than anything else after the Great Reunion. Now Ringers were aggressive in their pursuit of finding someone they believed to be a life partner. Once they did, they'd remain fiercely loyal for the rest of their days. It was their way of trying to stay safe, the way clan-families were ours, which made my and Rylah's fling a rare occurrence.

"Watch it, mud stompers!" a young boy yelled as he bumped into Zhaff.

I grabbed him by the wrist on his way by. I squeezed so that his fist came open, and in it, I saw Zhaff's false ID. Long fingers made Ringers excellent pickpockets. That was one thing I remembered about Titan that clearly hadn't changed.

"Let go!" the kid shouted.

I tore the ID out of his palm and shoved him along. "Watch your pockets, Zhaff," I said.

He nodded.

We were in a place no amount of training could prepare one for. I suppose that was what Luxarn realized when he decided Zhaff needed a partner.

The kid earned us even more attention. Faces peered out through cracked-open hatches of hollows, and masks covering everything but their eyes made them appear especially unwelcoming. I'd have felt much safer with my pistol.

Still, people kept their distance. Nobody tried to stop us, or ask what we were doing, or hold us up and take everything we had. I weirdly would've felt more comfortable if they had. Everyone just continued watching us with hateful stares, as if we were marching toward some sort of unsanctified ritual. As a collector, I was used to being treated with caution, even fear, but I wasn't used to being regarded with unbridled disdain.

"Remember to let me do the talking," I said to Zhaff when we arrived at the entrance to the Foundry. Two drunks stood to its side, glares piercing us like blades. They didn't say a word.

The Foundry was on the far side of level B5's central node, down a set of stairs above which its name was written in cool-colored neon lights. That was where Rylah had been holed up when I'd last dealt with her, so I hoped it was where she would be based on her message. We made our way down the set of stairs and into a broad tunnel wrapped in bands of pulsing blue light.

"And for heaven's sake, try to act natural," I said, taking notice of Zhaff's perfect, upright posture. I slapped him on his upper back to coax him into walking like a real person. It didn't work for long.

Two towering Ringer bouncers stood at the Foundry's entry. Both were armed with batons, though I found them far from threatening despite how far they had to look down to meet my gaze. Being born on Earth, I could crack their ribs in a single punch if I wanted to.

"IDs," requested the gruffer of two. He held out his palm. I did as requested and signaled Zhaff to do the same. The bouncer looked over our identifications, and when he was satisfied, he put on a wry grin and glanced toward his partner.

"One hundred credits to get in, for each of you," he snickered. His voice was muffled by a sanitary mask.

"You've got to be joking," I protested, trying to act the part of a harvester after a hard month's work. That was who our faux IDs said we were, after all.

The bouncer tapped his baton a few times. "You must be new around here, mud stomper. Now it's one fifty."

"You can't—" I sighed and turned to Zhaff. "Pay the man already, then. I need a drink."

Zhaff recognized my act. He handed over his credit chit for the bouncer to swipe. The other one came around behind us and patted us down. Zhaff's fists tightened as he confiscated our personal hand-terminals, but I sneaked him a shake of the head. I had a feeling he would've killed both of them in a heartbeat if I hadn't and brought the entirety of the lower ward upon us.

"Fancy hand-terminals," the more vocal bouncer admired. Mine was nothing too special, but better than most Ringers could afford. "Sorry, can't bring these inside. USF orders." He grinned as he tucked Zhaff's device into his belt and handed mine to his partner. "Have fun, Earther."

I let it go, resolving to come back for it later after we met with Rylah. They wouldn't be able to access our secured information unless they cut off our thumbs anyway.

"It's been a while, but I think I remember where she is," I whispered to Zhaff as we traversed a low tunnel carved into the deep bedrock of Titan and emerged into the Foundry. I was rarely ever sober in the club when I used to visit Rylah, so I had to think hard.

Colorful beams of light flashed throughout the mostly dim space, each one distorted by the layer of steam hanging over the floor. The electronic music was deafening. The Ringers had few, if any, real instruments when they arrived on Titan, so the music they cared for was entirely digitized. If there was a melody, I couldn't find it. All the sweaty Ringers, on the other hand, appeared to be on enough foundry salts to find a song in anything. Alcohol was also limited when they first arrived, so drugs were common on the Ring, made mostly from factory residue. That was fine with me. It helped us stay unnoticed.

I tried to gather my bearings amid the crazed dancers bumping into me. The Foundry was a reprogrammed factory, consisting of a network of gaping caverns. Vibrant, pulsating lights refracted through clouds of mist that spilled out through exhaust vents once meant for safety. Bars were built into stacks of machinery, colorful bottles filled with sythahol feeding through reallocated pumps to work the taps. Dancers in skintight plastic outfits lined machine belts that cranked along through the swelling crowds of Ringers. They may as well have been naked, but Ringers were always careful about being touched.

Beyond all that, a series of raised suites with broad, tinted translucencies faced the club on the far side. Once observation rooms for the factory, they were presently used as private suites for some of the Foundry's more distinguished guests.

"That's it," I said, pointing to one of the farthest suites. Zhaff nodded.

We traversed a sea of carousing that would've put New London to shame. I'll say that about the Ringers. The ones who are healthy enough to move sure make the most out of their nights. All the ways I imagined their ancestors used to stay warm during the early days of settling Titan had become completely ingrained in their culture, until we ruined carefree sex for them at least. A younger version of myself would've found it difficult not to join them.

A single sentry stood at the bottom of the staircase leading up to Rylah's suite. This one was a step up from the bouncers. He wore a white suit of composite armor with a tinted helmet that made his face difficult to see. It had no pale-orange circle inscribed on the chest plate, but he had no business wielding the automatic pulse-rifle he held. It appeared to be the same type as the one the Ringer on the *Piccolo* had.

Seeing it left no question in my mind that we were in the middle of something larger than a smuggling job. Luxarn was right to worry.

I pulled Zhaff over to the nearest bar and ordered a shot of some flavor of blue-colored sythahol. Most Ringers couldn't afford the real shit, so that was the best I could get. The bartender charged me another hundred credits and didn't say another word. While we waited, I leaned over the counter so I could talk to Zhaff inconspicuously, but with the sentry still in view.

"You should not be drinking while we—" Zhaff said before I cut him off.

"I'm trying to blend in," I said. "Check out the guard."

"He is wearing a similar model of armor as the Children of Titan combatant from the harvester, minus the orange circle," Zhaff determined.

"Same weapon too," I added.

"Agreed."

"Somehow, I don't think my girl is selling much information to people like us anymore."

"I can incapacitate him." Zhaff's eye shifted from side to side, planning a route of attack. It was nice to get an idea of his train of thought from that, as opposed to when he was wearing his eye-lens.

"Not yet. Rylah and I go back. She invited us to talk, so we'll talk first. But stay on your toes."

"Why would I stay on my toes?" Zhaff questioned.

"Never mind. Let's go." The bartender slammed down my drink, and I tossed it back before I could look down and see the spit that was probably floating in the center. It was unduly sweet, but it did the job. I got up and strode toward the sentry with a bounce in my step.

"Back the other way, Earthers," he said through helmet coms that made his voice sound deeper. He made no attempt to hide his contempt.

"We're not looking for any trouble," I responded coolly. "Just information."

"Lady Rylah is done talking to your kind. Back the other way or I'll paint the walls with your brains." He lifted his gun and aimed it at my head.

I raised my hands. "Charming. Tell her it's Malcolm Graves. We spoke earlier about a potential deal."

The guard lowered his rifle and raised his hand to a switch on the side of his helmet. After a brief moment of silence, he responded, "Come with me."

He stepped to the side so we could go first. Zhaff didn't need to say anything to confirm what we were both thinking: It was too easy.

We moved into the suite where two more heavily armed guards in white searched us. It was a fairly open hollow, with bare rock walls as if we were within an asteroid colony. The far side was entirely covered in a curved array of screens, similar to the surveillance center in New London except more extensive. A few of them displayed images of the club, but the others displayed views of every colony block on Titan, from both the outside and inside. Rylah stood in front of them.

"Ry, it's a..." I froze when she turned around. I'd forgotten how stunning she was. Her limbs were long and shapely, and her slender face may have been pale, but she had warm, rosy cheeks. If she was born on the Ring, then she couldn't have been more than second-generation. "Pleasure."

She got up and sauntered toward us, her violet dress hugging her lithe figure. I was expecting a hug at least, considering how we'd left things. Instead, she stopped a few paces away.

"Malcolm, it's lovely to see you again," she said, smiling widely. Zhaff was unfazed. He studied her the way he would anyone else, and as he did, I noticed him turn his body ever so slightly to reposition himself. Something was wrong.

"I told you I'd come back," I replied, keeping up appearances and returning the smile.

She rolled her eyes. "It took you long enough. How's that daughter of yours?"

"I couldn't tell you. We don't talk much these days. I'm working with someone else now."

"I can see that. Another lucky partner. I've been watching you two since you arrived at the Ring. I'm glad you decided to turn to me for help. Sorry about the guards, handsome. These are dangerous times."

"Yet you're still as beautiful as ever. I don't know how you do it."

"Always the flatterer."

"Some things never change." I flashed her a knowing grin. "So, like I said, I'm hoping you might be able to tell us something of value about the device we recovered. For old times' sake."

"It'll cost you."

As soon as the words left her violet-colored lips, Zhaff kicked me hard in the hip and sent me sprawling. A gunshot rang out, the bullet grazing my sleeve before speeding harmlessly into the ground. I rolled over to see Zhaff sweep the legs out from one of the guards and disarm him. Another was only able to get off a few inaccurate shots before Zhaff was on him too. The Cogent's hands moved so fast that my eyes couldn't keep up. He rendered both of them unconscious in short order.

I snapped out of my stupor as quickly as I could to strike the third guard from behind while he was taking aim. Titan's low g made me strong enough in comparison to send him flying. I pounced on him and punched through his visor, knocking him out and bloodying my fist.

Rylah bolted for her screens but didn't get far before Zhaff kicked one of the rifles up into his hands and shot her in the calf. No hesitation. He sprinted over to her as she squealed.

"Zhaff, calm down!" I shouted. I ran to pull him off.

"It is only a flesh wound," he informed me. He shrugged me off and knelt beside her. "Lock the entrance."

"Dammit, Zhaff! You've got to warn me next time you're about to do something like that."

"She was going to have us killed."

"I swear I wasn't!" she moaned, writhing in pain.

"She's lying."

"You're sure?" I asked. Without his eye-lens, I wasn't sure how good Zhaff was at reading faces, but he seemed as certain as ever.

"They... they did it!" Rylah claimed. Pain seeped into her voice. She had to force each word out. "The Children of Titan have been holding me hostage. I had no choice."

Zhaff leaned in to get a closer look at her face. "You are not a hostage," he said.

The absolute certainty in his words made Rylah's eyes widen. An information broker of her caliber wouldn't have been in the dark when it came to the Cogent Initiative like most people were. Dread gripped her as she realized what he was.

"I was!" she said. "I swear!"

I took a deep breath before I finally decided to walk over and lock the room's entrance. This wasn't how I'd intended things to go when I messaged her. There was no unusual commotion outside in the club signaling that someone had heard us. The gunshots must've blended in with the music's heavy beat.

"Mal..." she pleaded as I turned back toward her, attempting to wield her most seductive smile at me to rekindle old feelings. Her discomfort just made her look foolish.

"What are they paying you to work with them?" I asked as I approached her, struggling to keep my temper at bay. After all we'd been through, she'd tried to have me killed. It took every ounce of my being to stay focused on the job.

"I'm not."

"Lying," Zhaff said. He pressed a single finger down on her wound. She howled.

"Not officially!" she gasped. "They paid me to help with surveillance and dissemination. I'm just following the credits, same as you."

Zhaff removed his finger and turned to me. "She is happy to aid them. This is not the first time."

"I'm happy to earn credits helping my own people!" she said. "But I'm not one of *them*."

That answered my question of where she'd really been born. Her job must have been lucrative enough for her to purchase all the proper immunizations to stay clean, considering we'd shared a bed and she'd avoided the q-zones.

"A few nights together, and you try to kill me," I said. "I must have made quite the impression."

"That was a long time ago, Mal," she said. "It has nothing to do with that."

It was difficult to stay angry at her with the way the light of her monitoring screens reflected off her silky, glistening skin. Attempting to end my life, however, had a way of tempering any of the feelings I may have ever had for her.

"Offworlders," I said under my breath, with a few curses thrown in for good measure. I motioned for Zhaff to get off her. She grabbed at her bleeding calf the moment she was free.

"Look," I said, "we don't give two shits about your affiliation if you help us. There's no bounty on you... yet."

"If you're after Kale Drayton, I can't tell you where he is," she replied. "Even I don't know. They operate in cells. Most of their operatives don't know anything besides their current mission. That's the truth."

"So this Kale Drayton isn't their leader?"

She shook her head, then paused before shrugging. "I don't think so. But they barely told me anything."

I looked to Zhaff. He nodded. She was being honest.

"Fortunately for you, we're not after Kale yet," I continued. I reached down into my boot, pulled out the hacked hand-terminal with the symbol of the Children of Titan on it, and tossed it by her feet. "This device from the *Piccolo* is the only piece of physical evidence we have right now connected to what happened. So tell us what you know."

She bit her lip noticeably but didn't say anything as she attempted to avert her gaze from the hand-terminal.

"She helped them broadcast the recording," Zhaff said.

"Did she now?" I couldn't help but smirk. That was even better news than I'd expected. I turned my head toward Zhaff so I could gloat over how my decision to reach out to her had paid off, but I surprised myself by being unable to think of anything to say. It was hard to boast right after he'd saved my life. That wasn't all, though. I guess after all we'd been through so far, I was starting to realize that Luxarn Pervenio was right. Zhaff and I made a pretty decent team.

"I swear, I..." she began before dropping her gaze to the ground, apparently deciding it wasn't worth lying. "One hundred thousand credits, Malcolm. I couldn't have said no to them. So I helped them program that device, but I didn't realize it meant they'd leave it behind as a message and keep me under guard like I served them afterward. I didn't even know what it was for when I first helped!"

"A hundred thousand? I don't blame you." I reached down and placed my hand on her slight shoulder. The wound in her leg had her whole body shaking. "So you invited us down here to destroy it and remove me from the equation. Smart. I guess I did rub off on you."

"Mal, that's not—"

I placed my finger over her mouth. "Save it. This isn't about us. You or them, it doesn't matter. Help us now, and I'll try to pretend you weren't part of a plan to have us killed."

Rylah shot me a pained scowl. "After this, the Ring isn't going to see me for a long time. All those fanatics have brought to my life are problems. You aren't the first collectors they tried to shoot down in this room."

"Malcolm, that is impossible," Zhaff said. "She is in violation of—" I hushed him before he could finish. His single eye stared at me, but I urged him to trust me, and he remained silent. I needed Rylah on my side for the time being, no matter how I felt.

I lifted my hand off her and rose to my full, unimpressive height. "I'm guessing you heard about the bombing back in New London. A group of Ringers with the Children of Titan used it as a distraction to smuggle Pervenio equipment here from Earth. We need to find them. Considering your relationship, I'm figuring you might know something about that."

"I may have helped them here, but I had nothing to do with what happened on Earth," she asserted. "Titan is my only concern."

I looked to Zhaff quickly. He didn't shake his head or say a word, which had to mean she was being sincere.

"And I believe you," I said, "but whatever they're planning, it's about to concern all of the Ring. All you have to do is tell us where they may have run off to and we'll patch you up and be gone. Maybe you make the right decision afterward to stop helping these crazed Ringers, and this is done with, or maybe you don't, and I see your pretty face again all too soon."

Rylah stared at me, then at Zhaff before closing her eyes and breathing out. "All I know is that there's a Venta Co agent helping them. I've never seen him myself, but they call him the Doctor. That's it."

"The Doctor?"

"Yes. Like I said, I've never met the man. He only deals with the Children of Titan directly, so who knows what he's gotten into. Can't be good if you're here."

Zhaff validated her story with a nod.

"And you're sure he's working with Venta Co?" I asked.

"That's what I hear," she said. "Venta's been selling discontinued weapons parts to the people of Titan for years on the black. Those rifles over there, you take them apart, and you'll see that every piece came from them at one time or another."

"Even if that's true, helping with smuggling goods from Earth... that's a little more direct."

"Anything to cripple their rivals, right?"

"Yeah..." It wasn't the news I was hoping to hear. The definite involvement of another prominent USF-sanctioned corporation meant things were only going to get messier. We'd wind up handcuffed in our assignment while the real battle went on in boardrooms. We'd have to act quickly to avoid that.

"Well then, do you know where we can find this Doctor?" I asked.

"Not exactly," she said.

Before I could say anything, Zhaff was already bent down over her leg. He extended his finger and lowered it toward her wound. Rylah tried to scramble back out of the way, but I placed my palm on her chest and held her down with ease. She was no match for my Earther strength. I couldn't look her in the face as I did it, though. Apparently, there was still a heart beating in my chest.

"She knows where he is," Zhaff stated.

"I said not exactly!" she squealed before Zhaff's finger could get any closer. "I could tell you what I know, but only if you—"

Zhaff correctly predicted she would try to cut a deal, and had one of her guards' pulse-rifles pointed at her head before she could finish. "The price is your life," he said with the utmost sincerity.

Rylah swallowed hard as she stared down the barrel of the gun. She glanced over to me but found an equally unyielding expression forced onto my face. She exhaled.

"There are two Venta-owned hangars in the Darien uppers," she said. "I've heard about a special shipment coming into one of them sometime today. I'm not sure which, but I'm guessing it's what you're after."

I glanced over at her wide array of surveillance screens. "Can you show me?"

"Venta's very careful. I don't have cameras in the hangars." Zhaff moved the rifle closer to frighten more out of her. "But I can show you the outside!"

I brushed Zhaff aside and wrapped my arm around her. "That works for me. Zhaff, watch her hands and make sure she doesn't try to alert anybody."

"I'm not stupid, Mal," she groaned as I lifted her. I helped her over to her seat at the console that controlled the screens. I'd seen her operate her setup back when we were together, but it never disappointed and had doubled in size since. Her fingers flew across the keys as quickly as Zhaff's could, and all the images shuffled. She was tapped into so many views of the colonies of Titan, it honestly amazed me that there were hangars beyond her sight. I wouldn't doubt if she had an eye in every bathroom.

"Here's one," she said. "Hangar thirteen." The screen in front of her shifted to display a hangar entrance back at the docks. The door was wide open and the guard waiting there was with the USF. Paragraphs' worth of information popped up on the console in front of her. "Charter says the ship inside belongs to a USF assemblywoman and is being rented."

"And the other?" I asked.

Again, her fingers danced. "Hangar twenty," she said. The second hangar was larger, and we had a view within the adjoining lobby. Inside sat a receptionist as well as two guards in Venta Co blue posted by the sealed hangar entrance. The feed didn't offer the best angle, but I thought I recognized one of them. I leaned in over Rylah's shoulder to get a better look. She was breathing heavily.

"Trevor Cross," I said, sneering. He wasn't wearing his hat, but there was no question in my mind it was him.

"The Venta Co collector?" Zhaff asked.

"Yup. Man's useless in a fight, but no way they would waste credits putting him on guard duty unless it was important. How much do you want to bet he didn't run into us on Earth by accident?"

"I do not gamble, Malcolm, but it is a logical presumption."

"Well, if Rylah is right about what's behind there, then we're about to catch Venta red-handed backing the Children of Titan. Director Sodervall will be thrilled." I sat on the console so I was facing Rylah and patted her on the shoulder. "Now was that so hard?"

She gazed at me with her big brown eyes, hoping to win back my affection. "I told you what you want to know," she said. "Please don't hand me over. For old times' sake. They'll put me away for life for this."

"Sorry, Ry, but that's not up to me." I gestured toward Zhaff.

"She is already in violation of seven regulations that we are aware of," Zhaff stated. "She must be detained."

"Malcolm, please!" She turned to face me too fast, causing her to flinch in pain from her leg.

"I never thought I'd hear you beg," I said. "I'll tell you what." I rubbed my chin for a moment, just to keep her on edge. Zhaff's single eye focused on me. His lips cut a straight line, yet somehow I could tell he was displeased with the fact that I was even considering letting her go. But I had a fate in mind for her that was the nightmare of any person in her line of work. Something I felt would make us even for her trying to have me killed.

"We'll let you go," I said, "but only on these conditions. We're going to have you placed under constant surveillance. Try to flee the Ring, and you'll be put away for life. Try to warn that hangar we're coming or charge me for information ever again and you'll be put away for life. You work for Pervenio now in the operation against the Children of Titan insurgents, and if you let anyone else in on that secret, guess what happens."

"I get put away for life," she finished for me. I could tell by the way her voice uncharacteristically cracked that she was completely deflated.

"What do you think, Zhaff?" I asked. "The intel she can gather for Pervenio is far more valuable than having her sitting in a cell."

"Under those terms, I approve of the arrangement," Zhaff said, surprising me. I'd expected to have to explain more to him how having leverage over informants could be a collector's most useful tool. I like to think he was beginning to absorb a thing or two from being around me.

"Provided her information checks out, of course," I added. "Thanks, Ry. It's always fun when we get together." I stood and rolled her on her chair far away from her console. Then I used one of my bands to fasten her to a pipe. I also bound her legs.

"Really?" she grumbled, glaring at me with rancor as I stood.

"Hey, I could have gagged you." I'd considered it, but gunshots were louder than screams and nobody had heard those earlier. She'd had enough.

"You'd like that."

"Safety first." I threw a wink her way, then headed toward the exit. Zhaff followed, though he kept his gun aimed at her the entire way. I stopped to pick up the compromised hand-terminal.

"Pervenio will be holding on to this," I said. As I rose, I noticed the bodies of her unconscious guards in my path. "Oh, and I hope you don't mind, but we're going to borrow the armor from two of your friends here."

"Screw you, Mal." She spat in my direction. I suppose I deserved it, so I let her have that one little act of defiance. I always did enjoy her fire.

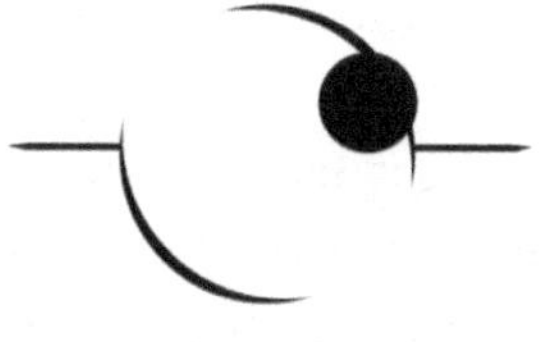

EIGHTEEN

ZHAFF AND I changed into the white armored suits Rylah's guards had been wearing. Mine had a fairly loose fit since it had belonged to a lanky Ringer, and the nano-fiber inlay had good flex to it. On such short notice, it would have to do. They were going to help us get as close to Trevor Cross and the Venta hangars as possible.

With the helmets on, it was also much easier to avoid the distrusting gazes of the Ringers throughout the lower ward. The disguise also got the Foundry's bouncers to hand over our hand-terminals with ease. I didn't even have to throw a punch. There was no question that the Children of Titan were the new, unspoken power of the lower ward.

As we walked, Zhaff used his hand-terminal to send in a report to the station about monitoring Rylah. Given his usual efficient manner, a team of officers were already entering the lower ward to head to her suite by the time we reached the lift. He was also able to ensure that no Pervenio security officers would bother us when we reached the upper ward, despite our suspicious suits.

We waited until we were back at the hangar we'd arrived in

to update Director Sodervall about what had happened. The situation was extremely sensitive, and Zhaff wisely didn't want to risk any other brokers like Rylah listening. Venta Co had full jurisdiction over their own hangars, even if Darien was Pervenio-run, and searching through their property wasn't exactly permitted.

"Not sure how we got lucky enough to stumble onto this one, but it seems Venta Co has definitely been helping the Children of Titan with their smuggling," I said to Sodervall as soon as his wrinkled face popped up on my hand-terminal. "My contact thinks the goods might be in one of their hangars here right now."

"As if I didn't have enough to worry about already," the director replied, exhausted. "That will surely complicate things. Our relationship with Madame Venta is rocky enough, considering her ongoing efforts to colonize Europa. Hold off until I speak with Mr. Pervenio before you do anything."

"He has already provided us with permission to proceed," Zhaff put in before I could say anything.

"*You* spoke with him?" the director questioned.

The fact that he didn't believe Zhaff let me know for certain that he didn't know who the Cogent really was. I wasn't usually keen on superseding a director's authority and causing myself trouble, but I had no desire to let anybody else in on Mr. Pervenio's secret and risk breaking my promise.

"We did," I said. Zhaff wouldn't lie, so with Luxarn Pervenio backing us, it didn't really matter if we hurt Director Sodervall's sense of pride. In fact, I found it a bit enjoyable, considering everything he'd put me through over the years.

"Fine, proceed," he grumbled. "You two aren't making my job any easier."

"It is not meant to be easy, sir," Zhaff said. Director Sodervall grimaced and ended the transmission immediately after.

I could hardly keep myself from chuckling. I knew Zhaff wasn't trying to be funny, but his words couldn't have been any more perfect. "Well said, Zhaff," I told him after gathering my breath.

He regarded me silently, lips straight as an arrow. Then a security officer arrived with our belongings, and he promptly attached his eye-lens. I grabbed my pistol and other effects, securing them to my belt. It felt good to be armed again.

"So what does the manifest say is going on in that hangar?" I asked him once we were ready. He pulled out his hand-terminal and swiped his fingers across the screen a few times. His eye-lens pored over the information, and I instantly missed being able to see the human eye beneath it. It helped me remember that he was human, at least physically.

"A Venta Co delivery ship from Mars arrived fifteen minutes ago at hangar twenty," he said.

"What are they supposedly delivering?" I asked as we turned to head back in the other direction.

"Various goods to be distributed throughout the shops they rent in Darien. Nothing out of the ordinary."

"Except for the collector out front. Unless Rylah made everything up and he's there for another reason, that must be our ship."

I didn't think she was—not with Zhaff listening to her—but I hadn't expected her to try to kill us either. There was enough bad blood between Venta and Pervenio to think they might make such a bold move if they thought they could get away with it, though. Plus, if Rylah was wrong, then we would've been completely out of viable leads. I never liked to consider that option while I was already knee-deep in an assignment.

Zhaff nodded, and we set off, still wearing the armor of Rylah's guards. Security officers throughout the hangar watched us attentively, but they kept their distance thanks to the order

Zhaff had circulated. I couldn't blame them for remaining wary based on what I'd seen on the Ring so far. The whole place was a powder keg waiting to blow.

With nobody to stand in our way, we were able to reach the closed lobby of hangar twenty in no time. We stopped in front of it, at a screen that displayed the receptionist inside. It didn't take long for me to recognize that it was the same view Rylah had and that she'd somehow hacked into that camera instead of placing her own.

"This is a private Venta Company hangar," the receptionist said through an intercom. "What is your business?"

"We're here on behalf of Lady Rylah," I responded as authoritatively as I could manage. "Care to make this quick?"

She bent over, held her hand to her ear, and said something inaudible. Then she looked back into the camera and said, "One moment."

A few seconds later, the entrance opened. Trevor appeared alongside another Venta guard. He held the pistol that matched my own, and the other wielded a top-of-the-line pulse-rifle, not like the crap they gave their Ringer allies. They wore full carbon-fiber suits of armor colored in the navy blue of Venta Co. No helmets.

We approached them slowly, their eyes scrutinizing us. Our disguises could only get us so far, considering that I wasn't tall enough to fill mine out. The clunky fit probably made me look absurd. I didn't have time to check a mirror. I did, however, make sure to approach from an angle so that Trevor wouldn't notice my pistol.

"I didn't hear about Rylah sending anyone up," Trevor said. "What does she want?"

Whether Rylah had helped with the bombing or not, there was no question she was involved enough with what was happening on Titan for a Venta Co collector to know who she was.

"She wants to speak with the Doctor," I said, voice distorted by my helmet so he wouldn't recognize it. "He's causing her trouble."

"What Doctor?" Trevor scowled and made his pistol more visible. "Sorry, boys, but we're under strict orders. Nobody gets in. We pay good money for this hangar, so tell her to come herself if she wants anything." He leaned in close and whispered, "If you two get caught sneaking around here again, you and that bitch are all dead."

I bit my tongue. It was usually advised that we try to avoid conflict with other powerful corporations. Trust me, it's amazing how one little gunfight can turn into a decades-long grudge. As I thought about what to say next, Zhaff must've seen an opening because he said, "I'm going to strike them, Malcolm."

He sprang into action, and before they could raise their weapons, he had torn them from their hands and had his pistol aimed at the side of Trevor's head on an angle that would allow him to take both of them out with a single shot. They extended their hands in surrender. The guard looked scared, like he hadn't seen much action in his life, but Trevor remained calm as a collector ought to. I knew beneath his stony façade, his heart was racing.

Knowing who Zhaff really was, I quickly realized that anything he did against Venta Co came with the highest level of permission. I had no problem playing along. I drew my weapon and aimed it at the receptionist, getting her to raise her hands so she couldn't alert anybody.

"Up," I said. "Away from the desk and against the wall." She listened. By the time she got there, she was in tears.

"You're going to pay for this, Ringers," Trevor growled.

I ignored him. *"'I'm going to strike them now,'"* I said to Zhaff, trying my best to mimic his flat voice. "Really?"

"You said to warn you first next time," he replied.

I smirked. "I suppose I asked for that."

"Hey!" Trevor raised his voice, clearly irritated that nobody was paying attention to him. It was going to make it all the sweeter when he found out who I was. "Do you know who you're messing with?"

"Now we do." I lifted the visor of my helmet and stared Trevor straight in the eyes. His expression was priceless. His jaw dropped, and the fear he'd been masking started to show. "How's your arm?" I asked.

"Graves? I knew there was something off about seeing a Ringer so short."

"Yet you still opened up. Like it's your first day on the job."

"Let me guess. That's your pet partner?"

I took a brief pause from watching the receptionist to grab Trevor by the chest, yank him forward, and punch him across the jaw. It felt good to release all the frustration of having to see Rylah again on someone who deserved it. Plus, only I was allowed to call her a bitch. I caught him before he fell and shoved him right back into position next to Zhaff's pistol.

"He prefers Zhaff," I said.

"C'mon, Graves..." Trevor moaned as he rubbed a cut on his lip. "Even you're not this stupid. Gonna start a war just because I called you both a few names?"

"No, but over what you're hiding back there I might. Why don't you let us in and we'll keep this civilized."

"We're not hiding anything."

"Lying," Zhaff stated. He pressed the barrel of his pistol against Trevor's head so hard it threaded his hair.

"You shouldn't lie to my friend here," I advised. "Open the

hangar, or he'll shoot you both down like the Venta scum you are."

"Sorry, Graves, no can do," Trevor said. "Best walk away now."

I stepped forward so that our noses were close to touching and glowered into his eyes. "Last chance, Cross. Open the hangar, or you'll upset him."

"When our bosses hear about this, they'll have you and your pet sweeping floors until he's as old as you are."

I decided to take a page out of Zhaff's book. I shot Trevor in the shoulder of the same arm I'd injured earlier, then returned to aiming at the receptionist. It was in the meat, but he fell over, screaming.

"Are you insane!" Trevor howled. "I'll have you both spaced!"

"Open it," I said to the other guard, who was staring as Trevor squirmed in pain. He was definitely rattled.

"Answer him," Zhaff ordered. He stepped around Trevor and took aim directly at the guard's head.

The guard took a deep breath before he glanced down at Trevor. "I'm not dying for them," he muttered. "There are Ringers inside. They paid a ton for safe transport from Mars. I don't know or care what they've got, but I'll let you in if you tell that one not to shoot."

I nodded in Zhaff's direction, and he grabbed the guard by the collar and dragged him toward the hangar entrance's control panel. "Enter the code," Zhaff said to him.

"Coward..." Trevor said through clenched teeth.

I knelt beside him, keeping my gun visible while we waited.

"You... you have him handling everything for you now, old man?" Trevor asked me, struggling to put on his usual grin. He was in too much pain. His armor softened the blow enough for his arm not to fall off, but a pulse-pistol round from that close meant it went clear through him.

"Impressive, isn't he?" I remarked.

He tried to sit up but failed. "You might as well kill me, Malcolm... because you signed a death warrant."

"I'm disappointed in you. Aiding terrorists? You should know better than that."

"I... have my... orders."

"So do I." The pain had him breathing heavily and looking ready to pass out. I leaned in close so he could hear me. "I'll see you soon, Cross. And for Earth's sake, would you buy a new pistol already?"

Before he could respond, I cracked him in the head with the butt of my gun, knocking him unconscious. "Get him help," I barked to the receptionist. "Now!" I shot her computer, causing it to burst into sparks so that it'd be useless to her. She ran frantically out of the lobby. As good as it felt to put him in his place, we were collectors. It wasn't my job to kill for free.

I got up and looked over at the hangar entrance. Zhaff had punched the guard across the face, incapacitating him as well. The heavy gate was unlocked and slowly rose into the ceiling. I hurried over to him.

"You ready?" I asked.

"Ready," he replied.

I reached into a pouch on my belt where I'd put Aria's Ark figurine, brought it to my lips, and gave it a kiss.

"Why do you do that?" Zhaff asked.

"For good luck. It was my daughter's. I like to think it reminds me of mistakes I've made, and not to make them again."

Zhaff nodded. We edged into the hangar side by side, pulse-pistols raised. A small ship was parked in the center, and four armed Children of Titan combatants in concealing white armor stood around the lowered cargo bay ramp. The same orange circle we had seen in the attack on the *Piccolo* was imprinted on their chests. Two storage containers stood upright among them, stamped with the Pervenio logo. The supplies stolen from New London, if I had to guess.

They quickly hand-signed something to one another before opening fire on us with the same model of outmoded Venta Co rifles as earlier. Zhaff and I dove behind the steely base of a decontamination chamber right before a spray of bullets riddled us with holes.

"Stand down, fugitives!" Zhaff shouted as he popped up to fire off a few shots of his own. I tried to do the same but was immediately forced back into cover. One of the bullets struck my spotters latched to my belt and shattered them.

"Damn!" I grunted. We were in a stalemate like that for about a minute, and being that it was a private hangar, there was no Darien security near enough to hear the scuffle through the colony block's dense metal walls.

Zhaff's eye-lens aimed at me and he motioned with his hand that he was going to try to make an approach.

"I'll cover you," I whispered, though it was probably closer to a shout so he could hear me over the gunfire.

We went to make our move, and an explosion shook the floor. I yanked Zhaff back and popped up to see a smoking gash in the outer plating of Darien, exposing us to the exterior. Freezing air whipped in and I could feel its bite even through my suit. Alarms wailed, red emergency lights flashed, and the entrance to the hangar sealed shut with a *snap-hiss*. If Pervenio security wasn't aware of the disturbances earlier, they were then.

That was when the combatants each grabbed the containers and raised their arms, revealing orange carbon-fiber wings extending between their arms and sides. They were promptly pulled through the breach and soared out across the sky of Titan until the haze of a violent storm rendered them invisible.

"Winged suits," Zhaff identified.

"You've got to be kidding me!" I shouted. "I thought those things were myths the locals told to scare new immigrants." Before being outlawed following the arrival of my people, it was said the Ringers once had suits allowing them to roam the skies as easily as birds do on Earth thanks to the low gravity and dense atmosphere of Titan.

"There are no such things as myths."

Zhaff sprang up and sprinted toward the opening. I stood to follow him, closing my visor as I did so my nose didn't freeze off. "What the hell are you doing?" I questioned, grabbing his shoulder before he leaped blindly through the opening.

"I have a read on their position. If we don't follow, we'll lose them. There is no time to deliberate."

"We'll freeze out there!"

"We are wearing similar suits," he replied. "They are capable of withstanding Titan's harsh environment for a substantial period and contain a suitable auxiliary oxygen supply in case of emergency."

"Are you sure?" I checked the seal beneath my helmet nervously. The rickety joints, especially in mine since it was so loose, had me worried that I wouldn't last more than a minute outside.

"Yes."

I took a deep breath. It's safe to say that I would've never trusted it without his nod of approval, but up to that point, he seemed to be very sure of things before he said them. And he never lied.

"Ready when you are, then," I muttered.

We sidled out to the edge, where even through my helmet, I could hear the wind howl. The ground wasn't that far below us, but beyond that, the visibility conditions were too poor due to a looming storm to see anything. Zhaff hopped off without hesitation and skated down the slick, angled surface of Darien's enclosure.

"I'm getting too old for this," I whispered to myself.

I shrugged, swallowed my pride, and tried to emulate him. I can't say I made it look as smooth, but my feet landed safely against the gentle slope of the translucent roof encasing Darien's hydro-farms. A layer of swirling sand made it impossible to see the green beneath.

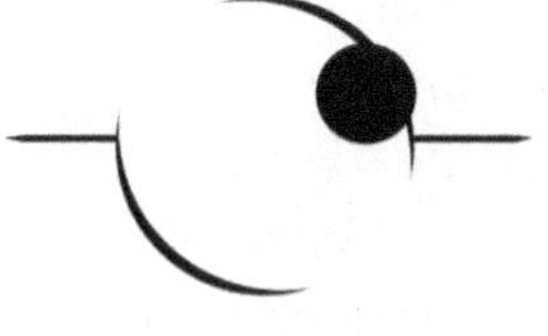

NINETEEN

I FOLLOWED Zhaff as he jogged headfirst into the storm. They were common on Titan, much as they were on the planet it orbited. I couldn't see more than ten meters in front of me with all the sand being whipped about, and without my spotters, I was blind. I had to rely completely on Zhaff's eye-lens to keep a reading on the smugglers, and his word that our suits would hold up.

"You're sure about these things?" I asked him again. We didn't have a com-link; I had to yell so my voice would project over the storm through my helmet's built-in speaker.

"Yes," he answered.

My whole suit bounced with every step, and I found it unsettling that I could hear the wind so clearly through it. I could even see my own breath against my visor because it grew so cold inside the helmet. Well below freezing, though that was admittedly better than the two hundred or so Celsius below it was beyond it.

After ten more minutes of slogging through the murk, the storm dissipated and Zhaff stopped. I moved next to him and gazed forward.

Based on the few times I'd been beyond the major settlements on Mars, I found the terrain of the worlds quite similar in appearance. The biggest difference was that even when it wasn't stormy, the sky of Titan was blotted by a rusty haze so thick that the location of the sun was impossible to determine. It made things not only dim but also frigid enough to freeze your bones in half a minute. Pervenio researchers claimed the terraforming efforts using cryo-volcanic eruptions across the surface to pump the atmosphere with oxygen had warmed average surface temperatures by a few degrees and even left trace amounts of the element permanently in the air. True or not, I wasn't about to test it. People loved to exaggerate.

Once we escaped the hydro-farms' roof, the fine-grained, ruddy sand that made up most of the region extended beyond my range of vision in every direction, with thousands of smooth, frozen rocks scattered across the flat landscape. Now that I could see them, it made it difficult for me to walk in a straight line, even in my weighted suit. They didn't seem to bother Zhaff.

In the distance rose a lonely white plateau beyond which the visibility remained extremely poor. The earlier storm had passed, but there another brewed. Bolts of lightning flashing throughout the dark clouds above them were enough to tell me that this one was going to be far worse. I didn't want to be caught in it.

"They went in there," Zhaff said. "The Darien Quarantine Zone."

He pointed toward the plateau. It didn't look special, but a tram line ran across the surface of Titan between Darien and it, entering an illuminated cave carved into its side. It was taking me a bit to gain my bearings, but he was right. Within it lay the quarantine zone where I'd never had any reason to go. Zhaff and

I shifted our path to stick to the shadows of its tram lines' towering stilts.

"Looks like we're on our own, then," I said. "No way Pervenio would risk the blowback of publicly sending Earther reinforcements into a quarantine zone. That's probably what the Children of Titan want them to do."

"You are correct," Zhaff replied. "I will inform the director of the situation." He typed into his hand-terminal.

"Fifty years since the Reunion," I said while I waited. "You'd think they'd have cleaned them out by now."

"The increase in immigration has helped keep sickness a constant threat to locals. All it takes is one missed micro-organism during decontamination or shipment to infect an entire block."

I remembered how sick the Ringer on Earth had looked. How he was coughing up blood before he took his own life. I'd never actually been to a quarantine zone, but I couldn't imagine a more depressing place in all of Sol. They were among the only places on Titan where the Ringers were granted some level of control, minus the legions of Pervenio security guards who monitored the entrances off the tram lines. Whatever this Doctor and his crew were up to, there were few better places in the Ring for them to hide.

All Ringers who showed signs of sickness were sent to quarantine, buried like ancient lepers within a mountain. It didn't matter what the diseases were either. Most of them had no labels, or did once, but no longer affected Earthers and had their names lost in the annals of pre-Meteorite Earth. All I knew for sure was that getting the proper medicines from any of the sanctioned USF corporations with a stake in the Ring was as difficult as it was expensive. They were almost exclusively produced on Earth by Pervenio Corp and its subcontractor and shipped all the way across Sol.

"Consider me lucky for not being born in this wasteland," I decided. "How'd they get in? The entrance to that rock can only be accessed through the tram line."

"Their signatures disappeared beneath it," Zhaff answered.

"Well, however they did it, I have a feeling that the Drayton woman who escaped got out the same way. We'll find it."

"We have to." Zhaff stored his hand-terminal and scanned the horizon. "The quarantine zone enclosure is approximately eight-point-seven kilometers away. We must quicken our pace in order to ensure we retain a safe amount of oxygen and do not freeze."

He'd conveniently left that part out earlier. I unconsciously cut down on how deep my breaths were, and we ran. He was decidedly faster, but I was able to keep close enough behind. Fear of suffocating had my adrenaline pumping and my legs churning despite how sore they were getting. If I was going to go, I'd prefer it to be in a hail of bullets or while I was drunk and fast asleep.

As we got nearer, the quarantine zone's plateau filled my vision from end to end, obstructing the subtle glow of the rusty sky. Not even a single translucency interrupted the uniformity of the rock for the people inside.

I was busy studying the tunnel entrance located many meters above where we were, when Zhaff suddenly stopped. A noisy tram raced by overhead, breaking the alien silence of Titan's surface that had prevailed after the first storm passed.

"What're you doing?" I yelled over the racket. I leaned over to catch my breath.

He didn't answer right away. As soon as the tram went by completely, the fizzle of gunfire zipped around my helmet, kicking up pockets of sand directly beside us. We rushed behind one of the tram lines' columns for cover. The barrage came from above, and it didn't relent.

I fired a few rounds blindly from behind the column to try to scare whoever it was before taking a quick peek around it. A group of objects darted across the ruddy sky, the flash of pulse-rifle muzzles giving away their positions. They were too small to be ships.

"They are attacking," Zhaff stated. "Three of them."

"Shit!"

Zhaff sprang up and sprinted toward the quarantine zone. I followed, weaving behind columns as they were peppered with bullets. We were halfway there when one glanced off my armored shoulder. The force of it knocked me off my feet, and a single winged attacker soared right over me. Zhaff somehow sprawled out of the way and got off a shot. It clipped the attacker's wing, causing him to sputter through the air and crack his head against the side of a column.

I rolled over anxiously and checked my shoulder. It was only a scratch, not enough to compromise the suit's integrity and expose me. Once I was sure, I hurried toward Zhaff.

He picked up the fallen attacker's body with ease and handed it to me. "Take him," he said.

I furrowed my brow at him, but as more fire whizzed by us, I quickly got his meaning. Without being dressed in a weighted suit, the Ringer's thin body was incredibly light in the low-g conditions. I hauled it sideways around my free arm and wielded it like a shield before Zhaff and I continued to run.

Zhaff fired calculated shots as we moved, but even those didn't strike our targets, which says a lot for the Children of Titan's flying abilities. I decided to show him how it was done. Projectiles deflected off the armor of the dead Ringer I held as I slowed down and aimed my pistol over his hip. I unloaded toward a blur of motion in the sky. One of the two remaining attackers plummeted, slamming into the ground a ways off, kicking up a cloud of sand. The last one promptly changed course and flew toward the quarantine, out of sight.

"Well-placed shot," Zhaff said flatly.

The praise had me grinning until I remembered I was reveling in a compliment from my teenage partner on his second official assignment. I forced my lips into a straight line and mustered my most serious tone. "We should hurry. We can't give them time to set up another ambush."

Zhaff agreed.

WE REACHED THE BASE OF THE QUARANTINE ZONE without any other attacks and skirted along its craggy base. According to Zhaff, the Children of Titan went beneath the plateau, so we figured there had to be some manner of secret passage. It was strictly forbidden for anybody deemed healthy, Ringer or Earther, to enter a quarantine zone without proper clearance, especially beyond the visitors' zone. I wished I still had my spotters so the thermal function might help me find it before Zhaff.

"See anything?" I asked Zhaff after a few minutes of searching. Everything looked the same to me. Sand and rock and metal.

He bent over, picked up one of the smooth stones, and scanned it closely with his eye-lens. After he placed it down, his head snapped to a nearby location. He got up and took long strides toward another cluster of rocks.

"It is here," he declared as he went to grasp one. There was a subtle flicker of light distortion as his hand passed right through it and a portion of the ground beneath it. "A hologram."

Once again, I had the chance to observe Zhaff's enhanced senses in action. The Children of Titan probably needed special scanners to locate the passage, even after knowing where it was. I didn't bother to ask him how he noticed the difference.

"Guns ready," I said. I couldn't kiss my lucky charm with my helmet on, but it's the thought that counts.

We stepped through the hologram side by side, down a steep ramp into a rocky tunnel lined haphazardly with flickering lights. It was dim, but I could make out a sealed hatch a short distance away. I kept my eyes trained down the sight of my pistol as I stepped cautiously along, scanning the walls for any concealed charges.

"They cannot risk the seal with explosives," Zhaff stated when he noticed my helmet turning from side to side. "That is an airlock ahead. Whoever dug this did so within the last decade, judging by the wear on the metal around the lights."

"The Children of Titan must be using this to hide right under Pervenio's nose," I noted.

He agreed, then stopped in front of the access airlock's control panel. "I can override the lock," he said. He withdrew his hand-terminal and rifled through commands. He was so fast I couldn't keep up with him. In no time, he sliced through the lock, and the heavy door of the outer airlock swung open.

I stormed into the dark cavern, my aim snapping from side to side to check my corners. It was empty. Zhaff stepped through calmly and shut the hatch behind him. There was a shrill whistle as the airlock resealed. My ears popped slightly, and then it got a little warmer inside my suit.

The inner seal opened in front of us. Expecting to meet a wall of gunfire, I rushed to the side of it and peeked around the corner. Again, I found nothing but an empty hall and a silence so cavernous that I could hear my heart beating inside my suit.

I switched off my oxygen supply and took in a gulp of the stale air. "I'll go first," I volunteered, mostly to make sure Zhaff didn't have another chance to handle everything on his own. I was getting tired of him striking first and making me look useless.

"I'll be directly behind you," Zhaff responded.

I wanted to tease him for being cowardly but thought twice. Courage had nothing to do with it. It meant that he wasn't sure what awaited us. He was being cautious and for good reason. Whatever we found, chances were better of one of us getting out if he wasn't shot first. The mission was primary. At every turn, I was beginning to better understand how his mind worked, and in my own bizarre way, I was also forming a greater level of respect for it.

I pressed on.

"Going right," I whispered sharply when I reached the end of the tunnel. The craggy ceiling of the large hollow beyond was filled with wavering light fixtures. I popped out first, pistol aimed high. Zhaff did the same in the opposite direction.

I guess Zhaff didn't think anything in the space we entered was much of a threat since he merely stated, "Clear," and delved farther in. What I saw stopped me dead in my tracks.

At first glance, it appeared to be a large, dug-out hollow below the quarantine zone. Hundreds of masked Ringers lined the space from end to end. They were laid out under tattered blankets against the corroded walls. Rustling, moaning, and coughing filled my ears from every direction. Most of them turned to gaze upon me with their bloodshot eyes, their slender necks hardly able to support their heads. All of them were so skinny that I could see the outline of their cheekbones through their sallow flesh. I turned around to see more poor souls strewn across the floor and lying atop chairless tables—men, women, and even children so young that they weren't as tall as my hips.

That was when I noticed the odor. The whole room stunk of body odor, sickness, and burned hair. My helmet's ventilation systems probably helped alleviate some of it, but it was still enough to make me gag. On the far end of the space, I saw the crackling flames of a furnace behind a makeshift glass enclosure. I didn't need to ask what it was for. I knew that infected Ringer corpses were burned to keep diseases from spreading, but the orange glow was enough to reveal the charred remnants of clothing filled by nothing but ashes.

Zhaff approached me, completely unfazed. "This hollow is clear," he said. "The quarantine zone is directly above us, but this is not part of it. The smugglers must be in deeper."

I'd been to the rotting sewer tunnels submerged beneath the Martian domes. I'd been to the most remote slums on Earth, and to the depths of asteroid mining colonies where being able to see the outline of your own hand in front of your face was considered bright. I've seen death all over and been on the end of the killing more times than I cared to count, but none of it could compare to this. Back on Earth, I lamented how thirty years of being a collector made me numb to suffering and bloodshed, but as I entered that new setting, apparently, I was wrong. *Quarantine* was a generous term. It was closer to a morgue.

In a trance, I stepped past Zhaff toward a blanket on a gurney right outside the furnace area. A motionless lump lay beneath it. A bony leg stuck out from the bottom, the skin mottled with inflamed sores. I peeled the blanket back from where I guessed the head would be with the tip of my pistol. Underneath lay a young female Ringer, her stringy hair matted against her damp forehead. Her jaw hung slack beneath her sanitary mask, and her glazed eyes stared blankly toward the ceiling, but I could hear that she was quietly wheezing. Alive, but barely.

A hand fell on my shoulder. I snapped around with my gun raised to find Zhaff bowing smoothly out of its line of fire.

"We must move quickly to apprehend the smugglers before we're swarmed," he said.

"There are so many of them," I whispered. The smell of the sick and dying together with the heat from the furnace made me dizzy.

Zhaff glanced down at the young woman, then up at the rest of the room. "Generations of offworld breeding has made them vulnerable to Earth's most basic microorganisms."

"I know that... I just never realized it was this bad."

"This space has been carved out below the actual quarantine operated by Pervenio Corp. This is what occurs when criminals attempt to operate beyond regulations."

I'd figured most of that out, considering the hidden entrance. "Somehow, I have a feeling the conditions above aren't much better. This makes the New Beijing sewers seem like paradise."

"The Quarantines used to be worse. Most of the medicines required stopped being produced by Earthers centuries ago due to our adaptation to the Earth's natural environment. Containment remains the safest option while research and production continue on Earth."

I glared back at the wheezing young woman. "My daughter was around her age last time I saw her." The thought of seeing Aria sprawled out to rot in the dark sent a horrible chill through my body. I took a step back and shook my head.

"There is no need to concern yourself. As only a first-generation offworlder, your daughter will have retained most of your immunities."

I didn't bother responding. I pulled the blanket back over the dying girl's head and tucked in her leg. Then I followed after Zhaff as he started off toward the other end of the refectory. The countless soon-to-be-cremated corpses had me thrown. Every time I heard a cough, my gun snapped toward it. Every time I heard incoherent rambling from a Ringer on the precipice of death, my trigger finger itched to put a bullet through their brain and end their suffering. I tried to ignore it by concentrating on breathing through my mouth.

"Up here," Zhaff said. "There is equipment running, and I am reading a collection of heat signatures." He tapped me on the shoulder and motioned ahead toward a tall passage at the short end of the hollow. Bright-white lights emanated from the other side.

He abruptly rushed forward and put his back against the wall on one side of the entrance as if he'd heard something. He signaled me to move to the other side. I listened, but once I was there, I opened my mouth to ask him what was wrong. He placed a finger on top of his helmet's visor over his mouth before I could.

A minute or so passed in silence before Zhaff sprang through the opening and pulled someone back. He slammed the intruder against the wall and nudged his rifle up under his neck.

He was a teenage boy, but definitely not a Ringer judging by his height. He wore a full hazmat suit for protection, but he appeared to be completely healthy. In fact, he looked familiar. I just couldn't place why.

"Who are you?" Zhaff asked before I could.

"I'm... only an assistant. I... I..." he stammered as Zhaff glowered at him with his eye-lens. "The Doctor wishes to speak to the collector."

I shot a look through the passage to see if anybody else was coming. It was clear except for the radiant, focused lights on the far side. "With me?" I asked. "Why?"

The boy staved off Zhaff's glare and gathered enough confidence to respond to me. "You must see for yourself, Collector."

"Why don't you tell us right here and save us the trouble?"

"I can't."

Zhaff released the boy. "He is telling the truth."

"My people will listen to the Doctor, Collector," the boy

said. "Your partner must wait here, but neither of you will be harmed as long as you hold your fire."

I pulled Zhaff aside. "He's just a kid. He might not be lying, but the Children of Titan were going to blow up Pervenio Station. They bombed New London. Do you really think they'll keep their promise?"

"I do not, but you must proceed. I will stay behind to make sure nobody attempts to escape."

"They'll only allow you to wait out here if you are placed under watch," the boy said.

"That is acceptable," Zhaff replied.

I was startled that Zhaff wanted to split up after being so adamantly against it back on Earth. "I'm not sure about this, Zhaff. I'd rather not wind up their prisoner."

"Do not worry. I will not hesitate." He nodded at me, the corners of his lips lifting subtly enough for me to know he'd developed a plan. I could almost mistake it for a grin.

"Are you sure?" I asked. He nodded again and backed away slowly. I was hesitant to follow the boy alone into the unknown, but I wasn't about to let that show. "Come on, then." I grabbed him by the collar and shoved him into the passage. When I glanced back over my shoulder, Zhaff had already vanished into the shadows.

"Wait. I must retrieve something," the boy said. I gave him the okay, and he hurried past me back into the hollow. I kept my pistol aimed at his chest while he did, and he returned quickly, rolling the gurney that the dying young woman was on. "This way, and, please, holster your gun."

"Do I have to?"

"Please. This is a medical facility."

I grumbled but reluctantly did as the kid asked. Then I followed him. Only two days before, when we'd arrived at the Ring, there was no chance I would've gone along with whatever it was Zhaff was up to. Against my initial intentions, however, I really was starting to trust the Cogent and all his heightened senses. His assurance wasn't enough for me to lower my pistol from the boy's back as he rolled the gurney forward into another hollow, but it was enough to get me going.

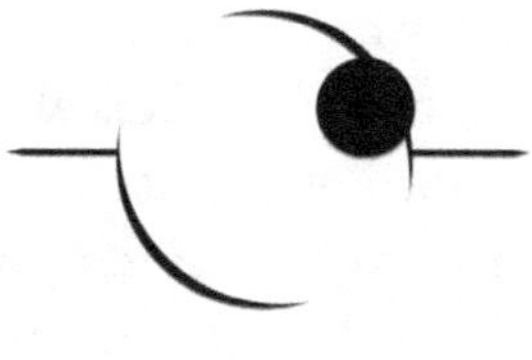

TWENTY

THE BOY LED me into a spacious cavern where two shadowy fighters slipped by us to keep an eye on Zhaff. More gurneys lined the rocky walls, divided by crudely hung curtains. Ringers lay on each of them, makeshift tubes sticking out of their bodies and attached to crude-looking monitors that beeped faintly. A middle-aged Ringer woman covered in rashes sat in one of them, her unsettling glare following me.

I quickly turned from her and looked toward the back of the cavern, where we were headed. Spotlights bathed a low table in front of a barricaded tunnel that led up toward what I assumed was the actual Darien quarantine that Pervenio operated. Someone stood beside it wearing a clunky hazard helmet on their head.

I peered up as we approached the table and saw at least a dozen white-armored soldiers watching from a carved-out balcony a level above. The outline of their suits' fabricated wings were tucked under their arms, and I could just make out the symbol on their chest plates—the same orange circle that the attackers, both on the gas harvester and in hangar twenty, wore. The Children of Titan.

"What are they doing?" I asked.

"They are watching over my instructor," the boy responded. He pointed to the person in the hazard helmet at the other end of the hollow.

My gaze fell back down on what I assumed was the Doctor. Other than the helmet, whoever it was also wore a winged suit of armor that was stained with blood. A Ringer lay on the brightly lit table nearby with a sanitary mask on. The young man's shirt was off, and he had a pale, chiseled body similar to those of the marble statues in Mr. Pervenio's office. He stared at me with intense loathing while the Doctor stitched up a fresh wound in his shoulder. I pegged him to be the one flying Ringer from outside who'd survived.

The Doctor's head turned to face me. "He came!" a distorted voice exclaimed, almost triumphantly. I couldn't see a face through the tinted visor. The Doctor snipped the end of a stitch and hurried around the table. "I mean, I knew that he would, but..."

The Doctor reached up and pulled off the helmet. Long, curly auburn hair came bouncing out, revealing that she was a woman. Then I saw her face—slim and freckled, but not quite white or long enough to belong to a Ringer. My heart began to race. She was older, but it wasn't a face I could ever forget. It belonged to my daughter.

"Thank you, Jordan. Go and tend to the patients," Aria said to the young assistant, who bowed before rolling the gurney with the woman on it over to an open medical station on the wall. She then turned back to me and said, "Hello, Dad."

It had to be a bad dream. I figured I'd dozed off on the shuttle down to Titan and had been dreaming ever since. But as I removed my own helmet, hoping to wake up, there was no denying it.

"Aria," I whispered. Words froze in my throat. My pistol very nearly slipped out of my hands. I reached out to make sure she was real, my gloved fingers grazing her pink cheek.

"He's grown, hasn't he?" she said. She no longer had the gentle soprano voice I recalled.

"I..." I turned back toward the boy and realized why he'd seemed familiar. He was Elios Sevari's son. The one I'd orphaned then never bothered to learn the name of.

"Aria, what are you doing here?" I asked.

"Everything I can, since nobody else will," she answered sternly.

"Where's the other collector?" the Ringer on the table snarled at me through his mask.

I peered down at him, startled by hearing someone else speak. All my focus had been on Aria. "My partner is waiting outside, just like you asked for," I said.

"I'm surprised to see you were willing to take on a new one," Aria said, suppressing a grin.

"So was I." In my peripherals, I couldn't help but notice the shadow of one of the Children of Titan operatives skulking around on the level above us. Never throughout the many years she was gone from me had I imagined her in a more dangerous place.

"Dammit, Aria, you shouldn't be here," I said.

"Neither should you," she countered.

I bit my lip, then sighed. "Would you mind telling your friends to lower their guns at least?"

"You killed my brothers," the injured Ringer growled. He sat up and slammed his fist against the medical table. "By Trass, you're lucky you're still alive!" The movement caused him to wince in pain. Aria placed her hands on his shoulder and helped lay him back down.

"Quiet, Nash!" she snapped at him. "After the stunt on Earth, Mr. Pervenio will keep sending more and more collectors until there are none of us left. If your former leader had detonated the bomb away from civilians where he was supposed to, then none of this would have happened. At least this is one collector I can reason with."

Nash muttered something under his breath before relaxing his head. He continued to hold his heated gaze fixed on me, however.

"I would love to work beyond the sights of guns, but in the end, we aren't Titanborn," Aria said to me. "It is their right to remain wary of me after all of this, no matter how much I help." She spread her arms, gesturing to the rows of gurneys filling the room. I couldn't help but notice how she'd used the term *Titanborn* freely.

"All of what?" I tried to get a good read on the workstation beside her table. Everything appeared to be medical equipment except for two familiar containers lying against a cabinet with the red-and-black logo of Pervenio Corporation stamped on the side. They looked just like the ones in hangar twenty and apparently had recently arrived since they were still closed. I approached them, finding it strange that nobody attempted to stop me from looking.

"Don't play games with me, Dad," she snapped, following close behind me. "Do you really think that after fifty years, Pervenio Corp couldn't help bring an end to places like this? Right now, we're buried a few dozen meters below the 'official' Darien quarantine, where sick people like this have no chance at receiving help because it costs a lifetime's salary to get the care they require. I bring the ones deemed 'too unfit to survive' here and care for them as best as I can. Many don't make it. Do you really think germs slip through decontamination only by accident? So long as Ringers fear being sent to places like this, Pervenio Corp will own the Ring."

"I never really thought about it." That was the truth. Like I've said countless times, I was never one to ask questions if the pay was right. As far as I was concerned, Pervenio Corp did what it had to do to secure a place in Sol and maybe one day, beyond. At least, that was how I'd gone about my life up until seeing Aria standing amid a terror cell and countless dying Ringers.

I leaned down and popped the lid off one of the containers, hoping with all my heart that it was merely a coincidence and she wasn't the smuggler I'd been hired to detain. There were no firearms, explosives, or any other dangerous technologies inside. All it held were filled vials and syringes, bottles, and small data pads with the Pervenio logo printed on them—everything a provisional medical center might need to start mass-producing cures. I quickly opened the other container only to find more of the same.

"Immunizations. Vaccines. Simple cures," she said. "Pervenio Corp has already discovered almost every disease that plagues the people of the Ring... or rediscovered to be precise. And while they are willing to waste billions commissioning Arks that may never reach their destinations, they keep all the medicine that isn't already paid for locked up on Earth to keep demand high. I've been working with the Children of Titan to get our hands on as much as we can."

"And Venta Co," I added.

She hesitated for a moment before nodding. "Yes," she said. "And them. They're helping me for the wrong reasons, but I took the best option I had. You taught me that."

I turned and gazed straight into her pretty green eyes. They looked like mine had when I was young and full of vigor, only she spoke words that an Earther never would. Sometimes I forgot she was an offworlder, but she was, through and through. I'd made her that way by never settling down. She was no longer the little girl who marveled at the Arks of the Departure.

"So that's where you disappeared to?" I asked. "You could've said something. I could've—"

"Done what?" she interrupted, a harsh edge to her tone. "Do you know what I had to go through to convince Venta to get involved? And still, Madame Venta only did it to hurt *your* employers. I've spent more than a year trying to get Titanborn out of quarantine zones all over Titan, and even still, I'm watched with rifles. That's how little these people trust anyone from beyond this moon. But can a real doctor let so many suffer and do nothing? Can she, Dad?"

I pictured the dead and dying Ringers outside in the refectory, recollecting how it felt like I was strolling through a graveyard. Even those in the quarantine above. They were enclosed deep under the orange moon's icy surface where nobody would ever see them, so that immigrants from Earth could arrive and continue to replace them with ease. None of the ads on Earth saying THE FIGHT TO ENSURE OUR SURVIVAL IS IN YOUR HANDS ever made mention of quarantines or furnaces.

"I don't know, Aria," I said. "But this isn't your fight."

"It is now," she replied.

I turned around to see the glinting armor and armed rifles of the Children of Titan fighters on the level above. I took a deep breath. "So what happens next?"

"Leave the supplies here for Jordan to continue administering. I've taught him enough. Pretend you never found it and take me in instead. I'll lead Pervenio to all the wrong places, and by the time they find out the truth, my friends here will be long gone."

I looked to the ground. "Aria, I can't..."

She grabbed me by the wrists and pulled me close. "I know what will happen."

I doubted she really did. They would stuff her in one of Pervenio station's famous cells. My standing with Pervenio wouldn't help either. In fact, I'd probably get thrown in with her and accused of conspiracy if her being my daughter came out. When she had nothing left to tell them, she'd be left there for life—or, worse, spaced with the trash for what she'd done. The suicidal ways of the Children of Titan had certainly rubbed off on her.

"You don't understand," I said. "I won't be able to lie. My partner—"

Right as the words left my lips, a chorus of gunfire rang out from the upper level of the hollow. I lunged forward, grabbed Aria, and pulled her back behind the workstation and containers for cover. That was when I noticed that none of the shots were aimed at me.

A muddle of screams and bullets ricocheting off rock greeted my ears. I peered over the workstation to figure out what was happening. I should've known immediately. On the balcony, shadows danced among bright flashes, and though I couldn't see him, I knew Zhaff was one of them. Apparently, his plan didn't involve waiting for me to discuss terms.

"Zhaff!" I screamed.

"Well done, Malcolm. These terrorists are in clear violation of fifteen Pervenio colonial regulations. The penalty for armed resistance is death. Secure the Doctor." Zhaff yelled at a relatively loud volume for him. It was precisely enough for his voice to project to me while retaining its usual evenness, as if he weren't currently taking on a cohort of Children of Titan operatives all by himself. He wasn't even breathing heavily. They didn't stand a chance.

"From ice to ashes!" one of the terrorists roared, his voice quickly trailing off into gurgles as a bullet shredded his throat.

I turned to see Aria, her eyes wide as they had been on that roof back on Earth. Her lips trembled, though whether it was with fear or sorrow, I wasn't completely sure. She'd seen enough gunfights as a child for me to imagine it was the latter.

For the first time in my life, I wasn't sure that I could follow through in completing a mission. It had always been so easy for me. Close my eyes, follow orders, and follow the credits that came along with doing so. I glared at the medical containers and then back at her. I must've repeated the motion at least four times before coming to a decision. I threw on my helmet, yanked Aria to her feet, and pulled her out from behind our cover. There was no time to second-guess.

"Put on your helmet and grab the containers!" I yelled to her. They might've been heavy on Earth, but on Titan, they were no more difficult to carry than two infants.

She nodded and did as I asked. I drew my pistol and stood. A bullet whizzed by me, somehow missing.

"I'll kill you!" the injured Ringer named Nash howled. Sometime during the fray, he'd rolled off the medical table to use it for cover. He had a rifle aimed at me from the ground and opened fire. I jumped out of the way just in time before getting off a shot of my own that struck him in the center of his chest, causing him to drop his gun instantly.

"No!" she gasped.

"Let's go!" I yelled, pulling on her arm.

She pulled back. "There's a better way!"

Bullets hissed by our heads, crackling against the floor around us as some of the rebels on the balcony who were still battling Zhaff noticed us and shifted their aim. "The Doctor flees!" one of them shouted from above. "Traitor."

"No, I'm not!" Aria shouted. "I—"

I was done listening. I grabbed Aria and ran as fast as I could with her in tow.

Shards of rock flew up all around us, but Zhaff carved through our enemies above with the artistry of a master painter and kept us from being hit.

"Get Katrina Drayton into the tunnels!" Aria shouted to Jordan Sevari as we passed. He was huddled under the gurney along with the middle-aged Ringer they'd been testing, terrified. It all made sense. Kale Drayton, the one thought responsible for the *Piccolo* attack, had his mom sprung from the quarantine right above us and into the healing arms of my daughter.

Aria was in too deep. I had to get her out, for both our sakes.

Somehow, we made it through to the first hollow unscathed. The many sick Ringers conscious enough to hear what was happening were either trembling or sobbing. Two Children of Titan operatives lay on the floor, their throats cut open by a sharp fragment of rock. Zhaff's handiwork no doubt.

"What was that?" Aria asked. She was struggling to catch her breath the same as I was. Pure adrenaline drove me.

"My partner!" I lugged her into the exit tunnel and keyed the airlock. Luckily, it wasn't locked from the inside. Once the sequence was complete, and the outer hatch was open, I shoved her through. Only then was I finally able to slow down.

"Turn on your oxygen," I panted.

She stopped and looked down at the containers in her grasp. "No! I won't let you return it all. We worked too hard."

I grabbed her by the helmet and switched her oxygen on myself. "Don't make me regret this."

She stared at me blankly for a few seconds. "Regret what?"

I remained quiet and nudged her along. It took me until the end of the long tunnel to completely gather my breath. Once there, I poked my head and my gun through the hologram-camouflaged exit to make sure the coast was clear. My eyes had to adjust to the brightness, and after they did, only Titan's murky sky was visible. The brewing storm couldn't be more than ten minutes out and appeared to be growing even more ferocious.

"Do you have anywhere to hide?" I asked. I couldn't believe the words coming out of my mouth. Thirty years and I'd only ever failed a handful of missions, let alone committed treason. But sometimes missions go off the rails and there isn't time to think things through. You have to react, improvise, and worry about the consequences later.

Aria appeared as astonished as I was. "What? I... Yes. The Children have plenty of sanctuaries buried under the ice."

"Can you fly your suit like they do?" She nodded.

"Good." I motioned for her to drop the containers. "You're going to have to shoot me now to slow them down."

"Dad, I..."

I handed her my pistol and took a few long steps back. "Aim right here," I said, pointing at my thigh. "Right in the meaty part. I'll tell my partner you escaped. I'll make a foolish attempt at lying to a Cogent." I couldn't help but picture that day back on the rooftop when I'd taught her to shoot for the first time. When things were simple.

She gawked at the weapon as if it were a foreign object. She was so busy trying to help people that I guess handling firearms was a skill she'd forgotten about. It was good to know that at least one of us still had a fully operational heart.

"If I puncture your suit, you'll freeze," she said.

I smiled. "My partner won't be long. I'll crawl back inside."

She examined the gun, and as she did, someone struck her in the back of the helmet, knocking her down. The pistol flew out of her hands and skidded across the sand. My heart raced even faster. This time, Zhaff didn't hesitate when I was about to be shot. Exactly like I'd asked him not to back on Earth.

"The interior has been secured, Malcolm," he said. "The child and a few survivors escaped into a tunnel and blew the entry, but the stolen supplies are accounted for thanks to you." His eye-lens angled toward Aria. "You couldn't handle one of them?" I could see his scarred, exposed eyebrow lifting behind his visor, as if he was making a joke. Any other time, I would've been proud to see him making progress as a normal human.

Zhaff bent down and pulled Aria's arms together behind her back. The blow had stunned her so badly that she was on her knees whispering something indiscernible. She didn't put up much of a fight.

I approached them cautiously.

"I sent a message while I was inside," Zhaff continued. "An airship should be dispatched soon to retrieve us once we are a safe distance from the quarantine so that we don't cause any unrest with the locals."

"Zhaff." The toe of my boot hit something hard. My pistol, lying innocently in the sand. "She's not going to hurt anyone."

"Not directly anymore. Pervenio will have many questions for her, however." He gripped her wrists and then looked up at me with his glowing yellow eye-lens. I thought I could see the corners of his thin lips curling into the early stages of a smile. "I will leave the fact that she disarmed you out of my report, if that is what concerns you."

"I'd appreciate it."

I swallowed hard, bent over, and slowly wrapped my fingers around the handle of my pistol so that he wouldn't notice. My heart beat so hard that it felt like it was going to burst through my rib cage.

I'd spent years of my life hoping I was still human enough to feel such an elevated level of apprehension again, but as it finally happened, I wished I never had. Zhaff was growing on me, but he would never defy orders. I knew that better than most. Until that moment, it was the one thing we had in common. The one thing I'd always respected. Difficult as he was, he was honestly the closest thing I'd had to a friend in far too long. I was no longer ashamed to call him my partner.

But it was either my daughter's life or that of Luxarn Pervenio's son. I'd given the richest man in Sol and his corporation everything up to that point, but I couldn't give him her.

"To ensure the safety of human propagation. Right, Zhaff?" I asked.

He stopped what he was doing and glared at me as if he realized something was wrong. His eye-lens angled toward my hand as my finger threaded the trigger of my pistol. I hoped that he wouldn't, but without hesitation, he reached for his holstered gun.

I was too slow on Undina. I was too slow in the wilderness of Earth. But I wasn't too slow then. I got my pistol up first and planted a bullet in his visor. He crumbled to his knees, but his own gun never left his hand. Not even when his body folded over.

Aria shrieked, and I took a few quick steps toward her before a sharp pain in my side caused me to collapse as well.

I knew what was wrong before looking down. Zhaff didn't get the shot he wanted, but he had gotten one off. It'd hit me in the quad, direct enough to pierce clean through my armor. As always, my partner was full of surprises.

I dropped my pistol and covered the wound with the palm of my hand, but the glacial atmosphere of Titan was already getting through. The pain began only as a tingle.

"You're hit!" Aria howled, snapping out of her state of shock. She stumbled over and bent down above me.

"I'll be fine!" I grated. I squeezed my eyes shut, trying to ignore the sting in my leg, which magnified rapidly.

"I'll get you back inside. You'll die out here!" She grabbed my arms and started dragging me back to the tunnel.

"There's no time!" I shook her off and pointed to the container with my pistol. Speaking was getting difficult. The area directly inside the wound got so cold that it burned like molten metal, the sensation quickly spreading up and down my limb without respite. An iciness I thought impossible sent my whole body into a shiver. Each word I spoke labored through long, winded breaths.

"They'll find me in there, and I'll be dead anyway for killing him," I said.

"Then I'll carry you with me!" She knelt and tried to dig her hands under my body, but I nudged her away with my elbow. She was likely strong enough on Titan to carry both me and the medical containers, but not to do that and fly as fast as she'd need to avoid the ships Zhaff had signaled for as well as the approaching storm.

"No, you have to leave," I whispered, clenching my teeth. "Just do me a favor first."

She pulled me closer. "Anything."

"Don't waste this chance. They don't come often. Get out of this life and take that kid with you. Don't do to him what I did to you."

I saw the internal struggle written all over her face, and I couldn't help but picture her as a little girl refusing to eat another yeasty ration bar. It was the same stubbornness that had likely led her to Venta Co and to helping the Ringers in the first place. I wasn't a stranger to it. It was what had kept me gallivanting around Sol for so many years.

But as I regarded her, I finally understood how that Ringer on Earth could pull the trigger on himself so easily. Standing for all those people in the chambers behind us, rotting for no other reason than being born on the wrong world, was a cause worth dying for. Just like dying to keep her alive was for me, no matter what the cost.

"Now get out of here before it's too late!" I yelled. One last order to the first partner I ever had. "And don't look back."

She peered back at Zhaff's body with wet eyes, then tightened her lips and nodded. "I won't forget."

I reached into my belt and removed her old Ark figurine, barely able to fit my quaking hand into the pouch. I placed it in her palm, which shook as much as mine was. She stared at the toy, and I stared at her beautiful face. "Aria... I was never the dad you deserved. I hope you can forgive me for... everything."

She placed a silencing finger over my visor. Her tear-filled eyes locked with mine for what seemed like an eternity. She leaned down until our visors tapped. A tear splashed onto the inside of hers as her eyes closed. Then, without further hesitation, she stood and picked up the two containers. There was another brief pause, and then I heard the whir of her winged suit as she took to the air.

She was gone.

I could no longer hold back the howl festering at the bottom of my throat. I released it as I attempted to drag myself back into the tunnel. The sting in my side was too painful. I needed one hand to cover the wound and didn't have enough strength with the other.

A pained laugh slipped through my lips as I reached Zhaff's body and gave up. "Maybe I really should have exercised more," I said to his body. "We would've made a hell of a team out here, I think—finding bombers, uncovering smugglers. We had a good run, my friend."

I grabbed his hand and squeezed it, and as I did, a tear rolled down my cheek. Maybe it was drawn out by the pain, but I couldn't be sure. It'd been an eternity since I could remember crying.

I rolled onto my back and turned my head toward his. My shot had gone straight through his eye-lens, and the change in pressure from his pierced visor had caused the pieces to try and rush out, jamming the hole closed. I was grateful for it; otherwise, I'd have had to see his head drained like an empty sack of fruits. The bullet entered at the top of his cheek, and with the eye-lens broken, I could see the color of his real eye one last time.

I wasn't sure what would happen when Luxarn Pervenio found his body outside a Ringer quarantine zone, but I knew he wouldn't think to blame his death on a loyal collector like me. He'd blame it on every Ringer in existence. If the hunger I saw in his face when we met wasn't only a mask he wore for show, then Luxarn would crash down upon the people of Titan like a god with a hammer. He'd condemn them or worse, invade the quarantine at my back out of vengeance. Then the Children of Titan would get the rebellion they so desperately craved. All in the name of credits and a son Luxarn was too proud to reveal to the world.

"Family..." I grumbled. "I hope you understand, Zhaff." I knew he wouldn't have.

Another wave of discomfort gripped me and caused me to clench my jaw. I turned toward the sky as it did. It was murky, just like I was used to where I grew up—no sun to be found. But there was something up there that I didn't anticipate. Something I've been told is as rare to see as a lunar eclipse on Earth, yet there it was. The storm drew ever nearer, but the area directly in its path was clear enough that I could see the silhouette of Saturn's Rings beyond the shroud.

For some reason, the sight was more striking from my unexpected vantage point than it ever had been from space. After a few more futile attempts at crawling into the tunnel, I rolled over and was happy to stare. It's rare for a collector to get a chance to really stop and appreciate a stunning view.

I grew faint, but even as my vision went blurry, I couldn't take my eyes off it. Not until the pain transitioned to numbness, my shivering stopped, and everything went black.

EPILOGUE

Luxarn Pervenio stared through the viewport of his office, watching as the orange orb of Titan passed by in orbit. He'd been waiting to hear word about the operation down there for some time. His best men were on the trail of the Children of Titan, and soon he'd be able to wipe them off the Ring for good and return operations to normal.

This was exactly the kind of mission Zhaff was trained for. It was the purpose he'd given him when his son's future seemed so bleak. A field trainer like Malcolm Graves was the final piece of the puzzle in getting him ready to help Pervenio into its next stage of expansion.

"Bot, get me a drink," he said to the spherical robot floating next to him.

"Yes, sir," it replied. It hovered over to his private bar. "What would you li... li... li..." A processing error caused the bot to lose control, float too far, and knock over a bottle. When it spun back, a red circle wrapped its viewing lens and started to blink.

Luxarn sighed. "Glitching again."

He was on his way to it, when a voice came through his desk

coms. "Mr. Pervenio, I have to speak with you immediately," Director Sodervall said.

Luxarn rubbed his temples between his thumb and forefinger. Sodervall was a loyal, hardworking man, but he'd been around for so long the sight of him brought up too many bad memories of affairs on the Ring. Luxarn kept thinking he'd retire and live out his life with all the wealth he'd earned, but the years came and went, and Sodervall stayed put.

It's time for some new blood, Luxarn thought.

"Go ahead," he said out loud.

"In person," Sodervall replied. "I'll be there shortly."

"Fine."

Luxarn popped open the control pad on the service bot's chassis and set its boosters to lower it to the ground. Then he raised his hand terminal to it and dug into its programming. He was nearly lost in the wonderful, organized chaos of coding when his door whooshed open.

"What is it, Sodervall?" Luxarn said without looking up. "I only have time for good news."

Sodervall rushed in, and the door closed behind him. He was short on breath. "It's agents Zhaff and Graves, sir," he said. "We made contact. They located a Children of Titan hideout burrowed underneath the Darien Quarantine where we believe the stolen supplies from Earth were taken. Zha—"

"Excellent! I trust that proper preparations are being made?"

"Of course. Sir, listen to me." He paused for a moment. "Agent Zhaff was found shot outside."

The breath caught in Luxarn's throat. "Is he all right?"

"I'm waiting for another update, but... it was in the head, sir."

Luxarn's stomach sank. A very human chill ran up his spine. He had to lean on the bot and turn away from the director. It was a feeling he hadn't experienced since his father died. Fear, doubt, a lack of control like when he was handed the reins to an empire.

"And Graves?" he said, voice shaking.

"We're still thawing him, but it doesn't look good." A longer period of silence passed until, finally, Director Sodervall intervened. "Sir, what do you want me to do?"

"My father should have let these inbred Ringers die off when we had the chance!" Luxarn punched the bot's control panel, shattering the screen. He drew his knuckles back, covered in scrapes and blood.

"I agree, sir," Sodervall said. "They're a cancer to Sol. But it's too late now. I need to know what you want me to do."

"To do?" The fury in Luxarn's tone was palpable. He stalked toward the director, making him shrink back in fear. "I want the Children of Titan exterminated, director! I want this Kale Drayton delivered to me in cuffs! Space every survivor from the *Piccolo* until one of them tells us the truth."

Sodervall recoiled further as spit spattered all over his face. "I...I'll get right to it, sir," he said.

"You damn well better! I don't care what it takes, but you will restore order down there. Tear that quarantine to pieces if you have to."

"Sir," Sodervall began. "I don't think that's—"

"Just do it, Sodervall! If you hadn't allowed things to get so dreadful down there, none of this would have happened. My s— Zhaff's blood is on your hands!" His lungs ran out of air, and he had to pause. Blood rushing to his head and shock nearly caused him to fall.

"Sir, are you okay?" Sodervall asked, taking his arm to keep him upright.

"I'm fine!" Luxarn screamed as he pushed him away. "Now find Kale Drayton and end this insurgency, or by Earth, I'll find somebody who can, and you can join the skellies in an airlock."

Sodervall swallowed audibly. "I'll handle it, sir." He swept out of the room without another word. The moment he got outside, Luxarn could hear him shouting at officers.

Luxarn made it to his desk and pressed all his weight against it. His breathing hastened, faster and faster until he started hyperventilating. He knocked a globe off as he scrambled for one of his drawers. He rifled through for a stress-reducing injection and jabbed the pack into his arm. A few short breaths later, he exhaled slowly through teeth and closed his eyes.

When he opened them again, Titan stared back at him through his viewport. On the back of its people, he'd grown Pervenio Corp into the most influential entity in all of Sol. But even all that impossible wealth couldn't purchase back the health of a bastard son he'd sent down to die on the world that had provided so much. A son barely a soul knew about but for the man who'd gone down with him.

Stars shone beyond the orange moon. He was so near to them now. Humanity was so near. But for the first time in his life, Luxarn wondered if the cost was more than he could bear.

THANKS FOR READING!

To ALL YOU wonderful readers out there, I hope you enjoyed this book. Even if you didn't, please consider leaving an honest review wherever you prefer to leave your bookish thoughts online. Reviews are the lifeblood of newer authors like me, and they help more than you could possibly imagine.

And if you enjoyed this story about the growing rebellion on Titan, continue reading the rest of the *Children of Titan Series*! Book 2, *Titan's Son,* will take you to the other side of the conflict, as Ringer Kale Drayton is drawn into the Children of Titan.

If you'd like to be updated about the series and its upcoming releases, as well as gain exclusive access to limited content, ARCs, and more, please subscribe to my monthly newsletter below.

Subscribe here: http://rhettbruno.com/newsletter

FROM THE PUBLISHER

Thank you so much for reading Titanborn by Rhett C. Bruno. We hope you enjoyed it as much as we enjoyed bringing it to you. We just wanted to take a moment to encourage you to review the book on Amazon and Goodreads. Every review helps further the author's reach and, ultimately, helps them continue writing fantastic books for us all to enjoy.

If you liked Titanborn, check out the rest of our catalogue at www.aethonbooks.com. To sign up to receive updates regarding all new releases, visit our website.

ABOUT THE AUTHOR

Rhett C Bruno is the USA Today Bestselling Author of 'The Circuit Saga' (Diversion Books, Podium Publishing), 'Children of Titan' (Aethon Books, Audible Studios), and the 'Buried Goddess Saga' (Aethon Books, Audible Studios); among other works.

He has been writing since before he can remember, scribbling down what he thought were epic stories when he was young to show to his friends and family. He currently works at an Architecture firm in Connecticut after graduating from Syracuse University, but that hasn't stopped him from recording the tales bouncing around inside of his head.

Rhett resides in Stamford, Connecticut, with his wife and their dog, Raven.

**You can find out more about his work
at www.rhettbruno.com**

SPECIAL THANKS TO:

ADAWIA E. ASAD	EDDIE HALLAHAN	KYLE OATHOUT
BARDE PRESS	JOSH HAYES	LILY OMIDI
CALUM BEAULIEU	PAT HAYES	TROY OSGOOD
BEN	BILL HENDERSON	GEOFF PARKER
BECKY BEWERSDORF	JEFF HOFFMAN	NICHOLAS (BUZ) PENNEY
BHAM	GODFREY HUEN	JASON PENNOCK
TANNER BLOTTER	JOAN QUERALTÓ IBÁÑEZ	THOMAS PETSCHAUER
ALFRED JOSEPH BOHNE IV	JONATHAN JOHNSON	JENNIFER PRIESTER
CHAD BOWDEN	MARCEL DE JONG	RHEL
ERREL BRAUDE	KABRINA	JODY ROBERTS
DAMIEN BROUSSARD	PETRI KANERVA	JOHN BEAR ROSS
CATHERINE BULLINER	ROBERT KARALASH	DONNA SANDERS
JUSTIN BURGESS	VIKTOR KASPERSSON	FABIAN SARAVIA
MATT BURNS	TESLAN KIERINHAWK	TERRY SCHOTT
BERNIE CINKOSKE	ALEXANDER KIMBALL	SCOTT
MARTIN COOK	JIM KOSMICKI	ALLEN SIMMONS
ALISTAIR DILWORTH	FRANKLIN KUZENSKI	KEVIN MICHAEL STEPHENS
JAN DRAKE	MEENAZ LODHI	MICHAEL J. SULLIVAN
BRET DULEY	DAVID MACFARLANE	PAUL SUMMERHAYES
RAY DUNN	JAMIE MCFARLANE	JOHN TREADWELL
ROB EDWARDS	HENRY MARIN	CHRISTOPHER J. VALIN
RICHARD EYRES	CRAIG MARTELLE	PHILIP VAN ITALLIE
MARK FERNANDEZ	THOMAS MARTIN	JAAP VAN POELGEEST
CHARLES T FINCHER	ALAN D. MCDONALD	FRANCK VAQUIER
SYLVIA FOIL	JAMES MCGLINCHEY	VORTEX
GAZELLE OF CAERBANNOG	MICHAEL MCMURRAY	DAVID WALTERS JR
DAVID GEARY	CHRISTIAN MEYER	MIKE A. WEBER
MICHEAL GREEN	SEBASTIAN MÜLLER	PAMELA WICKERT
BRIAN GRIFFIN	MARK NEWMAN	JON WOODALL
	JULIAN NORTH	BRUCE YOUNG

www.ingramcontent.com/pod-product-compliance
Lightning Source LLC
Chambersburg PA
CBHW051655180726
48284CB00006B/2003